Praise for this b...

'Gorgeously written eerie suspense . . . I loved it'
Karin Slaughter

'I was drawn into Karen Dionne's *The Marsh King's Daughter*
from its first captivating sentences. Troubling, sinuous and
powerfully told, you won't be able to stop turning the pages'
Megan Abbott

'Sensationally good psychological suspense – I loved this book'
Lee Child

'I don't use the word "brilliant" often, but no other
adjective feels adequate to describe this amazing novel . . .
It's an understatement to say *The Marsh King's Daughter* is
an exceptional achievement'
David Morrell

'Eerie and breathtaking, terrific and terrifying in the
best possible way'
Téa Obreht

ALSO BY KAREN DIONNE
The Marsh King's Daughter

THE
WICKED
SISTER

KAREN DIONNE

SPHERE

SPHERE

First published in the United States in 2020 by G.P. Putnam's Sons,
an imprint of Penguin Random House LLC
First published in Great Britain in 2020 by Sphere
This paperback edition published by Sphere in 2021

1 3 5 7 9 10 8 6 4 2

A CIP catalogue record for this book
is available from the British Library.

ISBN 978-0-7515-6744-1

Papers used by Sphere are from well-managed forests
and other responsible sources.

MIX
Paper from
responsible sources
FSC® C104740

Typeset by Palimpsest Book Production Ltd, Falkirk, Stirlingshire

Printed and bound in Great Britain by Clays Ltd, Elcograf S.p.A.

Sphere
An imprint of
Little, Brown Book Group
Carmelite House
50 Victoria Embankment
London EC4Y 0DZ

An Hachette UK Company
www.hachette.co.uk

www.littlebrown.co.uk

For Jeff,
For your unshakable faith in me and in my writing,
and for the germ of the idea that made
this book possible

Truth is like the sun. You can shut it out for a time, but it ain't going away.

—ELVIS PRESLEY

AUTHOR'S NOTE

Readers familiar with Michigan's Upper Peninsula will note that I've made a small adjustment to history for the sake of this story. While this novel takes place in the present day and Rachel's narrative unfolds as if the Newberry Regional Mental Health Center is currently in operation, the health center shuttered its doors in 1992 and the renovated buildings now house a medium-security prison.

1

NOW
Rachel

Sometimes when I close my eyes, there is a rifle in my hands. My hands are small; my fingers are pudgy. I'm eleven years old. There's nothing special about this particular rifle, nothing to distinguish it from any other Remington, except that this is the rifle that killed my mother.

In my vision, I am standing over my mother. The rifle is pointing at her chest. Her mouth is open, and her eyes are closed. Her chest is red.

My father runs into the front hallway. "Rachel!" he screams when he sees me. He drops to his knees, gathers my mother in his arms, looks up at me, his expression an unfamiliar jumble of shock and horror.

He rocks my mother for a long time, as if she is a baby. As if she is alive.

At last he lays her gently on the worn parquet floor and gets slowly to his feet. He takes the rifle from my trembling hands and looks at me with a sorrow greater than I can comprehend and turns the rifle on himself.

Not so, says the golden orb spider from the middle of her web in a corner of my room where the cleaners never sweep. *Your father killed your mother and then he killed himself.*

I don't understand why the spider is lying. Spiders normally tell the truth.

"How do you know?" I can't resist asking. She wasn't there when my parents died. I was.

The spider regards me solemnly from eight shiny eyes. *I know,* she says. *We all know.*

Her spiderlings skitter about the edges of the web as insubstantial as dust motes, and nod.

I want to tell the spider that she is wrong, that I know better than anyone what happened the day my parents died, and I understand the consequences of my childhood crime better than she ever will because I've been living with them for fifteen years. Once you've taken someone's life, it breaks you, shatters you into so many infinitesimal pieces that no one and nothing can put you together again. Ask any drunk driver who killed a pedestrian, any hunter who thought the friend or brother-in-law he shot was a deer.

Anyone who held a loaded rifle when she was too young to anticipate what was about to happen.

My therapists say I'm suffering from complicated grief

disorder and promise I'll get better in time. My therapists are wrong. I'm getting worse.

I can't sleep, and when I do, I have nightmares. I get frequent headaches and my stomach hurts all the time. I used to think constantly about killing myself until I realized that living in a mental hospital for the rest of my life is the greater punishment. I eat, I sleep, I read, I watch TV, I go outside. I breathe the warm summer air, feel the sun on my skin, listen to the birds chirp and the insects hum. Watch the flowers bloom and the leaves turn and the snow fall, and through it all, always, always in the front of my mind and deep in my heart burns this terrible truth: I am the reason my parents will never see, smell, taste, laugh, or love again. My parents are dead because of me.

The police ruled my parents' deaths a murder-suicide perpetrated by my father. All the news reports I've been able to find agree: Peter James Cunningham (age 45) murdered his wife, Jennifer Marie Cunningham (age 43), for undetermined reasons, and then turned the rifle on himself. Some speculate that I saw my father shoot my mother and that's why I ran away; others that I found my parents' bodies and this is what sent me over the edge. I would have told them that I was responsible if I had been able to speak. When I came out of my catatonia three weeks later, I made sure that everyone who would listen knew what I had done.

But to this day, no one believes me. Not even the spider.

2

I leave the spider to her offspring and check my watch, a cheap plastic model my aunt Charlotte bought at the dollar store after the last one she gave me was stolen, and head down two flights to the community room. One of the cable channels is showing the original *Star Trek* movie this afternoon and I promised my friend Scotty I'd make sure that nobody changes the channel. My footsteps echo in the empty stairwell. I'm wearing tennis shoes. Velcro fasteners—the only kind we're allowed. The ceramic floor tiles are cracked or missing, the plaster on the walls and ceiling flaked and peeling. My room is in one of the oldest buildings, which dates from the hospital's opening in 1895, back when it was called the Upper Peninsula Asylum for the Insane. "Newberry Regional Mental Health Center," as it's known today, is definitely better, but it still is what it is: one of two major adult psychiatric hospitals in the state of Michigan, this one in the Upper Peninsula, and the other in the Lower, where the mentally ill go to get better and the terminally insane live out their days. I fall somewhere in between.

I exit the stairwell into a wall of sound. The corridor is crowded. Patients, nurses, patients with nurses in lockstep beside them—because after a meal, bulimics can't be left alone. Orderlies, housekeepers, a doctor in a white coat. I hug the wall, keep my head down. I don't speak to anyone. No one speaks to me. My therapists are always saying that I should get to know my roommates and the others in my therapy group, but it's hard to see the point of making friends with someone who's only going to leave. I navigate the glass-enclosed passageway between the dormitory and the administration building that gets as hot as Hades on a sunny day—unbreakable plexiglass, the staff makes sure new arrivals know—and open the door to the community room.

The community room is as dreary as you'd expect for a mental institution that's over a hundred years old: dirt-stained cream-colored walls, worn green asbestos floor tile, heavy metal-framed, multi-paned windows so no one can jump out, vinyl chairs and couches patched with duct tape and bolted to the floor. It's also noisy, the television turned up far too loud so it can be heard over the conversations of visitors and patients who are talking much too loudly so they can be heard over the noise of the television. And it smells, a combination of stale cooking odors and disinfectant that my aunt Charlotte says reminds her of a nursing home overlaid with the stink of cigarettes. Practically everyone at the hospital smokes. Cigarettes are free; a clever ploy by the tobacco companies to get us addicted and make us customers for life, or merely another calming drug in the hospital's abundant arsenal, I couldn't say. It's lighters and matches we're not allowed, along with shoelaces, drawstrings, plastic grocery store bags, trash can liners, and dozens of other ordinary yet potentially lethal items that people who don't live in mental institutions get to use every day.

Even at that, there have been two successful suicides since I've been here. One girl unraveled a sweater and braided the yarn back together to make a rope, then tied the rope around her neck and threw the other end over a pipe near the bathroom ceiling and climbed up on the toilet and stepped off. Another drank a bottle of drain cleaner she stole from a cleaning cart when no one was looking. The cleaning woman lost her job over that. Still, when you consider that at least half the patients and probably more are here because they've either attempted suicide or have threatened to, you have to give the staff credit.

"Ur-sa!" Scotty calls from across the room when he sees me. He jumps up and flaps his hands. I smile and wave back. Scotty is a child in a man's body, big and broad-shouldered with arms that look like they could crush you with a hug, but who's soft as a marshmallow inside, with watery blue eyes and dishwater blond hair and a mental age of somewhere around nine. "Scotty" is not his real name, by the way; I only call him that because of his obsession with *Star Trek,* the same way he calls me "Ursula" because of my love for bears.

Scotty's brother, Trevor, is also waiting on the sofa. My stomach does its usual flip-flop when I see him. I knew he would be here, of course—he and I have an appointment to talk privately after the movie—but I can't help the effect he has on me. Trevor Lehto is twenty-eight, ten years younger than Scotty and two years older than me. Today he's wearing a lumberjack shirt with the sleeves turned up to his elbows, Converse sneakers, and jeans, which work well with his brown hair and eyes and a scruffy beard that manages to look both natural and groomed. I also have brown hair and eyes and am wearing jeans and plaid because this is practically the uniform for men and women in the U.P., but Trevor pulls off the look in a way that people tend to notice. I'm reasonably certain I'm not the only person at the hospital who has a crush on him.

"Long time," I say as I sit down on the other end of the sofa with Scotty between us. "You look good."

I'm not just being polite. Trevor is deeply tanned, and judging by the corded muscles in his forearms, more fit than I've ever seen him. I guess six months' backpacking in Northern Patagonia will do that for you.

"Thanks. I just got back. Of course, the first thing I had to do was come see this guy."

He punches his brother on the arm. Scotty grins and punches back. I can't help smiling as well. Scotty's smile is as pure and as genuine as his heart. It doesn't take much to make him happy, which is one of the reasons I like hanging with him. Some people think the reason I made friends with Scotty was so I could get close to Trevor, but this isn't true. I understand that our friendship might seem strange given that my I.Q. is 120 and Scotty's is maybe half that, but that's a big part of the reason our friendship works. Scotty accepts me for who I am and doesn't ask for anything in return. Most important, he doesn't ask questions.

"How'd he get the black eye?" Trevor asks me. "He won't tell me."

"I don't know. He won't tell me either, and no one else is talking."

While it's possible that Scotty fell down the stairs or walked into a door on his own, it's more likely that one of the orderlies hit or tripped him on purpose. Most of them are as big as football players, and some of them were before they blew out a knee or were otherwise injured and ended up here. Putting embittered, physically powerful people in charge of a powerless population is bound to end badly, and Scotty is an easy target. This is not the first time he's shown up with unexplained cuts and bruises, and sadly, it won't be the last. Trevor has been trying to find a decent halfway house near Marquette so he can keep an eye on his brother, but so far, nothing's turned up. There aren't many places willing to take a mentally challenged paranoid schizophrenic.

"Thhh," Scotty shushes as the movie begins. The room swells with a predictable chorus of groans and "Not this again!" and "Change the channel!" which is why I preset the correct channel earlier this morning and swiped the remote. I turn up the volume and stick the remote between the couch cushions.

The movie actually turns out to be a lot more enjoyable than I thought it would be, mainly because Scotty sits on the edge of the sofa leaning forward with his hands between his knees in rapt attention the entire two hours, while Trevor and I lean back against the cushions and trade eye rolls behind his back. Occasionally a woman across the room who is studiously pretending to read glances up from her book and looks pointedly from me to Trevor and back to me again, shooting daggers, which pleases me perhaps more than it should.

As soon as the credits are finished, Scotty gets to his feet. "May the Force be with you," he intones. To anyone else, Scotty's benediction would sound like gibberish: *Muh-ah-fah-ee-ih-oo*, spoken in a monotone with each word separated by a painful pause and forced out with great effort. I can't explain why I'm able to understand his mouth-full-of-marbles speech any more than I can explain my ability to understand the spider. I don't tell him that this is a line from *Star Wars*, and not *Star Trek*.

"Two weeks!" Trevor calls after him as Scotty pivots

on his heel and makes a beeline for his room in the men's wing. Scotty doesn't reply.

Trevor stands up and stretches. "Phew, that was brutal. Are you ready to get started, or do you need a few minutes first?"

"Let's do this." I wouldn't mind a pit stop before we sit down, but the public facilities on this floor are locked, and I don't feel like going down to the main office to beg for the key. I leave the remote on the sofa for whoever wants it and follow Trevor to an empty table as far from the television as possible. When Trevor called saying that he'd decided to make journalism his major and asked if he could interview me for one of those *Where are they now?* follow-up stories, I realized that the Universe had given me a gift. For fifteen years, the idea that my father murdered my mother has stood unchallenged. I am the only one who knows that he did not. This interview is a chance to do something good with my useless waste of a life—possibly the only one I'll get, since reporters haven't exactly been knocking down my door.

Still, I'm nervous. Telling an aspiring reporter that I killed my mother and letting him publish my truth is bound to carry consequences: skepticism and ridicule if I am not believed, followed by more therapy, more night-mares, more drugs; maybe going on suicide watch again if it turns out I can't handle the pressure, which I do *not* want to do, since I won't be left alone for a second, not even when I pee—or, if my story is believed, a police investigation, my father's exoneration, possibly jail time for me. Never mind that once Trevor knows I killed my mother he will never look at me the same way again. I've seen too many people spill their guts in group therapy believing that this will make them feel better, only to discover that revealing their deepest, darkest secrets invariably makes things a thousand times worse. Once you know that someone's uncle molested her while her stepfather recorded it so they could sell the videos on the dark web, or that the cute guy you had a crush on when you were fourteen spent the first seven years of his life believing he was a girl because that's how his mother dressed and treated him and at sixteen he was still struggling with gender issues, or that your new roommate's parents tracked every morsel of food that passed her lips and if she gained so much as half a pound, she had to work out for hours in an exercise room that was more like a torture chamber, it's hard to forget. I remind myself I *want* to do this. Trevor may have initiated this interview, but I am here by choice.

I sit. He sits. I wait.

"Okay if I record this?" He reaches into a green canvas messenger bag and places a digital recorder on the table between us without waiting for my answer. The bag looks new.

"Um, yeah. Sure," I say, though the thought of him carrying away a recording of our conversation makes me queasy. It hasn't been easy going from a terrified eleven-year-old so traumatized by what she'd done that she could neither move nor speak to where I am today, which—well, at least I can walk and talk. I'm told I was completely unresponsive to both verbal and physical stimuli when I arrived. I remember I could see and hear, but by the time I thought of what I wanted to do or say, speaking or moving just didn't seem worth the effort. I know that sounds odd, but that's the best way I can describe it. I wasn't bored, because I had no sense of the passage of time. Hours felt like minutes, days like hours, the three weeks I spent trapped in an uncooperative body fed by a nasogastric tube and drained by a catheter morphed into a single, interminable day. I could move but only if someone did it for me; then I'd stay in that position until they moved me again, which I imagine came in handy when it was time to shift me between my wheelchair and my bed.

More than anything, I remember an overwhelming weariness no child should have to know. At times, it seemed like too much effort even to breathe. I was lost in a swirl of thoughts and memories outside my control: *I am in the gun room. I lift the rifle to my shoulder. I shoot the lion in the great room. I shoot a zebra and a gazelle. I am a Big Game Hunter, and not an eleven-year-old girl who loves all creatures equally and wouldn't hurt a fly. "What are you doing?" my mother yells when she sees me. "Put the gun down!" and so I do. There's a big bang. My mother falls. She doesn't get up.* A scene that has looped in my head for the past fifteen years like a movie reel, unvarying in every detail.

13

He starts with a series of softball questions, which I lob back easily: What was it like spending my teenage years in a mental hospital (as bad as you'd think, and worse than you can possibly imagine); did I go to school (yes, we had classes, but I haven't gotten my GED because I'm not planning on leaving, so what would be the point— though I don't tell him that); do I have friends aside from his brother (none unless you count the spider, and calling our relationship "friendship" is a stretch in view of the way she constantly contradicts me, never mind that golden orb spiders only live for about a year and I've lost track of how many generations I've befriended); what would I like people to know about me that they don't already (the perfect opening to tell him I killed my mother, but it's a little early in the interview for that, so I merely shrug).

He shifts in his chair, signaling he's about to shift to another topic. I get ready. I am very good at reading body language. In a place like this you have to be.

"Now let's talk about your early years. Tell me what your life was like before you came to the hospital."

"Okay if I smoke?" I ask, buying time so I can choose my words carefully from the mental script I've prepared. There's so much riding on this interview. Trevor has to understand that my parents were as happy as any two people could be, that my father would no more kill my mother than Romeo would have killed Juliet. Once I establish that, I can tell him who did. Plus, I really do want a cigarette.

"Um, no. I guess not." He waves his hand at the haze hanging over the room. "I'll probably be dead from lung cancer by the time we finish the interview anyway."

I laugh along with him and shake out a cigarette, then raise my hand and keep it up until one of the orderlies sees me and comes over and lights it for me.

"Before I came to the hospital," I begin, feeding his exact words back to him, using the listening technique I learned from my therapists to send the subtle message that he and I are on the same page, "my childhood was very happy. My parents were one of those couples who truly loved each other. You know the kind I'm talking about: can't leave for work in the morning without a kiss—a real one, and not just a peck; holding hands when they walk down the street; sitting next to each other on a sofa when they're reading or watching television instead of sitting at opposite ends. My sister says our parents were more in love on the day they died than on the day they met, and I can believe it. We were both homeschooled, so we spent a lot of time together. The four of us along with my mother's sister lived in this amazing two-story log cabin built by my great-great-grandfather on four thousand acres southeast of Marquette back in the timber baron days—but I guess you know that," I add, thinking of the millions of words that have been written about us.

"It's all right. I'd like to hear it in your own words."

"Okay, then." I take a drag on the cigarette while I consider the best way to direct the conversation where

I want it to go, then tap off the ash into one of the thin aluminum ashtrays scattered around the room that are meant to be disposable but that the hospital never throws away because we're a state-run facility and chronically underfunded.

"My parents were wildlife biologists, as I'm sure you also know. Our property was surrounded by tall cliffs on three sides and a large lake on the fourth, very isolated, very pristine. My parents used to say that living and working in this amazing ecological microsystem was like heaven on earth. And because my father's parents owned the area my mother and father were studying, and my parents financed their own research, they didn't have to answer to anyone, so how they conducted their work and what they chose to study was entirely under their control. My father's focus was amphibians, while my mother studied black bears. They used to joke that my mother had twice as much testosterone as my father—because of their choices, you know."

Trevor smiles and writes my parents' joke in his notepad. "So, which did you prefer? Frogs or bears?"

"I loved anything that moved," I answer diplomatically, though the truth is, amphibians really don't do much for me, while I'm as crazy about black bears as my mother ever was, and always will be. "I used to go with my parents on their rounds. One day I'd be slogging around the ponds and creeks draped in mosquito netting and wearing hip waders like my father, collecting water samples and

16

counting tadpoles and scooping up frogs, and the next, I'd be crouching alongside my mother in her observation blind watching a five-hundred-pound black bear nosing around our bait station a few feet away."

"It sounds idyllic."

"It was."

I can't quite tell if he genuinely means this, or if he's challenging me to prove it. I hope I'm not overselling my childhood, and he thinks my memories are colored by wishful thinking and time. If anything, those years were more idyllic than I've described, as magical as a fairy tale: wild and beautiful surroundings, a hunting lodge as splendid as a castle in the middle of a mysterious, impenetrable forest; intelligent and loving parents who treated me like a princess, involving me in their work as if I were their peer while giving me the freedom to explore, learn, grow.

"So, you were comfortable wandering the woods by yourself?"

"I was. Tramping around the woods on my own was no different for me than the way a city kid learns to navigate the subway."

He nods as if I've confirmed something important, though I can't imagine what, then pulls his messenger bag toward him and digs through it and comes up with a plain manila folder.

"I want to show you something. This is a copy of the police report. No photos," he adds quickly. He riffles through the folder and pulls out a piece of paper and lays it on the table between us. "Right here." He taps the middle of the page. "This is where it talks about your disappearance."

Of course, he's zeroed in on the most sensational part of my story, though if he's hoping for a scoop, he's exactly fifteen years too late. Anyone can google my name along with "missing girl" and find plenty of articles about my disappearance, from tabloids to the national news. MISSING GIRL FOUND! and MIRACLE GIRL SURVIVES TWO-WEEK WILDERNESS ORDEAL—RETURNS TO CIVILIZATION UNABLE TO SPEAK, and my personal favorite: REAL-LIFE MOWGLI SAVED BY WOLVES?

"The report says that by the time police arrived, you'd already gone missing," he prompts, as if I don't know the details of my own story. "They set up a search, but by then the ground was too trampled to know which way you'd gone. Then that night, it snowed, which wiped out any chance of picking up your trail in the morning. Still, they searched for days—helicopters, tracking dogs, the works—though as more and more time went by, everyone had to admit that you were most likely dead."

"Right. Until two weeks later, a passing motorist found me lying beside the highway," I cut in, trying to hurry things along so we can move on to the topic I came to discuss.

"Lying beside the highway *unable to move or to speak*," he adds, which I'll grant *is* a fairly dramatic detail. "And yet aside from that and a few scratches and bruises, physically you were in remarkably good shape. But here's the thing, Rachel. I grew up in the Upper Peninsula. I know what the weather is like in early November. Temps below freezing at night, and with that fresh snowfall there's no way you should have survived those two weeks on your own. Yet somehow, you did. I know you couldn't remember anything at the time, but what about now? Is there anything at all that you can tell me? What did you eat? How did you keep warm? Where did you sleep?"

He looks so hopeful I'm tempted to make something up to satisfy him and his future readers. It occurs to me that I could tell him anything and no one could contradict me. Unfortunately, those days are as much a mystery to me now as they were then. Plus, I really hate when people don't tell the truth.

"Sorry, no. I still don't remember a thing. My therapists tried to help me get my memories back. I think they saw me as a personal challenge. I was this mystery girl, this wild child who turned up two weeks after she went missing with no idea of where she'd been or what she'd been doing. But eventually, we had to accept that those days are gone for good."

"But are they really? Don't scientists say we retain everything we've seen or heard? Those memories must be rattling around in your brain somewhere."

"Well, yes. Technically, that's true. I meant my memories are gone in the sense that I can't access them. Believe me, we tried. The thing you have to understand about memories associated with childhood trauma is that the brain processes these differently than normal ones, sometimes burying them so deeply a person doesn't even realize that the reason they're struggling as an adult is because of something that happened to them when they were a child."

What I don't tell him is that I don't *want* to remember those days, and never did, which no doubt was a big factor in my therapists' collective failure. If whatever happened during that time was so disturbing that my brain felt the need to erase it, I don't want to know.

"Could you just take a look? Please? Maybe reading the report will jog something loose."

I take the folder he's holding out to me, even though reading the details of that day is just about the last thing I want to do; basically, I'm throwing him a bone because he drove a hundred miles to interview me and we both know I haven't given him much. I scan the pages quickly, feigning interest until I come upon a line drawing of a child next to a picture of a massive rifle, and then I really am interested. I read the associated paragraph:

After the daughter was recovered, the M.E. examined the girl and found no evidence of bruising on her limbs or torso consistent with having fired a Winchester Magnum. Given the size of the weapon relative to the girl's height and weight as well as

*the lack of physical evidence, the M.E. ruled
that the daughter did not fire the rifle.*

My heart pounds. I place the folder carefully on the
table and wipe my hands on my jeans and stick them
under my legs to stop them from shaking. I don't understand. I shot my mother. I killed her—I *know* I did. I've
seen myself standing over her body with the rifle so many,
many times.

And yet there's no reason to think that this paragraph
is anything other than fact. Whoever wrote this report
couldn't have made this up. The details are too specific.
Too easy to disprove. Even I can see that the rifle in the
picture—which is *not* the Remington I see in my visions—
is so big, it would have been all but impossible for the
eleven-year-old me to pick it up.

*Given the size of the weapon relative to the girl's
height and weight as well as the lack of physical
evidence, the M.E. ruled that the daughter did not
fire the rifle.*

It's impossible. Yet the truth is right in front of me in
black and white.

I didn't kill my mother. I couldn't have. According to
the police report, I never even fired that rifle.

3

I close my eyes, sway, grab the edge of the table to keep from passing out. My throat is so tight I can barely breathe. Fifteen years. *Fifteen years* in a mental hospital serving a self-imposed life sentence for a crime I didn't commit. It's crazy. Nuts. Insane. I feel like a fool. Two sentences in the middle of a police report I never read prove my entire life has been shaped by a lie. *Defined* by it.

Memories of those wasted years crash over me in waves.

—*It's my twelfth birthday. I'm sitting cross-legged on the floor of a padded cell strapped into a straitjacket. My arms ache and my nose itches and I have to pee. My voice is hoarse from yelling for help. By the time an orderly slides back the viewing slot in the door, I have wet and soiled my pants.*

—*I'm fifteen. I'm lying on my back on a narrow gurney counting the fluorescent lights that pass overhead as I'm wheeled down a long hallway. My arms and legs are buckled into leather straps. My therapist has promised that this will be the last electroconvulsive therapy session I will need. I don't believe her.*

—Last week. I'm so doped up after yet another random medication change, all I want to do is sleep. An orderly wakes me up anyway and drags me out of bed to stand in line in front of the nurses' station with the other patients waiting for meds. Outside, the sky turns red and then green. Crickets chirp, while somewhere down the hall a violin plays. I dig at my arms until they bleed, trying to quiet the ants that are crawling under my skin.

"Are you all right?"

So many years. So much humiliation. So much suffering. *All of it for nothing.* I want to scream, smash my fist into the wall, rip up the police report and throw it in Trevor's face, climb onto the table and announce to the room that I don't belong here, and never did.

"Rachel? Are you okay? Talk to me."

He looks genuinely worried. I can imagine how I look to him: pale, sweating, shaking. He probably thinks I'm about to have a heart attack. Maybe I am.

"Actually," I say, "I'm not okay. I'm sorry. Must be a reaction to my new meds. Can we finish this later? Maybe by phone?"

"Of course. Do you want me to call someone? Is there anything I can do?"

"I'll be fine," I lie. "I'm just a little dizzy, is all."

"If you're sure . . ."

"I'm sure." I force a smile, put out my hand. "Thanks for understanding."

Of course he's disappointed, but I can't help that. He shakes my hand, turns off the recorder and gathers up his things, gives me his card, says it was a pleasure talking to me, hopes I feel better soon, promises to check back in a few days to see how I'm doing, tells me to call in the meantime if I remember anything important or if I just want to talk. Meanwhile, all I can think is *Hurry up, leave, go.* The second the door closes behind him, I cross my arms on the table and lay down my head.

Given the size of the weapon relative to the girl's height and weight as well as the lack of physical evidence, the M.E. ruled that the daughter did not fire the rifle.

How could I not have known this? Why do I not remember? When I came out of my catatonia, I told everyone I killed my mother. Why didn't anyone think to tell me not only that I *didn't* kill her, but that I *couldn't have*? I could have spent my teenage years at the lodge, gone to a university, gotten a degree, carried on my mother's research, fallen in love, gotten married. Instead, I've accomplished absolutely nothing, giving up my future in exchange for my parents'—a sacrifice I now know was entirely pointless and without cause. The perfect storm of misunderstandings and wrong assumptions that brought me to this moment makes me physically ill. After no one believed me when I came out of my catatonia and told them I killed my mother, I stopped talking about it. My aunt and sister never asked what was keeping me at the hospital because they thought my therapists were addressing my issues. My therapists didn't know the reason for my lack of progress because I never told them I still believed I killed my mother. And round and round it went. A tragedy of errors.

And yet . . . I know with absolute certainty that if I were to close my eyes right now, I'd see myself standing over my mother's body with the rifle. I have no idea why my brain conjures up this image, why I see it over and over, why my visions feel so real when, clearly, they are not. I understand that children sometimes think they are to blame when something bad happens; "magical thinking," it's called when two unrelated events are conflated in the child's mind and become inextricably linked: "I was mad at my mommy and she got in a car accident, so it's my fault she got hurt."

But I wasn't three or four or five. I was eleven—an intelligent, perceptive, well-educated, way-more-mature-than-most-kids-her-age eleven—certainly old enough to understand the relationship between cause and effect. *Something* must have happened to make me think I killed my mother. Maybe I came into the hallway after my parents were dead and picked up the rifle and stood looking down at their bodies. Maybe my poor traumatized brain took that snippet of genuine memory and twisted it until I became convinced that I pulled the trigger. Maybe . . . I can understand my brain wiping out my memory of that terrible day in order to protect me, but why would it replace the truth with something so much worse?

I sit up and drag a hand through my hair. The cigarette barely smolders in the ashtray. I use what's left of it to light another and lean back with my feet on the table and look around the room. It's strange to think that for everyone else, everything is continuing exactly as it was before, while for me, nothing will ever again be the same. For fifteen years, I was a bad person. I was the girl who killed her mother and caused her father to take his own life; who robbed the world of two talented and insightful scientists who could have gone on to make important discoveries; who was doing the only thing she could think of to make amends by living out her self-imposed penance in the worst place she knew. Take all of that away, and who am I?

I smoke and think and think and smoke until the dinner bell rings. The room empties quickly, not because people are in a hurry to eat the spectacularly bland and over-cooked cafeteria food, but because the community room is locked during mealtimes since there aren't enough staff to keep an eye on both places at once and we have to clear out. I stub out the cigarette and swing my legs off the table, then stick Trevor's card in my pocket and get to my feet, working my way against the crowd and back to my room like a salmon swimming upstream. No one stops me or questions where I'm going. Skipping meals is only a problem if you have an eating disorder, which I do not, though I'm thin enough it would be easy to convince someone I did if I had a reason to. For that matter, there are a lot of neuroses and psychoses I can fake. Mood disorders are the easiest, but I also do a mean schizophrenic. I used to pretend that I had a different disorder every time I got a new roommate, like trying on a new shirt or coat, which might seem manipulative or maybe even cruel, but was really just harmless fun. All my roommates were going to move on eventually, so what did it matter if they took the wrong impression of me with them? Making them think I was bipolar, or that I suffered from antisocial personality disorder, or obsessive-compulsive disorder, or paranoid personality disorder was better than telling them what was really wrong with me.

A diagnosis which apparently no longer applies.

I stagger up the stairs and collapse onto my bed like a drunk. I pick up the stuffed bear toy that's comforted me since I was a child and rub my thumb over the bald spot on the top of his head. When I first arrived at the hospital unable to move or to speak, my therapists tried to reach me using this bear. *Tell me what's bothering you, Rachel,* they'd say in a high, squeaky voice while they danced the bear in front of me and wiggled its arms surreptitiously with their fingers. *What are you afraid of? It's okay, you can tell me.* As if a confession to a stuffed animal could erase the memory of what I'd seen. What I'd done.

What I didn't do.

I sigh and look toward the corner. The spider wisely says nothing.

I roll onto my back and link my arms behind my head and stare at the brown stains on the mattress of the bunk above me. When I was little, I used to look for shapes in these stains the way other people see things in clouds: a bear, a whale, a man and a woman kissing, my father and mother—which, considering that these are merely urine stains contributed by countless bedwetters over untold decades, only shows how desperately I missed them. A kiss like you see in movies, a Rhett Butler–Scarlett O'Hara kiss, the kiss of two people who were madly and passionately in love.

Not the kiss of a man who was about to murder his wife.

My father killed my mother and then he killed himself.

I try the spider's words out loud. They don't feel real.

It was an accident. It had to be. Maybe my father was cleaning the rifle while my mother was nearby and he somehow pulled the trigger. Maybe the rifle went off all on its own. Maybe he was startled when a wood rat ran across the floor, or a fighter jet flew low overhead, or by a sudden clap of thunder. The accident could have happened in a thousand different ways for a thousand different reasons. All I know is that my father would never deliberately hurt my mother for all the reasons I was going to lay out to Trevor.

Trevor. I shudder to think how close I came to confessing that I was the one who killed her. That would have been the end of my credibility right there—assuming a long-term patient in a mental hospital has any credibility to begin with. He's probably kicking himself right now for setting up the interview, thinking how irresponsible I am for agreeing to talk to him and then almost immediately sending him away. I'm sure he only gave me his card out of politeness and has written off the story as a total bust.

At any rate, it doesn't matter what he thinks of me because there's no way I'm going to get in touch with him. Why would I want to help him work up a rehash of the same old Rachel's-father-murdered-her-mother-and-then-he-killed-himself?

My eyes fill. I was *so close*. I had everything figured out. After I proved my father's innocence, either through the court system or in the court of public opinion, I was going to take my own life. Not out of despair and hopelessness as my father took his (an act of selfishness I struggle with to this day; how could he leave me when I needed him most? How could he choose death with my mother over life with me?), but with courage and integrity as a final act of contrition. I'd even figured out how I was going to do it, something brilliant and original that no one at the hospital has tried before but that would absolutely work as I intended it to. Now what am I supposed to do?

I clutch my bear to my chest, burying my face in his fur and clinging to him as if he were an anchor, a lifeline, the only thing keeping me from sinking into an ocean of failure and despair so crushing I can barely breathe. Everything I sacrificed was to no purpose. Everything I believed was a lie.

I cry harder than I have in my life, harder than when I came out of my catatonia and realized my nightmares were true and my parents really were gone, great wracking sobs that turn my stomach inside out and convulse my entire body. I weep for the poor eleven-year-old orphan so traumatized by her parents' deaths she had to be committed to a mental institution, for the desperately lonely and suicidal teenager she became, for the twenty-six-year-old woman I am today, who was so convinced that her life had no value she believed that living in a mental hospital was the best that she deserved. I weep for my parents, for the tragedy that destroyed our family, for all the things that never were that should have been.

At last there are no more tears. I sit up and wipe my face with my shirtsleeve and go to the bathroom for a wad of toilet paper to blow my nose. My eyes are so swollen I can barely see. I lean over the sink and splash cold water on my face, then wet a washcloth to soothe my burning eyes and lie down again on my bed. It's hard to believe that for fifteen years I could have been so wrong. My visions are so persistent. So consistent. *So real.*

So, what if I am not mistaken? What if the medical examiner is wrong? I wish I'd thought to ask Trevor to leave his copy of the police report behind. There could be details in it that the police overlooked because they didn't fit the narrative the crime scene seemed to tell. Details that only I can understand the significance of because I lived at the lodge. These were *my parents.* I know things about them and their relationship that didn't even make it into the police report because no one ever interviewed me.

But then what? Combing over the report and identifying conflicting details and inconsistencies won't change anything because this is the report that convicted my father in the first place. And if reading the report triggers a memory, or I find something in it that I want to look into further, how am I supposed to investigate from here?

I am standing over my mother holding a rifle.

The M.E. ruled that the daughter did not fire the rifle.

Am I a killer, or am I not? There's only one way to find out. I have to go back to the happiest and most horrible place I know.

Home.

4

THEN
Jenny

I should have seen something. Heard something. *I should have known.*

If only I had looked out the window a few minutes earlier, I might have been able to pull our neighbors' son out of our pool in time to revive him. A few minutes before that, and I might have prevented him from falling in.

The police, the EMTs, my husband—even the Yangs say I did all I could. As soon as I saw the dark shadow at the bottom of our pool and realized what it was, I yelled at my daughter to run next door as fast as she could and tell Mrs. Yang to call 911. I sprinted across the yard and kicked off my shoes and dove into the pool and grabbed a handful of T-shirt and hauled the boy out and laid him on the pool deck and started CPR, though

I've never done CPR on a toddler and I had no idea if I was doing it right. I didn't stop until the EMTs arrived and took over, but it wasn't enough. By then, our neighbors' only child was dead.

I told the police officer who questioned me that I had no idea how the boy got access to our swimming pool. The pool is fenced, as anyone can see, and my husband and I are extremely conscientious about keeping the gate shut because we moved into this house two months ago and our daughter is only eight and doesn't yet know how to swim. Yes, the gate was open when I got there. No, I don't know how it got that way. No, I couldn't say exactly where our daughter was when the boy fell in. All I know is that when I finished whatever I was doing in the kitchen and went into the great room, Diana was sitting on the floor in front of the television watching a Disney movie.

The officer asked if he could speak with Diana in my presence. I told him sure. Diana confirmed what I'd already said, then sat down cross-legged on the floor at his request to demonstrate how she had been watching television with her back to the windows and her hands folded demurely in her lap. No, she didn't hear any strange noises coming from the backyard. Yes, the movie she had been watching, *Robin Hood*, is her favorite, though she also likes *Beauty and the Beast* and *The Little Mermaid*.

"Let me know if you remember anything else," the officer said kindly enough when he finished with us and gave me his card.

The card is stuck to the fridge. I have no intention of calling. Because as much as I wish it could be otherwise, in my heart, I know my daughter is somehow involved. There's just no way the Yang boy could have ended up at the bottom of our pool without her help. Whether she figured out how to open the gate and was playing by the pool and left the gate open when she came into the house and didn't see the toddler wander in, or she saw him fall and didn't think to come and get me, perhaps thinking that the boy could swim, I can't say.

What I do know, what I didn't tell the police officer, and what I absolutely won't tell my husband, now or ever, is that after I came into the great room and before I looked out the windows, I saw that my daughter's clothes were wet.

The police are gone, as are the EMTs, the fire department, the coroner, the reporters, our rubbernecking neighbors, and apparently everyone else in the city who either owns or has access to a police scanner. The action has shifted to the red-brick mini-mansion next door: lights blazing, cars choking the driveway and spilling into our cul-de-sac, a mountain of recriminating teddy bears and candles and flowers heaped against our shared fence; a spontaneous outpouring of grief and comfort and support to which everyone is welcome but us.

I'm tucked into a corner of the massive brown leather

sofa in the great room, a high-ceilinged, dark-paneled retreat at the back of the house with floor-to-ceiling windows that overlook the yard and the pool. It's dark. The pool lights are off. Moonlight reflects off the lethal water. Crime scene tape flutters in a light breeze.

Peter is sitting at the opposite end. Normally after our daughter has been put to bed and we finally get a chance to pour a glass of wine to relax and rehash our respective days we sit next to each other on this sofa; otherwise, it feels as though this cold, cavernous room will swallow us up. I much preferred the hundred-year-old farmhouse we rented when Peter was teaching in upstate New York, and the weathered Cape Cod in Swampscott during his stint at MIT. Even the tiny upstairs flat in the shabby bungalow in the declining Detroit neighborhood where we lived when we were first married had more character than this brick-and-limestone monstrosity. Each of those were humble wooden houses with small rooms and big histories: stairway railings polished smooth from generations of hands passing over them, stone walkways so dished from countless footsteps that after a rain birds would come and drink from their puddles. But the realtor promised that this time of year, housing in Ann Arbor was at a premium, and odds were good we wouldn't find anything else in our price range within walking distance of the university, and because all signs indicated that this was going to be a scorcher of a summer, who wouldn't want to live in a house with a pool?

I guess we know the answer to that question.

I lean forward and set the glass of wine Peter poured for me on the coffee table untouched. I'm already numb. *A child died in our swimming pool.* Every time I think the words, I feel like throwing up. Peter's lawyer friend says we could be charged with negligent homicide even though the boy's death was an accident. I hope we are.

I sit back and lean my head against the cushions and steal a glance at my husband. Peter looks as wasted as I feel. I try to imagine how we can possibly go forward from here; what it will be like tomorrow, and the next day, and the day after that, sitting on this sofa, looking out these windows—*seeing that swimming pool*—watching the seasons pass knowing that poor William Yang will forever remain a toddler because of us.

"We can't stay here," I say. "I mean it," I add when Peter doesn't respond. "We have to move."

He tosses back his drink—Jameson on the rocks instead of his usual glass of red wine.

"I understand why you feel that way. This is hard for me, too. But we can't move. This close to the start of classes, I doubt we could find so much as a room to rent."

"I'm not talking about moving to a different house. I'm talking about moving to a different city. Someplace where we can walk down the street or go to a park or a store or a faculty luncheon and nobody knows what happened. Where Diana can go to school without people whispering behind her back and pointing fingers."

"You know that's not possible. With my job history it's a wonder U of M took me on at all. This really is the end of the line."

"There has to be something we can do. I can't stay here. I just can't."

Peter studies the ice in his glass as if the cubes were a crystal ball that held the answer to our problem, then leans forward and puts the glass on the coffee table and sits back again in his corner. I wish he would slide across the sofa and take me in his arms and tell me that everything is going to be all right and that this too shall pass. I feel as fragile as the porcelain vase his grandmother gave us as a wedding present, which sits across the room on our fireplace mantel; brittle and insubstantial, as if the slightest puff of wind could blow me off and shatter me to pieces. The Howard Miller mantel clock she also gave us after she found out how much I love antiques ticks away beside it in the silence.

An idea begins to form.

"Maybe you don't have to teach," I say slowly, because my gut says this idea is a good one and I'll only get one chance to pitch it, so it has to be right. "Maybe you could do fieldwork instead. Up north. At your grandparents' place."

I let the words hang between us to give him time to come to the same realization: this really is our best option. Our only option. Peter loves the woods as much as I do. He's often said that the summers he spent as a boy at his family's hunting lodge in Michigan's Upper Peninsula wilderness are the reason that he became a wildlife biologist in the first place. We could be happy there. Or as close to happy as is possible after today.

"What about my classes?"

"You could cancel. Take the semester off and see how it goes. We can rent out the house or leave it empty if we have to. I don't want to live here. I really don't."

"You know there's no telephone or electricity at the lodge."

Of course, I know this. Haven't we spent every Christmas there with his family since before Diana was born? But I don't argue the point. He's only throwing out objections because he is not yet ready to admit that I am right.

I laugh. "You make it sound like that's a bad thing."

He shakes his head. "It's crazy," he says. A pause. "It's tempting," he adds.

My stomach tightens. He's almost convinced. "It's perfect."

"I doubt the university would agree."

"Then quit. We can live off our savings for a long time, especially if your grandparents don't charge us rent. Think about it. Your family owns this amazing, isolated chunk of pristine wilderness that's never been studied. Who knows what you might find? And you wouldn't have to answer to anyone. Imagine being able to focus on whatever you want without having to worry about grants and funding.

Then later, after you publish, you could have your pick of any university in the country. Assuming you want to go back to teaching at all."

"What about Diana?"

"I can homeschool Diana while you're in the field. Or she can go with you."

Or with me, I think, though I don't say it. It's been a long time since I've held a pair of binoculars in my hands. I put my career on the back burner when Diana was born with the understanding that as soon as she was old enough, I'd pick it up again. Unfortunately, our daughter turned out to be a difficult baby, and as she's gotten older, she's only gotten worse. The tantrums she throws over something as simple as either of us telling her to put on her shoes or to pick up her toys are epic—punching the wall until her knuckles bleed, kicking holes in her bedroom door—which obviously makes it a challenge to find babysitters and daycare centers that will take her. Diana's therapist says we give in to her too easily; that we are the adults and it's up to us to draw the lines if she is ever going to learn what is acceptable behavior and what is not. But her therapist doesn't have to live with our sweet, charismatic, highly intelligent, super-creative, ultra-manipulative, love-you-one-second-and-bite-you-on-the-arm-the-next daughter.

"That's not what I'm talking about," Peter says, and my heart sinks. I know exactly what he's thinking. It's all I've been thinking about, too. Whenever there's trouble, it seems as though our daughter is always at the center.

"Diana says she was watching television all afternoon."

"And you believe her?"

I can't answer. I want to believe, but our daughter lies so easily, so convincingly. After the paramedics took over and I went into the house—ostensibly to change out of my dripping clothes, but more important, to change my daughter's—and I asked her how she got so wet, Diana claimed that she had been playing swimming pool with her Barbies in her bathroom. But when I looked in, expecting to find a pile of wet towels and water all over the floor, the tub and sink were dry.

"Mommy? Daddy? Are you going to tuck me in bed?"

We turn around at the same time. Diana is standing at the top of the stairs, all blue eyes and chubby cheeks and golden curls, wearing a pair of Disney princess pajamas that are far too small for her, but are the only pair she'll put on without a fight. A sick feeling washes over me. After today, how can I look at my daughter the same way again?

"Your turn," Peter says.

I'm pretty sure it's not, but I don't have it in me to argue. Diana's nighttime routine is exhausting. We try to make a game out of placing the water glass on her night-stand just so and filling it with precisely the right amount, and tucking the bedcovers around her tight, but not too tight, and reading her favorite bedtime story three times in its entirety even though we all know this particular fairy tale by heart. The last thing I want to do is play her game tonight.

I disentangle myself from the sofa. Diana doesn't smile when she sees me coming toward her, doesn't run down the stairs to meet me or hold out her arms in anticipation of a kiss or a hug as I imagine other children do. All she does is stand at the top with her arms folded across her chest and wait for me to come to her.

As I start up the stairs to go to my daughter, suddenly, I am afraid.

5

I got what I wanted.

Peter, Diana, and I are driving north on I-75 at this very moment on our way to our new wilderness home. I don't even want to think about the amount of work it took to get us to this point: convincing his grandparents to let us live at the lodge year-round, finding a therapist for Diana within a hundred miles of our new home who had room for her in his schedule, renting the house, boxing up our household goods and putting them into storage, loading the U-Haul we're pulling with our clothes and books and toys and other can't-do-withouts—all in a little over a month. I should be ecstatic that we're on the road at last. Instead, I'm exhausted.

It doesn't help that Peter has barely spoken since we pulled out of the driveway. I know he's upset. "One more step down the ladder," he joked grimly when he tossed the university's termination letter on our dining room table and walked away. We both knew there was only the slightest possibility that they would keep him on after he put in a request for a sabbatical and canceled his classes. But seeing their decision in black and white must have stung. I know he'll forget all about it once he gets caught up in his research and realizes how much he's missed working in the field. I just wish he knew it, too.

Diana has been passed out behind us in the middle seat practically since we left, thanks to an old prescription for sedatives I found when I was cleaning out the medicine cabinet. I have another dose with me in case I need it after she wakes up. I realize that drugging my child in exchange for a few hours of peace and quiet probably makes me seem like a terrible parent. But Diana is so easily bored, and boredom for her inevitably leads to rage; I guarantee the best outcome for all of us would be if she slept the entire nine hours. Maybe if we made this drive more than once a year, she'd be a better traveler. We skipped Christmas the year she was born because no parent in their right mind would bring a six-week-old baby to a remote wilderness cabin. We also missed the Christmas Diana was six because she'd been suspended for biting one of her classmates and we were trying withholding a reward to get her to modify her behavior. It didn't work.

Neither have any of the other methods we've tried. We've read all the books: *The Defiant Child*, *Parenting the Strong-Willed Child*, *Raising Your Spirited Child*—all promoting different parenting strategies that seem to work just long enough to get our hopes up before everything goes back to the way it was. I keep telling Peter that we need to accept our daughter for who she is, and that whatever idealized version he's carrying in his head of what he thinks a little girl should be is not our reality. Diana was never a sapling that could be shaped and bent; she was born a tree, roots planted firmly in the earth, thick trunk, sturdy branches. Intractable, immovable. Asking her to change would be like asking a rock to get up and walk. Her therapist thinks Diana has some form of antisocial personality disorder because of her out-of-control rages and her complete lack of remorse. But what eight-year-old isn't impulsive and self-centered? I have to believe that things will get better as she gets older. Meanwhile, I am not going to let anyone slap a label on my daughter that will define her for the rest of her life.

"We should stop for gas before we cross the Bridge," I whisper as quietly as I can after we pass a sign that says we will arrive at the Mackinac Bridge in thirty miles. There's no need to specify which bridge I'm talking about; everyone in Michigan calls the Mackinac Bridge "the Bridge," as if the state had only one, and no wonder: the five-mile-long suspension bridge that connects Michigan's Upper and Lower Peninsulas is truly spectacular, even more impressive than the Golden Gate, arching two hundred feet above the Straits of Mackinac, the longest two-tower suspension bridge in the Western Hemisphere. "Diana will be upset if she misses it. And I could really use a bathroom."

"Whatever you want."

I bite back a sigh. This has been essentially the sum total of our conversation for the entire drive. *"Where would you like to stop for lunch?"* *"Wherever you want."* *"Would you like me to take a turn driving?"* *"Whatever you want."* *"Okay if I turn on the radio?"* *"Whatever you want."* I never would have guessed that Peter could turn so passive-aggressive. I'll admit, I may have pushed too hard for this move. (A man convinced against his will is of the same opinion still, my mother used to say.) But it's not my fault a child died in our swimming pool. I just can't stay in a place where my family is vulnerable. The police ruled the Yang boy's death an accident, and it looks as though we're not going to be charged, but Peter's lawyer friend says we're balanced on a knife edge. Anything untoward, even something as minor as a traffic ticket, could lead them to reopen the investigation. As long as that possibility is hanging over us, hiding out at a hunting lodge in the middle of four thousand wilderness acres sounds just about perfect to me.

Diana stirs at the sound of our voices. She blinks herself awake and pushes against her seatbelt as though it were a straitjacket.

"Hi there, sleepyhead," I say. "Did you have a good nap?"

"I haveta go potty."

"There's a rest area up ahead." Peter points to a big blue highway sign in the distance.

"I haveta go *now*." Diana gets that look that warns she's about to explode.

"Maybe we should pull over," I suggest.

"She can wait," Peter says firmly, clearly determined to be the adult in the room, though I notice he's pressing harder on the gas pedal. "Two minutes, tops."

I unbuckle my seatbelt and twist around to reach between the seats and pat her knee. There was a time when we thought our daughter might be autistic, but the fact that she can tolerate being touched ruled that out.

"Just a little longer, sweetheart. We're almost there."

To my surprise, Diana stops struggling and relaxes. I give it a few more seconds, then sit back and refasten my seatbelt and share a score-one-for-the-parents look with Peter. Moments later I hear the sound of trickling water.

"Oh, Diana, honey. What did you do?"

"Did she?"

"She did."

"Oh my God. I can't believe you let her do that."

"I *let* her? *I* let her? You're the one who wouldn't pull over."

"I wasn't about to have my eight-year-old daughter dropping her pants in plain sight of the highway. She's not a toddler."

I choke back my retort and dig through the snack cooler for napkins and paper towels to soak up the mess. Diana smiles smugly, as if she knew her actions would provoke an argument and Peter and I are doing exactly as she wanted. Not for the first time, I wonder how our daughter has managed to wrest control of our family. I have no doubt that she wet herself deliberately to punish us, but for what? Making her endure a long car ride so we can bring her to a place where she can be happy?

We ride in silence. Peter pulls into the rest area and parks. I get out and slide open the rear passenger door. The back seat reeks. Urine darkens her jeans. The seat is soaked, as is the carpet on the floor.

I hand the towels to Peter. "Wait here with Daddy," I tell Diana as I go around to the back of the U-Haul to look for a change of clothes. "Don't move."

Of course, she takes off like a shot, running up the sidewalk toward the bathrooms without an ounce of shame over the fact that her entire rear end is sopping wet.

"Diana! Get back here!" Peter shouts.

"Wait for Mommy!" I call.

She stops in the middle of the path and cocks her head, then spreads her arms wide and twirls, a butterfly in a sky full of unicorns and rainbows. A grandmother walking toward her car grins at Diana's obvious delight, then notices Diana's backside and smiles ruefully in sympathy. I shrug my shoulders and force a smile in return; two mothers commiserating over the trials and tribulations of raising children. As if there could be anything remotely charming about an eight-year-old who deliberately wet herself.

Peter strides toward our daughter, truly angry. I grab

the first items of clothing I can find and hurry after him. Neither Peter nor I have ever hit our daughter and I don't expect him to now, but if any of the dozen people watching our little drama decide that we are being in the least way abusive, it wouldn't take much for someone to call the police.

"It's okay," I hiss when I catch up to him. I put my hand on his arm. "People are watching. Just let me get her cleaned up and we can get out of here."

He takes a deep breath, then looks down at me and shakes off my hand. "Whatever you want."

He turns and heads for the bathrooms. I take Diana by the hand and follow. It's all I can do not to cry. I feel like I'm being punished for something I didn't do. All I *want* is to get Diana away from the people who don't understand her, so that no one can hurt her, and so she can't hurt them. Later, when she is older and has settled down and has hopefully grown a conscience, we can go back to civilization if Peter wants to. For now, I am absolutely convinced that our self-imposed exile is the right thing to do. A wild child living in the woods. What could be more appropriate?

It's dark when we finally arrive. At least, I think we're nearly there. It's hard to tell for sure because there's no sign marking the turnoff from the highway. Not even a mailbox. Peter's great-grandfather's secret Shangri-La is difficult to access in the summer, almost impossible in the winter; a four-mile drive down a narrow dirt road cut through a gap in the cliffs the only way in or out. We thought we got an early enough start this morning that we would arrive while it was still light out, but thanks to Diana's multiple demands for bathroom breaks during the second half of the trip, which we knew were most likely faked, but which after her earlier stunt we didn't dare deny, here we are. In hindsight, I should have given her that second dose of sedative when we stopped for supper, but after the near disaster at the rest area, I just didn't have the heart to travel any farther down the bad-parenting road.

Peter has been driving slower than I could walk for the past ten minutes trying to spot the turnoff. It's maddening to have to go this slow when we know we're so close. But after fourteen hours on the road, the last thing we want to do is drive past it.

"Is that it?" I point to what looks like it could be an opening in the brush fifty or so feet ahead. Or it could be a rock, or a shadow. We've made this mistake twice already.

"Maybe." Peter swings wide into the opposite lane so he can angle the minivan's headlights toward where I'm pointing. The first time he did this, I was sure that an unsuspecting driver was going to appear over a hilltop in front of us or come up on us from behind and smash into us. Then I realized that at one o'clock in the morning on this remote stretch of county road there is exactly zero traffic.

"Are we there yet?" Diana asks for perhaps the hundredth time.

"Almost," I respond as I have for the other ninety-nine. "Do you see anything?" I ask Peter.

"Nothing."

He pulls back into the right-hand lane and keeps going. I rub the condensation from my window with my shirtsleeve, then roll down the window and squint into the darkness. A wall of trees slides past in an unbroken line. It's hard to believe that somewhere in this dense climax forest of pine and mixed hardwoods is our new home. All we have to do is find it.

"This is it," Peter says at last, and I can hear the relief in his voice. "I'm sure of it. I recognize that big white pine. The access road is just past it."

Sure enough, when he pulls into the opposite lane and angles the headlights one more time, two faint tracks lead from the highway up and over a small rise. Anyone who didn't know better would think this was just another anonymous logging road, and a barely used road at that. No one would have any idea that anything of any consequence waits at the end. Which I suppose is the point.

"We're here!" I announce excitedly for Diana's benefit, then laugh when all three of us heave a simultaneous sigh.

Peter jockeys the trailer around until we are exactly perpendicular to the highway. "Ready?"

I check to see that Diana hasn't unbuckled herself again, then grip the edge of my seat. "Ready. Hold on!" I call over my shoulder.

Peter guns the engine and the minivan leaps forward. We hit the shoulder in a spray of gravel. The hill isn't terribly tall, but it's steep, the ruts deep and sandy, the hump in the middle covered with dried grasses that scrape against the undercarriage as we plow forward.

Halfway up, we lose momentum. The tires spin. Peter hunches over the steering wheel as if willpower alone could keep us moving. I can't help leaning forward as well. Even Diana rocks back and forth.

"Make her stop!" Peter barks.

"Diana! Sit still! Daddy's trying to drive."

We slow even more. It's so dark, with no point of reference I honestly can't tell if we're still moving. If we get stuck, if the trailer pulls us backward and we slew sideways and end up in the ditch, there's no way we're getting out without a tow. Assuming we can flag down one of the nonexistent cars traversing the highway and convince the imaginary driver to help us.

And then, miraculously, the road levels out and we crest the top. A few moments later the trailer does as well. Just as I am about to congratulate my husband on his most excellent off-road driving skills, the trees swallow us up and we careen blindly down the other side.

"Slow down!" I can't help yelling, though Peter is already jamming on the brakes as the trailer pushes us faster and faster down the hill. The minivan slams into an unseen pothole and bottoms out. Branches scrape the sides and lash my face. Quickly, I roll up my window.

When we come to a stop at the bottom, I have no idea if we're on the road at all. Peter peels his fingers from the steering wheel and takes a deep breath. His hands are shaking. So are mine.

"Again!" Diana squeals. "Do it again!"

We can only shake our heads. Clearly, our daughter's utter fearlessness and oversized sense of adventure are going to serve her well here. More than ever, I am convinced that moving to the lodge is the right thing to do. I've been calling this move "Our Grand Adventure" ever since our plan was conceived, which Diana thinks is funny and Peter thinks is overblown, but this really is going to be an adventure. Our friends think we're crazy to leave the comforts of civilization and move to a remote wilderness cabin. But conditions aren't going to be nearly as challenging as everyone seems to think. While it's true there's no phone line at the lodge, we can drive out to the highway and on to the nearest pay phone when we need to make a call. And we won't be entirely without electricity; we'll generate our own twice a day, morning and evening, just as Peter's family does at Christmas, which means we can cook on a regular stove and use a refrigerator and washer and dryer. We'll also have running water and indoor toilets thanks to the gravity-feed water tower and the pumphouse by the lake. And while for all practical purposes wc won't have central heat—I know from personal experience that in the dead of winter, the ancient oil-fired furnace in the basement can't begin to compete with the size of the rooms—we can layer on extra clothes and use kerosene space heaters as needed.

On the plus side, the scenery is going to be spectacular. It's hard to believe that tomorrow we could be tramping around in our very own woods, leaves crunching underfoot and squirrels gathering acorns while the chickadees chatter, maple and beech trees glowing red and gold against an azure sky. We can take out the canoe on our very own private lake whenever we like, catch perch and rock bass for our dinner, spend long winter evenings in front of a roaring fire, sipping drinks and reading Hemingway and Dostoyevsky while Diana sleeps on a bearskin rug at our feet, her cheeks flush with heat, while outside the wind rattles the windows and the snow blows.

Okay, so maybe I am a bit of a romantic, as Peter often claims. Realistically, I know our lives won't be nearly as idyllic as I'm making it sound. There will be firewood to cut, mosquitoes and black flies to deal with, rain and wind and cold. But weighed against the advantages, these are mere inconveniences. The only thing that matters is that we will be living in a place where our daughter will be able to thrive and grow.

We navigate the next four miles with only the light from the quarter-moon to guide us, the minivan's headlights slicing across the tree trunks like a laser, bare branches reaching for us like zombies in a horror movie. I'd forgotten how rough the road is, and how narrow. Peter's parents argue about the condition of this road all the time. His father wants to bring in a bulldozer to knock down the hills and straighten the curves and fill in the low spots with gravel. His mother wants the road to remain as it is. I used to take her side in the debate because I love the way that the lodge has been frozen in time, but now, as we lurch along in near-total darkness, Peter clenching the wheel and me digging my fingernails into the armrest and the edge of the seat, knowing we'll have to deal with the condition of this road every time we want to drive in or out, I begin to understand his father's thinking.

By the time we come to the security gate that spans the gap in the cliff, the clouds have moved in and what little moonlight there was is gone. If I hadn't known better, I'd have sworn we'd been kidnapped and driven to a secret rendezvous in the middle of nowhere—which is actually a fairly accurate way to describe our acreage now that I think about it. Peter's father had the gate installed three years ago after the lodge was broken into and vandalized. I used to think that this gate was an abomination, the chain-link fencing strung with concertina wire more suited to the entrance to a mental hospital, or a prison. Now I think it's beautiful. On the other side is quite possibly the only place on earth where my family will be safe.

"Are we there?" Diana asks yet again when we come to a stop.

"We're here," Peter says with a grin. He opens his door to get out and unlock the gate, then sits back down and reaches across the console and takes my hand.

"We did it, Jenny. We made it. We're home."

I squeeze his hand in return. Peter doesn't let go.

6

NOW
Rachel

Fifteen years in a mental hospital serving a self-imposed life sentence for a crime I am now almost certain I didn't commit is so far beyond the pale, to say I feel massively cheated and betrayed doesn't begin to cover it. It's hard to know who is the most deserving of my anger— my family, my therapists, or myself. Right now, I'm fingering my family. I can't believe they let me languish at the hospital all these years. I honestly can't recall a single instance in which Diana or Charlotte brought up the possibility of me getting out. I have no idea which of them is ultimately responsible for my unjust incarceration or if they are equally to blame, but I guarantee there are going to be some hard discussions with my so-called loved ones the minute I get home. If my therapist knew what I am planning, she'd say I need to let go of what happened in order to move on. But maybe I don't want to go forward. The answers I need don't lie in my future; they're buried in my past.

I tuck my stuffed bear into a corner of my duffel and zip the bag shut. White Bear is my constant, my most precious possession, the only thing that has traveled with me from home, to the hospital, and now back home again. White Bear is also the reason I spent my twelfth birthday in a straitjacket after one of my roommates took him while I was sleeping and hid him inside one of the toilet tanks in the community bathroom and I shoved her into the wall after she showed me where she'd stashed him. I didn't mean to give her a concussion. That said, having a reputation as someone who is not to be trifled with has definitely worked to my advantage. The incident has been blown all out of proportion over time—I've heard whispers that I put the girl in a coma or worse—but I don't care what people say about me as long as they keep their hands off my stuff.

I stand up and sling the duffel over my shoulder. The bag is heavy. Inside are my books: more than fifty Berenstain Bears titles, given to me by my therapists on special occasions over the years after my passion for bears became clear, along with two books of fairy tales I stole from the hospital library because I'm the only one who checks them out, so who's going to miss them? I've loved fairy tales since I was old enough to read them—the darker, the better—and I especially love the tales that feature bears: "Bearskin," "The Willow-Wren and the Bear," "Goldilocks and the Three Bears." Not the G-rated story everyone remembers from kids' books and cartoons, but the 1831 version in which the bears set Goldilocks on fire and drown her.

These along with a suitcase full of secondhand clothes Aunt Charlotte picked up for me at thrift shops and yard sales are all I have in the way of worldly possessions—not counting, of course, the acreage and the lodge. I've thought about signing my half of the property over to my sister more than once since Diana is the one living there and I had no intention of going back. Now I'm glad I didn't.

I pause in the doorway and take a last look around the room. The spider watches me warily from her corner. If she knows that something is different about today, she doesn't let on.

"Goodbye," I whisper. I don't tell her I'm not coming back.

I also didn't tell Scotty that I was leaving. I wanted to see him one last time, wanted to grab one final hug, wanted to remind him to brush his teeth every night so his breath doesn't stink and to steer clear of the orderlies who have it in for him. But Scotty will never understand why I get to go home and he does not, and the thought of trying to explain why it might be a long time before we see each other again is just too painful. I'm hoping that I can come and visit him before he forgets all about me, but the next days and weeks are so uncertain, I'd rather say nothing than make a promise I can't keep.

I head down to the lobby to sign out for the last time. It turns out it's easy to discharge yourself from a mental hospital if you're the one who put yourself there, which luckily for me I did when I recommitted myself after Diana's guardianship ended the day that I turned eighteen. All you need to do is tell your therapist you want to leave. Fill out the paperwork, wait three days in case you change your mind, then pick up your discharge instructions along with any prescriptions for your current meds, and you're good to go. Whether or not you're actually cured apparently isn't a deciding factor, which makes me wonder about all the people in similar circumstances who are walking around outside these hospital walls who shouldn't be. It took me longer to arrange for my ride than it did to arrange for my discharge.

Outside it's cold, mid-April, maybe forty-five or fifty degrees, with the occasional wind gust blowing across what's left of the snowbanks that cuts through me like I'm not wearing anything at all. My tennis shoes and jean jacket are nowhere close to adequate for the weather, but I'd rather take my chances with hypothermia than spend a minute longer than is absolutely necessary inside. Growing up in a mental hospital is every bit as *One Flew Over the Cuckoo's Nest* as it sounds—locked rooms, leather restraints, electroshock therapy, mood-altering drugs—but that was the point. I was warehoused.

Forgotten. I didn't so much fall through the cracks as willingly jump into them.

Now, of course, all of that has changed.

Instantly, my anger boils up thick and hot. I dial it down to a simmer and shelter against the building to shake out a cigarette. I've been thinking a lot about what I'll do if it turns out I didn't kill my mother. It's hard to know where to start. Most women my age have a job, a house or an apartment or a condo, a 401(k), a car. I don't even know how to drive. I can't cook or sew. I have no idea how to do a load of laundry or iron a shirt or hang a picture or run a dishwasher. I've never made a budget, or rented a movie, or shopped for groceries, or bought something online. Until last week, I'd never even made a phone call.

This is not to say that I am without skills. I know which wild plants are safe to eat and how to fix them, how to find my way in the woods without the sun, moon, or stars. I can swim like a tadpole, climb a tree like a bear, sit as still as an opossum. I can look at a set of tracks or a pile of scat and know immediately which animal made it and how long it's been since the animal left it behind. I know the differences between a mouse and a vole and a shrew, between a grass and a rush and a sedge, between a marsh and a bog and a fen, and the list goes on and on. I'm not helpless. I just need help.

At last the dark green late-model Jeep I'm expecting turns in at the end of the long driveway. I toss the cigarette on the sidewalk and wave. Trevor rolls down his window and waves back. He looks happy, as he should. I've promised to give him full access to the crime scene along with all the photos he wants to take in exchange for this ride. I may have also hinted at the possibility of an interview with Charlotte or Diana, though I have no idea if they'll agree to this, so I was careful not to promise. Either way, the level of access I can give him should be enough to take his story from a local-interest piece to a full-length feature article he can possibly place with a major newspaper or a national magazine. I'm his ticket to fame and fortune; he's my passport to the outside world. I think it's a fair trade.

The Jeep comes to a stop directly in front of me. Trevor gets out and goes around to open the back. "Is this everything?"

"This is it." I wave my hand dismissively at my luggage as if my lack of material possessions is a lifestyle choice and not something imposed on me by the life I chose. He loads my suitcase into the cargo area while I slide into the passenger seat with the duffel between my feet.

"You sure you don't want to put that in the back?" he asks as he gets in behind the wheel. "There's plenty of room."

"I'm good." There's no logical reason to keep my duffel bag close except that knowing White Bear is near enough to touch him if I need to makes me feel less nervous about what I'm about to do. And yes, I realize my therapist would have a field day with that.

"Suit yourself." He puts the Jeep into gear and we're off. I don't look back.

It feels strange to ride in a car, stranger still to ride in a car with a man who is for all practical purposes a stranger. I've known Trevor for years, but only in the context of the hospital, and always with Scotty around. I know he's Scotty's legal guardian, and I know he was casting about for a decade trying to figure out what he wanted to do, which is why he's only just now going back to school, and I know he loves wild places as much as I do, but that's about it. If he's read even half of what's been written about my family, he knows far more about me than I do about him. I'm not sure how I feel about that.

"I was surprised to get your call," he says as we pull out onto the highway. "Feeling better?"

At first, I don't know what he's talking about. Then I remember. "I'm fine, thanks. Those medication changes can really do a number on you. I appreciate your coming to get me."

"It's no trouble."

Given that he's about to put three hundred miles on his car today as a favor to me, I doubt this is the case, but I don't call him on it because—obviously—he's doing me a favor.

A housefly buzzes against the window glass. *Let me*

out! Let me out! it says over and over. I crack open the window and cup my hand over the fly and guide it gently to the opening. It takes off without so much as a thank-you. Flies aren't the best conversationalists. For that matter, neither am I. It's hard to know if keeping my thoughts to myself is something I learned because of all the hours I spent with my mother sitting silently in her observation blind, or if I would have been this reticent no matter how I was raised. I do know that I discovered early on that choosing when to speak and what to say was one of the few aspects of my hospital experience that I could control. I actually haven't spoken a word in group therapy in years—not out of stubbornness, as my therapists no doubt assumed, but because I had no interest in getting better. Aside from Scotty and Trevor, the only ones I spoke to regularly were the spiders. If Trevor is hoping that this car ride will turn up some juicy details for his article, he's going to be disappointed.

"Did you bring your copy of the police report?" I ask.

"It's in my bag in the back."

"Okay if I have a look?"

"Help yourself."

I twist around to reach between the seats and take out the manila folder and read the report carefully straight through. I'm looking specifically for references to me. Aside from the paragraph I focused on last time, there's not much. After I was found beside the highway, I was brought to the local emergency room, where doctors patched me up and gave me fluids and kept me for observation. Apparently, it took them a while to realize that the reason I didn't speak or move was not because I wouldn't but because I couldn't, though to be fair, mine was probably the first case of catatonia they had seen. They brought in a psychiatrist, who checked me out and sent me on to the Newberry Regional Mental Health Center for evaluation, and as far as the police report is concerned, my story ends there.

I page back to the photograph of the murder weapon. *Alleged* murder weapon, I correct, because before I can accept that this is the rifle that killed my parents, I need to understand why I see a different one in my visions. This Winchester Magnum is a monster; the kind of rifle a hunter would take on safari if she was planning to shoot dangerous game at close range. Definitely not a rifle an eleven-year-old girl could fire without doing herself serious injury, as the report rightly concludes. If I had fired this rifle, there would have been evidence of massive bruising on my shoulder, even after two weeks. The recoil alone should have broken my trigger finger and possibly my wrist or my arm—unlike the much lighter and smaller Remington I see in my visions, which any eleven-year-old with a minimum of instruction is perfectly capable of holding and firing properly.

And yes, as it happens, I do know quite a lot about rifles. The display cases in the gun room were empty when I lived at the lodge, but when the family came for Christmas

I used to sit on my great-grandfather's lap while we pored over photos from when the cases were full and he taught me each rifle's name and what it was used for: .22 long rifles for small game, Winchesters and Remingtons for medium game, larger rifles for wolf and deer, all the way up to a Mannlicher-Schoenauer big bore capable of bringing down a rhino—proof of which stood on a raised platform in the middle of our great room.

"Anything?" Trevor asks.

"I'm sorry?"

"Just wondering if anything's coming back. About those missing days," he adds when it's obvious I'm still not getting it.

"Oh. No. Nothing."

"Maybe you'll remember more after you get home."

"Maybe."

I don't tell him that regaining my memories is exactly what I'm hoping will happen, though the question of how I survived those two weeks is a long way down my priority list. I want to stand in the place where my parents died. Close my eyes and experience my vision in surround sound, high definition, on-the-spot-and-in-the-moment Technicolor. I want to see or hear something new, some critical missing detail that will put all my questions to rest, no matter how painful the answers might be. If it turns out that the Winchester is indeed the rifle that killed my parents, I am ready to accept that I didn't fire it. But just because I didn't shoot my mother doesn't mean that I am not responsible for setting in motion the events that destroyed my family. There has to be a reason I took the blame, even if I didn't pull the trigger. All I need to do is remember.

I slide the report back inside its folder and return the folder to Trevor's messenger bag. There's another reason I am not yet ready to accept its findings, a glaring omission that could have turned the official conclusion on its head if anyone knew.

Not only do I know a great deal about hunting rifles, I am a very good shot.

7

THEN
Jenny

The first thing we did when we moved in was clear out the gun room. For one thing, we don't need guns for protection. Black bears may be the top predator on our acreage, but they are also among the most timid and least aggressive bear species on the planet. And while we know we have at least two wolves hanging around because we've heard them howling on three separate occasions, we've never seen them and don't expect to. There's a nearly infinitesimal possibility that because of our acreage's unique configuration and extreme isolation it could be home to a passing cougar or a wolverine, but these animals are so rare in the Upper Peninsula—only twenty confirmed cougar sightings over the past decade, and wolverines quite possibly never lived in the state at all despite Michigan's nickname as "the Wolverine State"—that the odds of Peter or me stumbling across either are essentially zero. Bottom line: we're here to study the wildlife on our property, not to shoot it.

More to the point, there is no way we are going to allow so much as a single rifle on the premises as long as our daughter is in the house, let alone fifty-six. (Fifty-six!) It doesn't matter that the gun collection was kept in locked display cases, or that the ammunition was stored in locked drawers beneath, or that many of the rifles are rare and valuable museum-quality antiques that under any other circumstances should have been on display; children far less inquisitive than our daughter manage to get their curious little hands on deadly weapons all the time. It would be just our luck for Diana to find the one rifle in the single unlocked case that happened to have been put away loaded and accidentally shoot herself or us.

Peter and I documented everything with photos against the day that we might have to put it all back, then boxed up the rifles and ammunition and carted them off to a storage unit we rented in Marquette. When Peter's family came up for Christmas and his grandfather saw what we had done, I thought he was going to have a heart attack. But after Peter explained that it was this or install a security gate across the gun room's wide arched open doorway, which he knew his grandfather would have had a fit about because he had already made it clear that we were not to make any physical changes to the lodge, his grandfather backed down. I think the other relatives were secretly pleased. As far as I know, there's not a hunter in the bunch.

The second thing we did after we moved in was convert half of the old barn into his-and-hers office space. Luckily, Peter's grandfather's decree didn't extend to the outbuildings. We also set up an office for Diana between ours so she wouldn't feel left out, and so we can keep an eye on her while we're working. It's a beautiful space, the kind of dedicated learning area I would have killed for when I was her age, furnished with an antique child-sized desk and chair we found in one of the bedrooms along with an overstuffed armchair for reading and floor-to-ceiling shelves crammed with what might quite possibly be the largest collection of stuffed animals in the entire Upper Peninsula, and all the DK and *National Geographic Kids* nature books I could find. Peter thinks the NASA-approved star maps I plastered on the ceiling and the highly detailed mobile of the solar system I hung in the middle are a bit much, but we don't yet know which field of study will catch Diana's interest. The key to making this work, we both agree, is keeping our daughter occupied with interesting and challenging projects. There's nothing Diana hates more than being bored.

So far, it seems to be working. Naturally, there have been a couple of hiccups along the way, as you'd expect after making such a major lifestyle change, but aside from a dozen shredded stuffed animals, we made it through the winter without any major blowups or disasters. (Diana claimed she was dissecting her stuffed animal collection, which is actually rather charming and precocious when you think about it, considering that both of her parents are wildlife biologists—never mind that the toys she destroyed cost several hundred dollars to replace.) All in all, I think she's doing better.

I wish I could say the same for Peter. In hindsight, September was a terrible time for us to move because the amphibians he was planning to study were about to go into hibernation. Sure, there was wood to chop and snow to shovel and gas for the generator to fetch and groceries to purchase and books and scientific journals to catch up on along with an assortment of household repairs to keep him busy, but for a highly intelligent and creative person like my husband, these were hardly a satisfactory trade-off for teaching. Add in the fact that last winter was especially brutal, with fewer sunny days than normal and twice the average snowfall, and it's no wonder he got depressed.

To be honest, I'm struggling, too. I should have realized that moving four hundred miles from the place where William Yang died wouldn't be far enough to purge me of his ghost. I think about him every day. Every time Diana runs into a room, or slides down the stairway railing, or rides her bike around and around in our circular gravel driveway, or bumps her head, or skins her knee, I think about how these are things that William Yang will never do and my heart breaks all over again. At times the weight of his death is so crushing I think maybe I should go for counseling. I understand I wasn't responsible for what happened. No one could have foreseen that the boy would wander into our yard and fall into our pool, and if that lack of foresight means that I am to blame, then his mother is, too; how did her son find his way into our backyard in the first place, and why didn't she keep a closer eye on him? Yet I still feel as though I need to somehow make amends. I read in his obituary that William's favorite toy was a stuffed teddy bear, so I decided to study black bears in his honor. Peter thinks I should study the half-dozen bald eagle breeding pairs that nest in the swampy area by the lake, but I've always loved bears, and I honestly feel that my research into their numbers and habits will make an important contribution. A healthy population of top predators indicates a healthy ecosystem, but all around the world, balanced ecosystems are becoming increasingly rare as wildlife comes under pressure due to environmental destruction and human encroachment that force animals who have no business living in close proximity to get along. The opportunity to study an area that's been in ecological stasis for decades offers a unique and valuable perspective, and this isn't only my opinion; the biology professor at Northern Michigan University I consulted, and who agreed to act as my ad hoc advisor, thinks so, too.

Which is why, after reading everything about *Ursus americanus* I could get my hands on over the winter, Diana and I are crouched behind a large boulder near the base of the east cliff on this chilly April afternoon waiting for the bear Diana named "Rapunzel" to come out of her den. Technically, Diana is supposed to be with Peter today per our agreement that she would split her days equally between us now that we are both back in the field, but Peter says her noisy footsteps and nonstop chatter scare his frogs away. I guess my bears are more tolerant.

The day is sunny but cold. All the snow has melted except on the shady side of the boulder we're hiding behind. My feet are frozen, but I stand as still as possible and keep my binoculars trained on the opening. The den is dug beneath the roots of a large pine growing partway up the side of the cliff. Because of the late start last fall, this was the only den I could find before all the bears on our acreage holed up for the winter, which means that this is the only bear I was able to collar while she hibernated in her den, and thus is the only bear I'll be able to track throughout the spring, summer, and fall—an inauspicious start to my research project by anybody's standard. Next year, I'm going to have to do a lot better.

"I'm cold," Diana whines, and not for the first time. "I'm tired. I'm hungry. I want to go home."

I lower the glasses and squat down beside her to give her a hug. Her nose is dripping, and her cheeks are red.

"I know you're hungry, sweetie. Mommy is, too. But you know we can't bring anything to eat when we're in the field."

A bear's sense of smell is seven times more powerful

than a dog's, and bears can pick up a scent from as much as a mile away. After feeding off her own fat reserves for six months and nursing any cubs, I guarantee this bear is a lot hungrier than we are. Even something as insignificant as a granola bar or a handful of nuts in a ziplock bag could make us a target.

"Just a little longer, I promise. You want to see Rapunzel's cubs, don't you?"

Diana nods.

"And you remember Mommy promised that if you stay very still and don't frighten her cubs, you can name them?"

Diana nods again. "How many babies does she have?"

"We won't know until they come out of their den."

Which is another lesson learned. If I had waited to collar this bear until after she'd given birth, not only would I know how many cubs she'd had, I would have been able to weigh and measure the cubs and take blood samples for DNA testing to begin establishing their family tree. Still, crawling into this bear's den while she slept and putting the radio collar on her knowing that she was capable of killing me with a single swipe of her paw was such an amazing experience, I think I can be forgiven for being overeager.

I train the glasses on the opening again. Black bears commonly give birth to between two and four cubs, but the number of fertilized eggs that implant in the mother's uterus after she mates in June depends on how much she weighs the next fall when she goes into her den. Black bears will eat almost anything: blueberries, strawberries, raspberries, thimbleberries, Juneberries, buckthorn berries, blackberries, and dogwood berries; wild cherries and apples; acorns, beechnuts, and hazelnuts; grasses, leaves, and clover; bees, ants, and hornets. Normally their varied diet affords them plenty of opportunity to bulk up, but the summer just past was very dry. From all over the Upper Peninsula there were reports of hungry black bears raiding gardens and bird feeders and beehives and garbage cans—even killing a chicken or a lamb when the opportunity arose. This bear was so underweight when she went into her den, we'll be lucky if she has even a single cub—a possibility I have been extremely careful never to mention in front of Diana.

At last, I see movement. I tap Diana's arm and hand off the binoculars. "Shh. Get ready. She's coming out."

Diana lifts the binoculars, which are far too big and heavy for her, and squints through them like a miniature naturalist. She looks so cute, my heart swells. I make a mental note to pick up a smaller pair for her as soon as I'm able to get to a sporting goods store.

"I see her! I see her!"

"Shh. Remember, we have to be very quiet."

Even without the binoculars I can see that this bear has lost a great deal of weight. She stands in the opening for a long time, blinking as if she is surprised to discover this bright new world of color and light, then slides down the rocky scree not fifty feet from the boulder we're hiding behind and lumbers toward a patch of fresh, green grass.

"Where are her babies?"

"Shh. Just wait."

"I don't *want* to wait. I want them to come out *now*."

Diana stomps her foot and smacks the binoculars against the boulder, then plunks down on the ground with her arms crossed and her back toward the den. I snatch up the binoculars. Thankfully, the rubber field casing did what it was supposed to do. I grit my teeth. It's all I can do to keep from smacking her. I understand she's cold and hungry and tired; that Diana is not a naturalist, but rather a nine-year-old girl with a short fuse and a penchant for throwing temper tantrums. Expecting her to watch and wait with me for hours is too much to ask.

She sticks out her lower lip and refuses to look at me or to speak. As I train the binoculars on the opening again, I can't help but smile. Diana has no clue that in giving me the silent treatment she is doing exactly as I want.

I watch and wait for a long time. Just as I am beginning to think that my prediction has come true, and there will be no cub for Diana to name, I see movement. I can hear whimpering from inside the den as Rapunzel ranges farther and farther away.

"Diana. Come here." I pull her to her feet and point her toward the opening and hand her the binoculars as Rapunzel's cub gathers the courage to leave the only home it has ever known and crawls into the sunlight.

"Oh!" she exclaims. "Look!"

Quickly, she claps her hand over her mouth. But I don't scold her for her outburst. I am just as surprised.

The cub is white.

White. I can hardly believe what I'm seeing. Albino bears are extremely rare. I can't recall a single sighting in the Upper Peninsula, possibly not in the entire state. An albino black bear was shot by a hunter years ago in Pennsylvania—which, unbelievably, was perfectly legal— and a mother black bear and her albino cub were spotted walking along a highway in Ontario more than a decade before that, but these are the only instances that I'm aware of. There's a subspecies of black bears in British Columbia called "Kermode bears" in which twenty percent of the population is white, but their coloring is the result of a genetic mutation and not true albinism. Outside British Columbia, the odds of seeing a white bear drop to some-thing like one in a million. *One in a million.* Incredible to think that such a rare and special bear cub was born right here in our very own woods.

"Is it a ghost?" Diana whispers.

"It's an albino. This means Rapunzel's cub was born without any coloring in its skin or fur, like the pictures in your coloring books before you color them. Native Americans call white bears 'spirit bears' or 'ghost bears,'" I add, which makes her smile.

"I'm going to call him 'White Bear.'"

"White Bear is a great name. Here. Let Mommy have

a look." I reach for the binoculars, and in the awe of the moment Diana gives them up without a struggle. The cub looks like a small white cloud against the den's opening: pure white fur, pink eyes, tiny pink nose. It seems healthy, maybe five or six pounds, well within the range I'd expect for a cub that was born while its mother slept last January. I have no idea what its albinism will mean for its future. Certainly, its coloration will make it easier for me to spot it, but it will also put the cub at a distinct disadvantage. Up to half of all cubs die during their first year anyway from drowning, den cave-ins, hypothermia, starvation, and infections from injuries. That this cub is white will make it particularly vulnerable to the biggest threat facing young bears: other bears looking for a quick and easy meal.

I hand the binoculars back to Diana and take out my camera. Peter is going to go nuts when he sees these pictures.

Suddenly, a rock flies into the camera frame. The cub startles and shies away. Before I can process where the rock came from and why, there is another.

I whirl around as Diana is about to throw a third.

"Diana! What are you doing? Stop that!" I drop my camera into my pocket and grab her arm to pry the rock from her fingers. She pulls loose and throws the rock anyway. The cub squeals from the unlucky hit and tumbles head over heels down the slope. Diana laughs and claps.

"Why did you do that?" I yell as the cub scrambles to its feet and runs off squealing to its mother. "That wasn't nice. You could have hurt the cub. You could have killed it!"

"Mommy. Look." Diana points behind me.

I turn around. The cub's mother is staring straight at me, wagging her head slowly from side to side and growling a warning.

Quickly, I push Diana behind me. "Stay absolutely still," I hiss. "Don't move."

The bear runs several paces toward us and stops, swinging its head and chuffing. I scoop up Diana and plop her down on top of the boulder as the bear raises up on its hind legs and paws the air, then drops down on all fours and lands with a heavy *thwump*. I swear, I can feel the ground shake.

"Is she dancing?" Diana sounds more curious than afraid.

"It's a warning. She's telling us to leave her baby alone and go away."

The bear runs forward again. I step out from behind the boulder and stand as tall as I am able. The key to facing down a black bear is to make yourself look and sound as threatening as possible. Lie down and play dead, and you will be. Or so I've read.

"Go on! That's enough. Get back! Go away!" I shout and wave my arms.

"Go away!" Diana echoes.

"That's right. Good girl. Make as much noise as you can."

We clap and yell. The bear raises up on its hind legs

again and opens its mouth wide and roars. Saliva drips from its jaws. We're so close, I swear I could count its teeth. This bear could easily snatch my daughter off the boulder if it wanted to. But to do that, it's going to have to go through me.

"Mommy?" Diana says in a small voice. "Is Rapunzel going to eat us?"

"Not today," I reply through gritted teeth. I run straight toward the bear, yelling and flapping my arms. "Go on! Get out of here! Leave! Go!" If I had a rifle, I swear I'd shoot it.

The bear drops to all fours. Behind it, the cub mewls. The bear looks from me to the cub and back to me; then with a final warning chuff, it turns and stalks off into the forest. The cub follows.

I sink down with my back against the boulder. My hands are shaking, and my legs are so weak I don't think I could run from a kitten. If Peter finds out about what just happened, I'm going to be studying bald eagles whether I want to or not. First thing tomorrow, I'll start construction on a bait station with an observation blind. It's just too dangerous to observe bears out in the open. Or at least it is as long as my daughter is around.

"Can I get down now?"

"Of course. Scooch over here to Mommy."

I get shakily to my feet and hold out my arms as Diana slides across the boulder and jumps into them. I hug her until she squirms, then set her on her feet.

"Did you see her, Mommy? Did you *see* her? She was so *mad*!" Diana shifts excitedly from foot to foot. Her eyes dance.

Once again, I am in awe of my daughter's fearlessness. Diana has to know that this wasn't a game, that we were in real danger, that things could have turned out very differently if the bear had decided to attack.

"Diana, why did you throw rocks at the cub? He's just a baby. You could have hurt him. How would you like it if somebody threw rocks at you?"

"It was a speerment. I wanted to see if the cub would run and he did!"

An experiment. Fury replaces terror. I can't believe she threw rocks at the cub for no reason other than she wanted to see what it would do if she did. What kind of person even thinks of such a thing? Where is her compassion? Her empathy and fellow feeling for a creature smaller and weaker than she is? What in God's name is *wrong* with my daughter?

I take a deep breath and stash my camera and binoculars in my backpack. "Come on. Rapunzel and White Bear aren't coming back today. It's time to go home."

As Diana trots along cheerfully beside me, it occurs to me that once again, my daughter has gotten exactly what she wanted. Maybe the real reason she threw rocks at the cub was to make the bears go away so we would go home. Or maybe I'm giving her too much credit. Either way, I can't have her interfering with my research like this again.

I gave up my career once because of her, I am not going to do it a second time. I refuse to spend my days at the lodge supervising my daughter while Peter is in the field. There has to be a way to work things out. Diana's a smart girl; she can learn.

She'll have to. Because this spring and summer, I am going to spend all my waking hours in the field and then some. I need to get as much work done as I can over the next six months, because while I won't be able to confirm it until I can get to a drugstore, I am 99.9 percent certain that I am pregnant.

8

NOW
Rachel

I've been thinking a lot during this drive about what I'm going to say to my sister. Our relationship has always been complicated. Part of the reason is the nine-year age difference. But the bigger part, I think, is that we are just so different. We may share the same genetic material, but our DNA definitely came together in two distinct and disparate combinations. We don't even look alike. Diana is the classic fair-skinned, blue-eyed blonde, while I'm your typical brown-haired, brown-eyed girl. Diana is tall, lithe, and beautiful as a model. As for me, let's just say I'm not the kind of person anyone would notice in a crowded room, and leave it at that.

Despite our differences, we spent a lot of time together when we were growing up because we had no one else, though it was hard to find things to do that interested us both. A board game that was suitable for a thirteen-year-old can't be played with a sister who's only four. As a result, we often made up our own games. Many of the games we played were based on fairy tales, which—considering that we were two children living virtually alone in a vast and nearly impenetrable forest—was not a stretch. Acting out Hansel and Gretel was an obvious choice. We also liked Rapunzel and Red Riding Hood. Once when I was pretending to be Robin Hood and Diana was chasing me as the sheriff of Nottingham, I lost my grip on the rope swing that hung from the branch of a sturdy maple that extended over a deep ravine and broke my arm. Looking back, I can see that the games we played often had an element of danger to them, but that was what made them so exciting. I can honestly say that the times when I was alone with my sister were the only times that I felt truly alive.

Aside from fairy tales, the only other interest we have in common is our fondness for bears. During my early years at the hospital, whenever Diana and Charlotte would come to visit, we'd go to a fast-food restaurant, or to a movie if the Tahqua Land Theatre in Newberry was showing something G-rated. But after we went to Oswald's Bear Ranch the summer that I was fourteen, there was never a question as to where we'd go. We'd bring along a bag of apples and take turns tossing them over the tall double chain-link fence. I liked feeding the yearlings best because they were more energetic than the adults and would stand up on their hind legs and beg. Once I had my picture taken with a cub.

I understand that a lot of people have mixed feelings about keeping wild animals in captivity, and I do, too. But Oswald's is strictly rescue, no breeding. The cubs live in one enclosure, the yearlings in another, and the males and females each have their own. Naturally, I would have preferred to see the bears roaming free. But when an animal isn't capable of living in the wild by itself for whatever reason, short of euthanizing it, which I am adamantly opposed to, what are you supposed to do? You'd be surprised how often a neglected or abused bear, or an orphaned cub, needs a home.

That the largest bear rescue facility in the entire United States was only ten miles from the hospital where I was incarcerated always seemed miraculous to me. I used to dream about going to work for Oswald's, either as a paid employee or as a volunteer—I didn't care which. I'd sell tickets, or stock the gift shop, or collect food scraps from the area's restaurants and grocery stores and schools and hospitals as feed for the bears— I'd even clean the restrooms if that was what they wanted me to do as long as it meant that I could be around bears.

But as I got older, I realized that this was never going to happen. How could I do anything that would bring me pleasure knowing it was my fault my parents would never enjoy anything ever again? I lost my right to personal indulgence the moment I pulled that trigger.

Unless, of course, I didn't.

Once again, my anger threatens to boil over. My therapist would say that anger is a negative emotion that needs to be eliminated or kept under control. But I know better. My anger fuels me, propels me, gives me the motivation to do what I have to do. *Fifteen years*. I repeat the words over and over in my head like a mantra.

"There's a roadside park up ahead," Trevor says. "Do you need to stop?"

"I wouldn't mind a smoke."

He turns in and parks. Ours is the only car. Later in the season this roadside park will be crowded with picnickers and tourists, but for now, it's just us. My family had a picnic here once. We were on our way to Tahquamenon Falls and had been planning to eat when we got to the park, but we stopped here even though we were only an hour from home because my sister kept complaining that she was hungry.

I walk over to the picnic table where we sat that day and shake out a cigarette. Diana's and my names are carved into the top. I remember my mother scolded my father for defacing the table, but I think she only did this because she was our mom and she thought she had to. There were plenty of other names cut into the tabletop, so what could it matter if our father added two more?

I brush away a winter's worth of pine needles and run

my fingers over the letters. We were sitting at this table eating our sandwiches and tossing potato chips to the chipmunks who came to beg when a man came up and asked if we'd seen his little girl. She was about my age and height, he said, only she had long blond hair instead of brown, and she was wearing pink leggings and a pink fleece jacket and pink mittens and a pink scarf.

We stashed our lunch in the car so the chipmunks couldn't get to it (though I emptied the bag of chips beneath the table for them first) and joined the impromptu search party, which soon became a formal search and rescue when the Michigan State Police arrived after someone called 911. The girl was found eventually beneath a pile of brush at the bottom of a steep gully. Everyone assumed she had been running and didn't see the drop-off and that was why she fell, though how she ended up almost completely covered in leaves and branches was a mystery.

Seeing her lying on the ground with her eyes open though she wasn't moving made a big impression on me. Until then it had never occurred to me that someone my age could die, or that the woods might not be safe. Of course, I had no way of knowing then that in a few short weeks, my parents would also be dead—or that I too would be lost.

Trevor comes out of the bathrooms carrying two cans of Coke. He waves when he sees me. I raise my hand to let him know that I see him and that I'll be there in a minute, then take a last drag on my cigarette and toss the butt on the sidewalk. A flock of sparrows scavenging along the walkway scatters and regroups. I could listen in on their conversation if I wanted to, but right now I'm more concerned with what's going on inside my own head. I haven't thought about that girl in years, yet I remember every detail of that day. I remember the dead girl's father was wearing blue jeans and a red plaid shirt, that he had a salt-and-pepper beard, and that he was bald. I remember thinking that it looked like his hair had slid down off the top of his head and gotten caught by his chin. I remember my mother and father and sister were eating ham and cheese sandwiches while mine was peanut butter and jelly. I remember that Aunt Charlotte didn't come with us even though I'd wanted her to because she had plans with the man I called "Uncle Max," though he wasn't really my uncle. I remember my mother telling me that I had to finish my apple before I could eat my brownie, so I ate three bites and dropped it on the ground on purpose. I remember I talked to the girl before she died. She had a jump rope and wanted me to take a turn. I remember she ran into the woods crying after I told her I didn't want to. I remember her eyes were open when we found her, but she wasn't looking at anything. I remember her pink scarf was gone.

And yet I remember nothing about the day my parents died. I asked my therapist once if she thought I was cursed like in a fairy tale because so many people I knew had died. "Do you think you're cursed?" she'd asked, which I didn't answer because by then I'd learned that answering a question like that only led to more and it wasn't a subject I wanted to dissect. If I had, the answer would have been yes. I used to wonder how the girl's family was dealing with her death. I hoped they were doing better than me.

Back at the car, Trevor hands me one of the Cokes. I appreciate the gesture because I don't have any money. There was no need for cash at the hospital, and theft was a serious and constant problem. Diana and I have a joint bank account, but I don't know how much is in it, and she's the only one with an ATM card. To be honest, I've never paid much attention to the reports our financial advisors send over. I'm thinking that it's time for me to get more involved.

Trevor finishes his Coke and tosses the empty in the back of the Jeep, and we hit the road. Two hours down, one hour to go. I stare out the window as the miles roll by. Trees, trees, and more trees, until at last, the landscape starts to look familiar. The trees are bigger than I remember, and the brush alongside the road is taller and denser, but call it instinct, or muscle memory, or just a gut feeling—somehow, I know we're close.

"Slow down. We're almost there. We're looking for a big white pine. The entrance road is just past it."

And then the tree is exactly as I remember, looming above us. Trevor turns where I point, and the Jeep takes the hill without breaking a sweat. My parents liked to tell a funny story about how they almost didn't make it up this hill the first night they arrived at the lodge because they were driving a minivan and pulling a heavy trailer loaded with all their stuff. They were so afraid they were going to get stuck that the next day, when my father went to Marquette to return the rental trailer, he came back driving a four-wheel-drive Suburban. He always called the experience their "baptism by woods road," and laughed when he said it, though I didn't understand what he meant until I grew up.

We follow the road's twists and curves, dodging potholes as big as duck ponds and staying away from the edges in the low places that look like solid ground but will suck your vehicle in up to its axles if you're not careful. "My father taught me how to drive on roads like this," Trevor says after I remark on his expertise. "All of my friends knew how to drive before we were old enough to get our licenses."

I nod, thinking: *My father never got the chance to teach me*.

We stop when we come to the security gate. "What is this place? Fort Knox?" he asks, which happens to have been another of my father's jokes. "I hope you remember the combination."

"I do if they haven't changed it."

I get out and enter a combination of my and my sister's birth dates and the gate swings open. Motion sensors close and lock the gate automatically behind us.

The road smooths out when we near the shore. The lake is just visible through the trees, a thin strip of silver sparkling in the afternoon sunlight. I roll down the window and drink in the long-forgotten smell of pine needles and rotting leaves. This lake belongs to me, as does every rock, every bush, every tree. Or more correctly, half of it does. Still, it's amazing to think that this beautiful, pristine forest is mine, and I can do with it as I wish. Native peoples never bought into the idea of land ownership, but I can understand its appeal.

We rumble across a mossy wooden bridge that spans one of the feeder streams that empty into our lake, pass through a double row of pin oaks my great-great-grand-father planted to form a green tunnel in the summer worthy of a Southern plantation, and turn onto a hard-packed circular gravel driveway.

"Wow," Trevor breathes when we come to a stop. He rolls down his window and sticks out his head and looks up. "I've heard about this place, but, just—wow."

After fifteen years, even I'm impressed. My childhood home looks straight out of a fairy tale, a mist-shrouded castle, mysterious and otherworldly, and so at odds with its wilderness setting, it seems to have been designed and placed by a cosmic hand. People say you can't go home again because all the things you remember from your childhood will seem diminished and small, but the hunting lodge my great-great-grandfather built is impressive by anyone's standard: a massive two-story log cabin made of

Oregon pine he had trucked in so he wouldn't have to cut a single native tree, with wide fieldstone steps and stained-glass casement windows and a magnificently extravagant weathered green copper roof.

Inside there is a kitchen and a dining room and a library and a game room and a music room and a great room with a matched split-fieldstone fireplace at one end and a wide balcony at the other. Ten bedrooms, four big bathrooms that used to be bedrooms, three porches, a carriage house, a tennis court, and the old barn where my parents had their offices. Every inch sown with memories: the screened-in side porch where Diana and I used to play on rainy days, the sleeping porch above it where we would retreat to on hot summer nights. The Michigan basement under the back half of the lodge with its low ceiling and packed-dirt floor and scaling limestone block walls that we used to pretend was a dungeon, the oil-fired furnace in the middle with its big round belly and protruding arms our fire-breathing dragon.

The lodge where I grew up.

The lodge where my parents died.

My home.

"Where do you want me to park?" Trevor asks.

"Here in front is fine." I could direct him around to the side and go in through the kitchen door, but I'm going to have to face what happened on the other side of this door sooner or later, and I choose sooner. If Diana and

Charlotte have managed to figure out a way to live with the family tragedy, then so can I.

Still, just looking at the front door makes me ill. Charlotte says the oak parquet floor where my parents bled out has been torn out and replaced, but I don't need to see the bloodstained boards to see myself holding the rifle, my parents' ruined bodies, blood on my hands and on my clothes.

I am standing over my mother with the rifle.

The daughter did not fire the rifle.

Either I shot my mother with the Remington, or my father shot her with the Winchester. Both can't be right. I *have* to know which is true. All I need to do is remember.

I take a deep breath, walk purposefully up the steps, and open the front door.

9

THEN
Jenny

Two weeks until Christmas, our second since we moved to the lodge, and I think I can honestly say that I've never been dreading the holiday more. I'm not a purist when it comes to holiday traditions by any stretch of the imagination; many is the winter I've wished we were jetting off to a Caribbean island instead of driving north to join Peter's extended family for Christmas at the lodge yet again. But now that Peter and I are hosting the festivities instead of merely attending them, it's fallen to us to get everything right.

We've spent the past two weeks doing nothing but decorating. It's a good thing my and Peter's research subjects are asleep. The chandeliers in the great room have been draped with fresh pine boughs that Peter cut in the surrounding woods. Considering that each of the three cast-iron and deer-antler chandeliers is eight feet in diameter and hangs sixteen feet above the floor, this decorating was no small feat. The stairway railings have been wrapped with more of the same, the hand-forged iron curtain rods above all the windows and doors festooned with swaths of cedar and red holly berries that Peter gathered from the boggy area down by the lake. I've popped enough corn to feed an army to make garlands for not one, not two, but three Christmas trees—one in the great room, another on the stairway landing, and a third outside in the yard—and strung miles of fresh cranberries we bought at the grocery store because we forgot to gather the wild cranberries from our bog and there was no way I was going out in a foot of snow and fifteen-degree weather to try to collect them. (Though if anyone asks, Peter and I are prepared to say that this is exactly what I did.) My fingers are so sore I can barely hold a needle. The linens in all ten bedrooms have been washed and pressed—Peter's grandmother insists that the sheets and pillowcases be ironed—and the everyday coverlets exchanged for the red-and-green Christmas-themed quilts his great-grandmother made. All the furniture in the great room has been dusted, as has the taxidermy, to which Diana added a sprig of holly behind each of her favorites' ears.

We went through this same routine last year, of course, but this year I'm doing everything with a two-month-old baby. Fortunately, my sister is coming this afternoon, because there's still a ton of cleaning to do. The lodge was nowhere near spotless when we moved in, and it will never lose that musty old-cabin smell no matter how much we air it out, but now that we are living here full-time, I feel as though I should at least try to chip away at the decades-long accumulation of dirt.

I'm standing on a stepstool brushing down the fireplace mantel with a feather duster so I can set up the hand-carved olive-wood nativity scene that Peter's grandfather brought back from Jerusalem when the front door opens. A chill sweeps the room. Peter comes in carrying an armload of firewood and drops it on the growing pile beside the hearth. Diana adds the two small pieces she's carrying as well.

"You look whipped," he says as he brushes himself off. Sawdust and wood chips rain down on the floor. "Why don't you go upstairs and lay down until Charlotte gets here?"

"You don't mind taking over?"

"Of course not. Take all the time you need."

"Mommy is whipped?" Diana asks as I hand Peter the feather duster. "Who whipped her?"

"'Whipped' means Mommy is very tired," Peter patiently explains.

I leave my husband to instruct our daughter in the finer points of English idioms and head for the stairs. Diana is so cute when she takes things at face value. Peter and I have learned not to tell her it's time to hit the sack, or that she should keep her eye on the ball, or that we're going to run to the store, or that it's raining cats and dogs. Poor Diana was so disappointed after that last one when she ran to the window expecting to see actual kittens and puppies falling from the sky, she threw a book through the glass. That part wasn't so cute.

My bed is calling to me—another saying I will never speak in front of my literal-minded daughter—but I stop first at the room we set up as a nursery to look in on the baby. The baby is sleeping peacefully, as I knew she would be. Our second daughter is an absolute joy, perfect in every way: sweet rosy cheeks, tiny bow of a mouth, a tuft of baby-fine hair sticking straight up on the top of her head, and with the cutest scattering of tiny red freckles across her cheeks; quiet, calm, happy. I can't resist stroking one cheek with my finger. Her eyes remain closed, but the corners of her mouth turn up in a sleepy smile.

Not for the first time, I marvel at her even temperament. If I had done something like this with Diana, she'd have woken up screaming. This baby is the exact opposite of our first daughter in every way, as if the Universe realized it messed up big-time and was trying to make amends. When Diana was this age, her screams were so loud, our ears would ring. When this baby is hungry or needs her diaper changed or is just feeling lonely and wants to be picked up, she squeaks. I used to nurse Diana to sleep in my rocking chair, then dislodge her oh-so-carefully from my breast, carry her gently to her crib, lay her down as softly as humanly possible on the genuine sheepskin that was supposed to promote sleeping, and slowly, ever so slowly slide my hands out from beneath her while holding my breath and praying that she would stay asleep—only to have her wake up screaming the second my hands broke contact. This baby I could literally drop into her crib after nursing her to sleep and she'd snuggle happily into her blankets. (Not that I would, but I could.) I used to think that Diana's difficulties were my fault because of my inexperience, and that I was a bad mother. It's nice to know the problem wasn't me.

I leave my sweet baby to her sweeter dreams and draw the window shades in the master bedroom, then kick off my shoes and collapse on top of the bed. My to-do list swims in my head: sweep up the sawdust and woodchips Peter left by the hearth, hang the front door wreath, wash the mountain of dishes that have been accumulating on the kitchen counter for days, go to the post office and pick up the box of antique ornaments I ordered to replace the ones that Diana broke and cross my fingers that they are similar enough that Peter's grandparents won't notice. But gradually, my thoughts become less organized. I am washing dishes at the big farmhouse sink while Diana dries. Diana is using the sheepskin she slept on as a baby as a towel. The sheepskin turns into an actual sheep that jumps out of her hands and *baa*s as Diana giggles and feeds it bite-sized pieces of leftover chocolate cake.

I wake to the sound of Diana's laughter coming from

the baby's room. I sit up groggily and swing my feet over the side of the bed and scrub my hands over my face. The wind-up alarm clock on the nightstand says I was asleep for half an hour, but if anything, I am more tired now than when I lay down.

Diana giggles again. Of course, if she's playing with the baby, this means that the baby is also awake, which means she will need to be changed and fed whether she complains about being wet and hungry or not. I slip my feet into my shoes and start for the door.

"Jenny!" Charlotte exclaims when I step into the hallway. "Peter said you were asleep. I wasn't going to wake you—I was just going to sneak a peek at the baby."

"Char! Oh, wow—it's so good to see you! You look great. It's been way too long."

We embrace, then stand back and look each other over, then laugh and sink into each other's arms again. Charlotte smells of fresh air and snow and cold. The long blonde hair I remember has been buzzed short on the sides and streaked with pink on top. The lip stud is also new. She's wearing a cream-colored natural wool Highlands-style cable sweater with an Inca-look peasant skirt paired with hiking boots and thick woolen socks and huge dangling found-object earrings I have no doubt she made herself.

"I like your look," I say when we pull apart again. I reach up and touch one of the earrings, which sets it jangling.

"Thanks. Wish I could say the same for yours."

"Hey, no fair. I just woke up. Wait till you see me after we dress for dinner tonight. The servants have a wonderful meal prepared."

Charlotte laughs and we embrace again. It's hard to keep my hands off her. When we were younger, we were never close. My sister was always the creative one, the wild child, while I was as responsible and mature as you'd expect of the older sibling. Now that we are adults, I like to think that my sensibleness has tempered her lack of self-control and that some of her exuberance has rubbed off on me. Her wild side still gets her into trouble; Charlotte's just off a bad breakup with an abusive misogynist she had no business hooking up with in the first place. She also recently gave up her receptionist job at an insurance agency to make a living selling her jewelry, a plan I am one-hundred-percent certain is going to fail, though I would never tell her. At any rate, the fact that she's not working means she's able to come and visit, so there is that. I'm hoping to talk her into staying on indefinitely. While I would never admit it to Peter, after more than a year with only the three of us rattling around this big, empty house, I'm lonely. I have no idea if wilderness life will suit my bohemian sister, but we certainly have the room.

"Come see the baby," I say when Diana laughs again.

I lead Charlotte into the nursery. For a fraction of a second, I think that Diana is tickling the baby. Then I see the pillow she's holding over the baby's face.

"Diana! *What are you doing?*"

I rush across the room and grab her arm and push her away and snatch the baby out of her crib. The baby is limp, her lips and skin tinged blue. I collapse into the rocking chair and pound the baby's back and pinch her cheeks until her coloring returns to pink. She draws a deep shuddering breath, then looks up at me and reaches for a strand of my hair and coos.

Charlotte drops to her knees beside me. Her shocked expression no doubt mirrors my own.

"My God. That was awful! Is the baby all right? Why did Diana do that?"

"Diana is—unpredictable," I manage. I look at my daughter standing next to the baby's crib with the pillow still in her hands, watching us as calmly and unconcernedly as if she hadn't just witnessed me bring her sister back to life, and shudder. If Diana had held the pillow over the baby's face a few seconds longer . . . if Charlotte and I had lingered a bit more in the hallway . . . "I don't know why she did that. Sibling rivalry, I guess."

"That wasn't sibling rivalry. Sibling rivalry is when you used to pinch my arm or pull my hair. Diana was trying to kill her."

"Oh, I'm sure she didn't mean to. I doubt she even understands what could have happened."

It can't be as bad as it looked. Maybe Diana was only going to put the pillow under the baby's head, and I came in at precisely the wrong moment and misunderstood what she was doing.

I hand the baby to Charlotte and pull Diana onto my lap.

"Diana, honey, why did you put the pillow over your sister's face? Don't you know you could have hurt her? She could have stopped breathing."

She nods. "I know. I like it when she stops breathing. Her face changes colors."

"Her— You've done this before?"

She nods again. "Lots of times. Am I in trouble?"

Fear, revulsion, and horror sweep over me. I honestly thought that Diana would get better in time; that if we showered her with love and affection, her hard edges would soften. But what she did wasn't a mistake—this was a deliberate attempt to see how close she could come to killing her sister. The marks on the baby's face that I thought were freckles aren't freckles at all—they're burst micro-vessels from a chronic lack of oxygen. Diana *has* done this before, not once but many times. In my darkest moments I used to wonder if we should send her away, but how can we? She's our child. We're her parents. We love her.

Now I wonder if whatever is wrong with my daughter is something that all the love in the world can't fix. I can't bear to think of her locked away in an institution, but what else can we do?

Yet how can I sacrifice one daughter to save the other? Maybe there's a new drug that will help her keep her dark urges under control, or a behavior modification program we haven't yet tried. Maybe it really is sibling rivalry, but an extreme form. Maybe Peter and I need to triple the amount of attention we give her to compensate for the attention we give the baby. For nine years, she was an only child. Naturally, she sees her new sibling as a threat. Diana's therapist's office is closed for the holidays, but I'll make an emergency appointment as soon as I can get through to them.

Until then I promise that I will do everything in my power to make sure that my daughters are never left unsupervised when they are together.

10

So, this is where things stand:

I'm standing on the front porch of my childhood home with my duffel over my shoulder and my hand on the doorknob. Trevor is behind me with my suitcase. The door is open. Inside it's dark and quiet. There's no sign of life; no smoke coming from the chimneys, no cars in the driveway, no activity from Charlotte's and Diana's studios in the barn. It figures that after priming myself for a showdown during the entire three-hour drive, I've managed to come back at a time when no one is home. As half-owner of the lodge I have every right to show up unannounced and uninvited and to go inside if this is what I choose to do. Yet I can't bring myself to step over the threshold. I thought I would be able to walk boldly across the place where my parents died. I was wrong.

A raven calls: *Cr-r-ruck tok, cr-r-ruck tok, cr-r-ruck tok, cr-r-ruck tok.*

I search the trees. The raven is perched on the topmost spike of a tall white pine. The spike is bent from its weight. Ravens are massive birds, much bigger than crows: two feet long and with a four-foot wingspan, with a black beak, black eyes, and glossy black feathers.

I shiver. That the first forest creature to greet me upon my return is a raven has to be a sign. All over the world, ravens are viewed as harbingers of death. Some cultures believe that ravens are the souls of wicked priests; others that ravens are the incarnation of damned souls or even Satan himself. Some say that when a raven croaks at night it's because the raven is really the wandering soul of some poor person who was murdered who didn't get a proper burial. Native Americans worshipped ravens as the creator of the Earth, moon, sun, and stars, but they also viewed them as tricksters and cheats, though I've never had a problem with them.

The raven looks down at me. I look up at it. *All will become known,* it says after it is certain that it has my full attention.

"What?" I whisper as quietly as I can because Trevor is standing right behind me and if he knew that I was talking to a bird, he'd stuff me into his Jeep and drive me straight back to the hospital. "What will become known? Is it about me? Is it about my parents?"

All will become known, the raven says again. It opens its wings wide and flaps away.

I feel like picking up a stone and chucking it after it. I hate when animals use enigmatic sayings to pretend to wisdom. That this raven spoke to me is not unusual; birds often serve as messengers from a higher realm in fairy tales and legends, assisting heroes and heroines by offering them wise advice. Unfortunately, I can't tell if this raven's message is a warning or a promise.

"Rachel? You don't have to do this, you know. There must be another door that we can use." Trevor knows as well as I do what happened on the other side of this one.

"I'm fine."

And as if speaking the words out loud has broken the spell, suddenly, I am. I take a deep breath, walk quickly across the place where my parents died, and stop at the entrance to the great room to give my eyes time to adjust. The room is so big, and the windows so tree-shaded and narrow, coming in from outside on a sunny day is like being struck blind.

"Can we turn on some lights?" Trevor asks.

"No, sorry. I mean, yes, we do have electricity, but we only run the generator twice a day, morning and evening. We won't be able to turn on the lights until my sister and aunt come home."

"Ah, gotcha. That's okay." He takes out his cell phone and uses the flashlight feature to light the room. "Holy crap. This looks like the set of a horror movie."

I burst out laughing. I've never heard anyone describe my home quite like this. Most of the scientists and former work colleagues of my parents who came to visit gushed over the lodge's construction and décor. The *Architectural Digest* article my grandmother had framed and hung on our dining room wall calls our great room "an over-the-top extravaganza; the definitive example of lodge style gone amok," which pretty much covers it. Sixty feet long by forty-five feet wide, with a twenty-four-foot-high vaulted ceiling and three massive cast-iron and deer-antler chandeliers and a fieldstone fireplace that's so big, there are two benches inside where you can sit. Plank oak floors, leather furniture, Tiffany lamps, Navajo blankets, animal-hide rugs, and enough taxidermy to open a natural history museum, which in the half-light look every bit as menacing as Trevor's remark implied: a beaver gnawing on a stick on one end of the fireplace mantel, a mink and a martin posed to look like they're fighting on the other end, a pair of Canada geese on the wall above with their wings spread as if they are perpetually flying south, a wild turkey beside the fireplace displaying his tail feathers for a nonexistent female, and on and on. Native animals mix with exotics: a snarling gray wolf beneath a majestic Cape buffalo head, a black bear beside a leopard, a crocodile posed as if it's trying to decide between a bighorn sheep and a white-tailed deer.

"Aren't some of these endangered?" Trevor asks as his light falls on a juvenile mountain gorilla that I happen to know has been on the critically endangered list for decades. My parents hated trophy hunting and made sure that Diana and I understood what the animals we grew up with represented.

"If they are, I guess we have my ancestors to thank."

"I'm sorry. It's just that—well, you told me how much you loved animals when you were a kid. How could you stand living surrounded by all of this?"

I shrug. "You know how it is. Kids accept whatever they grow up with as normal." I don't tell him that every time I passed through this room I whispered an apology to its unwilling inhabitants for my ancestors' collective bloodlust.

Trevor switches his phone to camera mode and shoots a panorama despite the miserable lighting, then walks around the taxidermy taking close-ups. I'm not sure I like him poking his critical eye into every corner of my home knowing that his readers will one day see these pictures and pass judgment. On the other hand, I opened this can of worms when I invited him here, and I can't very well put them back.

"Come on. I'll give you the grand tour." The sooner we get this over with, the sooner I can do what I came to do. I bring him first to the gun room. If Trevor is going to make a big deal about my ancestors' trophy hunting, then I want him to see that the gun cases are empty, so he understands how much my parents disapproved.

"Okay, now this is definitely impressive. What are we looking at? Maybe fifty, sixty rifles?"

"Something like that," I manage. I put out a hand against the doorjamb to steady myself. The sheer quantity of weaponry in this room knocks me back. I feel as though I've stepped into a past that I recognize but never knew. All of the weapons from my great-grandfather's stories have been returned to their places, exactly as I remember from the pictures: a Winchester 1894, according to my great-grandfather the most-sold sporting rifle in American history; the classic Winchester Model 70, which every young hunter saved for; a Remington 770, one of the most accurate mass-produced rifles in American manufacturing and the rifle I see in my visions; and so many more.

And there is another addition. In the middle of the room is a large glass display case filled with birds. I borrow Trevor's phone to go in for a closer look and quickly identify most of them because these are all species that live on our property: sandhill cranes, great blue herons, peregrine falcons, short-eared owls, bald eagles, brown-headed cowbirds, pileated woodpeckers, American goldfinches, and common crows—a male and female of each, all expertly mounted and preserved. My sister always did like birds. Fortunately, there are no ravens.

Trevor is standing in front of one of the cases with his hand pressed against the glass as if he wants to stroke the rifle behind it, a Pre-'64 Winchester Model 70 that is in such high demand among shooters and collectors my great-grandfather said it was worth five thousand dollars. I swear, he's all but drooling. I can only imagine how Trevor would react if I were to show him the most expensive gun in my family's collection, a Colt .45 revolver my great-grandfather said used to belong to Wyatt Earp. I'm about to point it out to him when I realize that the place where the revolver should be is empty. A Winchester Model 1873 Carbine saddle ring that was worth seventy thousand the last time it was appraised and a factory-engraved Winchester Model 42 shotgun worth about the same are also missing. I wonder if they're on loan to a museum.

"Do you hunt?" I ask.

"Some," he answers. "Deer mostly, though I've gone out with my buddies a couple of times for bear. But we didn't get anything," he adds quickly, remembering where he is and who he's with.

"Come on. I'll show you the rest of the house." I lead him back through the great room and stop at the bottom of the stairs. If anything deserves to be featured in his article, the stairs are it. Twelve feet wide at their base, the main staircase splits halfway up at a landing that's big enough for a pair of armchairs with a table and a lamp between them. The stair railings and stiles are made of intricately woven branches; the treads are birch logs split in half with the bark still on them, their ends painted in fantastically detailed fairy-tale scenes: Hansel and Gretel breaking off a piece of the witch's gingerbread roof; Red Riding Hood skipping blithely down a woodland path while the wolf lurks in the trees; Rapunzel in her high tower waiting for her prince; Rumpelstiltskin pointing his finger accusingly at the princess who weeps at her spinning wheel next to a mountain of straw. Twenty-eight steps, fifty-six scenes in all, well-known tales and obscure, each so intricately detailed I used to spend hours studying them and still find something new. It's no wonder *Architectural Digest* put them on their cover.

I lead him up the stairs and pause at the top so he can take photos of the great room from above, then head down the bedroom hallway. Two faint squares spilling from two open doors are the only light. Judging by the paint-spattered jeans draped over the back of an antique pressed-wood rocking chair, Diana has taken over our parents' master bedroom with its view of the lake. Charlotte appears to be using the same room she did when I was a child. The rest of the bedroom doors are closed. There's no reason to heat rooms you're not using.

I open the door to the bedroom that has the sleeping porch because I used to wish that this room was mine. I drop my duffel on the bed, then unzip the bag and sit White Bear in the place of honor in the middle. Trevor follows with my suitcase.

"Was this your room when you were a kid?"

"No, mine was at the top of the kitchen stairs. It and the room across from it used to belong to the servants back when the lodge had a full-time staff. When I was little, I liked to sneak downstairs before anyone was awake, pretending that I was Cinderella and it was my job to stir up the fire while my lazy stepsister slept. But that was as far as my fairy-tale improv could go, since I had two loving parents, and I couldn't very well assign the role of wicked stepmother to my favorite aunt."

"Cute. So, you loved fairy tales when you were little?"

"I did. My sister used to read them to me all the time, though some of the stories were pretty gruesome. Looking back, I'm surprised my parents were okay with it."

"I know what you mean. Cannibalism, murder, poisonings, chopping off feet and hands and heads. But the stories are so satisfying, aren't they? Everything is black and white, good and evil. And there's always the reversal at the end, where the good guys get to live happily ever after."

"You're into fairy tales?" I don't know why I'm surprised. I guess because fairy tales were such an intimate part of my childhood, I never really thought they could be equally important to someone else.

"I just signed up for a class on the influence of fairy tales on modern literature. *The Lord of the Rings* and *The Chronicles of Narnia* are the examples we're going to be studying, but there are so many more that draw on classic fairy-tale elements, like Goldman's *The Princess Bride*. Have you read it?"

I shake my head.

"Not even seen the movie?"

I shake my head again.

"Oh, man, are you in for a treat. We're going to have

to figure out a way for you to watch it. Meanwhile, I'd like to get a picture of you in your old room if you don't mind. Assuming it's unchanged."

"Let's find out."

I lead him to the end of the hall and open the door to my childhood bedroom and step back in time. The room is exactly as I remember it: the crazy quilt my grandmother made, so named because no two fabric squares repeated, and if you tried to find a match, allegedly, it would drive you crazy, the room-sized braided rug also made by her, the toys and books on the low shelves my father built beneath the windows, the artwork created by yours truly on the walls. Details I'd forgotten: the pencil marks on the doorjamb that marked my growing height; the twin knotholes in the pine paneling next to the closet that I used to think were monster's eyes until my father painted them into rabbits. The room is a time capsule, frozen at the exact moment that my life fell apart. I stand in the middle and turn a slow circle. Everywhere I look, I see my parents: the whimsical bear sculptures my father whittled for me, the early reader nature books my mother gave me, a crayon drawing of my happy little family made by me.

"Good, good," Trevor murmurs as he circles me with his camera as though I were a fashion model. "I like that pensive look."

"Where do you want me to stand?"

"Just do whatever feels natural. Pretend I'm not here."

I take him at his word and go over to the window seat.

I used to sit on this cushion for hours watching the pair of ravens who built their nest in a nearby pine. It pleases me to see that the nest is still here. The nest is huge: five feet across and two feet high, with a nest cup inside made from smaller twigs and branches and lined with mud and grasses. When I was little, I used to wish we had a ladder tall enough that I could climb inside and sit. I remember wondering if I did, if the birds would feed me. I wonder if this nest belongs to the raven who greeted me. Ravens live for up to seventeen years in the wild, and mate for life, so it's possible.

As if in answer, a raven swoops down with a large stick in his beak and perches on the side of the nest. Moments later his mate settles beside him.

"Do you remember me?" I whisper as quietly as I can.

The female cocks her head and turns one shiny eye toward me and puffs up her feathers.

We remember.

I can't begin to say how happy this makes me—not only that this is the same pair I loved when I was a child, but that I can now understand their speech and they can understand mine. I used to try to teach this pair to talk. "Nevermore," I'd say over and over again because my dad said it would be a good trick if my ravens could learn to say this, though they never did. I wonder what my father would think if he knew we were having an actual conversation.

The male drops his stick where I can see it as though he's brought me a gift.

"Thank you," I whisper.

All will become known, he says again.

I purse my lips. I still have no idea what this means. What will become known, and how, and when?

Then it hits me. *Ravens live up to seventeen years.* If this pair are the same birds who nested here when I was a child, this means that they were alive the day my parents died. The raven is saying that I don't have to struggle to regain my memories. *They* will tell me what they saw. What they know. Obviously, the testimony of a pair of ravens is never going to hold up in a court of law, but if they can point me in the right direction, I can present any new evidence I find myself.

I nod to show that I understand. "Later," I whisper.

"What's that?" Trevor asks.

"Nothing. I was just thinking about how late it's getting."

"I guess it is. I'm almost finished. Just keep looking out the window. But don't smile."

I hadn't realized that I was. But how can I not? I've never told anyone that I can understand the languages of insects and animals. To be honest, I don't fully understand the whys and hows of my ability myself. I was eleven the first time a spider spoke to me. This was shortly after I came out of my catatonia. *You can talk if you want to,* the spider who lived in a corner of my hospital dorm room told me, and while my therapists had been trying for days to get me to speak, for some reason, the spider's simple logic made sense. I picked up my book of fairy tales and read aloud the story called "The White Snake," by the Brothers Grimm, because I knew that this was a story about another person who could understand the languages of all living creatures after he took a bite of his master's special dish. My voice sounded strange to my ears, rough and scratchy from disuse, but the spider was right; I *could* talk. I wondered if perhaps I too had eaten a piece of white snake, and this was why I could understand the spider. Possibly one of the cooks put a piece in my soup or stew. At the time, it seemed as good an explanation as any.

Fifteen years on, the best explanation I can come up with is that I'm like those people who have a special affinity for a particular animal—dogs, say, or horses—and are able to communicate with them on such an instinctive level, to anyone else it seems like magic. The difference between me and them being that I don't have to guess at what the various species are thinking or feeling; I really can understand what insects and animals say. Also, my ability seems to run across all species. Naturally, I don't listen in on every conversation, but only when I choose to; otherwise, the collective cacophony of hundreds of insects and birds and animals all yakking away at the same time would be too much to bear.

All I know is that I've been talking to insects and animals for almost as long as I can remember. And I'm not crazy.

11

THEN
Jenny

Diana's therapist's office is on the second floor of an old wooden building on a side street in downtown Marquette. Most of the buildings are far more substantial. The Marquette County Courthouse is the most famous, a beaux arts and neoclassical red sandstone structure in which Otto Preminger's movie *Anatomy of a Murder* was filmed in the same courtroom as the original murder was tried. Marquette is the largest city in the Upper Peninsula, which sounds impressive until you realize that Michigan's Upper Peninsula is such a big, empty place, its entire population could fit inside a city the size of Pittsburgh or Cincinnati.

Still, the city has everything we need: shopping, a movie theater, restaurants, concerts, a bowling alley, a craft brewery, along with the Peter White Public Library, the research library at Northern Michigan University, and a bookstore on Dr. Merritt's building's first floor. Every month, I pick up the books I ordered the last time I was in town and place an order for more. Most of the books I purchase are work-related, but occasionally the owner talks me into picking up a novel. It's not that I'm against reading fiction; it's just that there are already so many books at the lodge, many of them classics, some of them no doubt rare and valuable first editions, I'd need a hundred lifetimes to get through them all.

Normally, driving to Marquette and spending the day in the city is a welcome treat. But there's nothing normal about today. Today, all I can think about is that accursed pillow. I can still see Diana leaning over the side of the crib and pressing the pillow against her sister's face, the baby's little arms and legs kicking and flailing as she fought to stay alive. But it wasn't only the pillow and what Diana was doing with it that chills me. It was her expression. Serene. As if she knew exactly what she was doing and understood what might happen and didn't care.

I check my watch. Peter, Charlotte, and I have been waiting for Dr. Merritt to finish with Diana for close to an hour. When the door to his inner office opens at last, Diana darts out from behind him and runs into the waiting room and plunks down next to Charlotte on the sofa. She grabs a book off the coffee table without looking at it and thrusts it into Charlotte's hands.

"Read me a story!"

Charlotte laughs and pulls Diana close. "Big dogs and little dogs. Black and white dogs," she begins, somehow making the simple story sound engaging enough for a nine-year-old who reads at a tenth-grade level. My sister is so amazing. I never would have made it through the holidays without her. Char was an absolute lifesaver; plying Peter's family with food and drink, cheerfully washing their dishes and doing their laundry, taking Diana sledding during the day and working jigsaw puzzles with her in the evenings while I walked around like a zombie, pretending that everything was fine and that this Christmas was no different from any other, not sleeping, barely eating, stealing an occasional glance at my husband and seeing my anguish reflected in his eyes. I swear, we could have won Academy Awards for our performances.

"Mr. and Mrs. Cunningham?"

I stand up and shift the baby on my hip. I feel as though I'm walking toward a guillotine. Because we're here to discuss not only what Diana did to her sister and what we can do to keep it from happening again. When I finally got through to Dr. Merritt's office after the holidays, the receptionist told me that Diana's test results were back.

I was against the idea of testing from the beginning. Whatever is wrong with my daughter isn't something that can be weighed and measured. Diana's previous therapist wanted to run tests as well, but I couldn't see how putting a name to her condition was going to help us. The only reason I agreed this time was to placate Peter, who agreed with Dr. Merritt, who said that refusing the tests only puts off the inevitable. Now I'm sorry I did.

"There's no easy way to say this," Dr. Merritt begins after he's seated behind his desk and Peter and I are settled in the guest chairs opposite him. A single manila folder waits ominously on the desktop between us.

Then don't, I silently plead. *Don't do this to us. Don't ruin our lives any more than they already have been.*

"Go ahead," Peter says. He sounds calm, but I can tell he's nervous because the muscle in his jaw is twitching like it always does when he's upset.

"As we discussed, I've used a combination of psychological examinations and family rating scales to evaluate Diana," Dr. Merritt begins, "all designed to measure predatory conduct associated with adult psychopathy."

Psychopathy. I close my eyes against that terrible word. I knew this was coming. I'm not stupid. I've spent enough hours researching what might be wrong with my daughter to know that this was where we were going to end up. But hearing the word from Dr. Merritt's professionally objective lips cuts to my very core. My daughter can't be a psychopath. She just can't.

"I also asked one of my colleagues to verify the results, and her findings agree with mine," he goes on. "Diana tests at two standard deviations outside the normal range for callous-unemotional behavior. This puts her on the severe end of the spectrum."

"It all seems a bit—arbitrary," Peter manages, and I'm grateful that he hasn't lost the ability to speak, because I don't think I could squeeze a response past the lump in my throat if my life depended on it. "I mean, I'm not questioning your judgment, Doctor. It just feels as though you're relying more on opinion than on scientific method."

"I don't disagree. Unfortunately, there is no standard test for psychopathy in children. And to be perfectly honest, many psychologists believe that psychopathy can't be identified in young children at all. But a growing number, including me, believe that psychopathy is a distinct neurological condition and that the primary traits can be identified in children as young as five. The most significant factors we look for are what we call callous-unemotional traits, which distinguish fledgling psychopaths from children with ordinary conduct disorders who are also impulsive and who exhibit hostile or even violent behavior. To the best of our current understanding, the results are conclusive. Diana is a psychopath. I'm sorry."

I look at Peter. Peter looks at me. He gropes for my hand and squeezes my fingers so hard it hurts. *Our daughter is a psychopath.* Such an ugly word. So loaded with negative connotations. Such a cruel label to assign to a child.

"You're sure?" Peter asks.

"Diana's behaviors fit all the criteria." Dr. Merritt ticks them off on his fingers. "C.U. children tend to be highly manipulative. They also lie frequently—not just to avoid punishment, as all children do, but for any reason, or for none at all. Callous-unemotional children are also unrepentant. They don't care if someone is mad at them, and they don't care if they hurt someone's feelings. If they can get what they want without being cruel, they will. But at the end of the day, they'll do whatever they must to achieve the result that they want. However, it's important to understand that in real life, psychopaths are nothing like you've seen depicted on television and in movies. Diana isn't some deviant heartless soul bent on doing evil. She just doesn't understand the ramifications when she does hurt someone—nor does she care, as when she put a pillow over your baby's face to observe the color change."

"So, what do we do? How do we fix this?" Peter asks.

"Sadly, there is no cure. Diana was born this way, and there is nothing that you or I can do to change her. It's also important to understand that her condition is not your fault, no more than if Diana had been born with any other non-heritable birth defect. However, I and my colleagues believe that confronting the problem early on may present an opportunity to help children like Diana change course, if only slightly. We believe that the capacity for empathy might still exist weakly in callous-unemotional children, and that it can be strengthened. This is where your baby can help."

I grip my daughter more tightly in my arms.

"Naturally, I'm not suggesting that you do anything that would put your baby in danger. But as Diana sees the two of you showing affection toward her sister and loving the baby and responding to the baby's needs, she can learn empathy from your example."

"Helping Diana is as simple as soothing the baby when she's crying?" Peter asks.

"Essentially yes. Believe me, I'm not minimizing the crisis that brought you here today. It's essential that Diana and the baby never be left unsupervised when they are together. Still, I believe there's hope. A sliver instead of a slice perhaps, but hope, nonetheless."

Hope. Such a meager consolation for people who have no way out. It's impossible to imagine what our lives will be like going forward. Will Diana always be a threat to her sister? Will we have to supervise their interactions for years? Decades? Their entire lives? Will Diana get worse as she gets older? Will she ever have any semblance of a normal life, or is she doomed to be the outcast, the monster the villagers surround with pitchforks, the demon roaming the darkest parts of the forest that everyone fears?

"I realize this is a lot to take in," Dr. Merritt says. "Do you have any questions?"

Peter and I shake our heads. I'm sure I'll have a million after we leave the office, but right now, I just want this to go away.

"Then I'll leave you two alone. Take all the time you need."

Dr. Merritt shakes Peter's hand and squeezes my shoulder, then lets himself out a side door into his private office. I can't help feeling jealous. He gets to go back to his life, whereas he just destroyed ours.

The minutes tick by.

"A psychopath," Peter says at last. "I guess we should have named Diana 'Norman Bates' or 'Baby Jane.'"

"Don't. Don't you dare say those names alongside our daughter's."

"It was a joke."

"It's not funny."

Peter drags a hand through his hair, then turns his chair around to face me and leans forward and puts his hands on my knees. "I understand you're upset. So am I. This is terrible news. But attacking each other isn't going to change anything. I'm as stunned as you are."

"I know. I'm sorry."

Peter hands me a wad of Kleenex from the box placed conveniently on Dr. Merritt's desk. I wonder how many boxes his office goes through in a week.

"We can't tell anyone," I say after I've dried my eyes and blown my nose. "Not a soul."

"Not even Charlotte? She knows what Diana did. She has a right to know why."

"Not even Charlotte. I mean it, Peter. The only way to keep this a secret is to keep it to ourselves. As bad as this is now, if people find out about Diana's diagnosis, it will be a thousand times worse. Everyone will start looking at her sideways—if they're willing to be around her at all."

Peter purses his lips. I can tell there's more he wants

to say, but at last he nods. "All right. We'll do it your way. We will never speak that word again."

"Thank you."

The victory feels hollow—not because I don't believe that Peter is sincere in granting me this concession, but because of the dreadful circumstances that sparked the battle. If Diana had a visible handicap such as cerebral palsy or muscular dystrophy, or if she was missing an arm or a leg—even if she had a better-understood psychological condition such as schizophrenia or if she was bipolar, it'd be different. There are support groups for families dealing with these issues. People would understand. They'd offer help.

But no one is sympathetic to the mother of a psychopath. To the mother of a girl who tried to kill her infant sister. A girl who let a toddler drown in a swimming pool.

Or did Diana push the boy in?

12

NOW
Rachel

It's six o'clock. Trevor and I have been sitting in the pair of leather armchairs in front of the fireplace in the cold and the dark for what feels like hours. I don't know if he's hanging around because he's still hoping to interview Diana and Charlotte, or if he's lingering so I won't have to wait for them alone. Either way, at this point, I just want him gone. I understand that's not a particularly gracious sentiment on my part, but the day has been so unsettling: checking out of the hospital, seeing the lodge again after so many years, walking across the place where my parents died, dealing with the flood of memories that being here evokes, and talking to the ravens—I really need time alone to process it all. It wasn't until I pointed out that it's entirely possible that Diana and Charlotte could be traveling and might not come home tonight at all that he finally gave up.

Now as I walk him to his Jeep, it's so dark I can barely see the pair of ravens circling overhead. Ravens don't normally fly at night, which makes me think that this pair are as eager to talk to me as I am to talk to them.

"Thanks for the ride," I say, perhaps a little too quickly as he slides behind the wheel. It isn't only the ravens. At some point as I was showing him around the lodge, I realized I'd caught a break by coming home when my aunt and sister aren't here. Explaining why I'd suddenly shown up unannounced was going to be awkward enough, never mind explaining why I also brought along a reporter. Trevor and I came up with a cover story during the drive about how he's doing an article on Michigan's ten most beautiful log cabins, and from there he was going to work the conversation around to the day my parents died, but now, unless the Fates are conspiring against me and he and Charlotte and Diana pass one another on the road, I won't have to use it.

"Are you sure you'll be all right?" he asks. "I really don't like dropping you off and driving away."

"I'll be fine. I'll just grab a bite to eat and go straight to bed." I should have offered Trevor something to eat while we were waiting, I realize now, but it's too late to do anything about it. Clearly, I'm going to have to work on my social skills.

"Okay, then. Now that I've seen this place, I'd like to do some more research on it and come back in a day or two. Maybe get some pictures when the lighting is better. Hopefully talk to your aunt and your sister."

"You're welcome anytime. Just remember there's no phone service at the lodge, so I can't promise they'll be here when you come back."

"Understood. Meanwhile, I look forward to seeing you again."

Something about the way he says this makes me think he's not just being polite. That there could one day be something between us makes my stomach flutter. Occasionally someone at the hospital would show an interest in me, but I never let it go anywhere because I had no future, and also because two people with mental problems hooking up really didn't seem like a good idea. Now I wonder what it would be like to have both a future and someone to share it with. If it turns out I didn't kill my mother, my life will be a blank slate, and I will have the only piece of chalk, an idea that is both empowering and intimidating considering the many possibilities. It's not just the big things like where I'll go to school if I want to go to school, or what I'll do for work if I want to work, but the thousand and one everyday decisions that even now are entirely under my control. I could go into the kitchen right now and eat peanut butter straight out of the jar if I wanted to or take a bag of cookies to my room without having to worry about somebody stealing it and keep it there until the cookies are gone. I can get up when I want, go to bed when I want, go for a walk or read a book or sit around doing absolutely nothing if this is what I choose to do. Fortunately, I have a plan.

I stand in the driveway and wave until Trevor is out of sight, then hurry inside and up the back stairs to my childhood bedroom. I should probably look for something to eat before it gets too dark to see what I'm doing, but I have a date with a couple of ravens.

I open the window and stick out my head. "Hello? Are you there? Are you awake? Can we talk?"

Nothing.

"Hello?"

No answer. Not the slightest ruffle of a feather. Stupid ravens. Stupid Trevor for hanging around so long. Stupid me for thinking that the answers I seek will come as quickly and easily as a single conversation.

I leave the window open a crack and shake out a cigarette. The lodge is absolutely silent, the crackle of burning paper and tobacco the only sounds. The hospital was never quiet; bells clanging, trays clattering, footsteps echoing, patients screaming and crying. This feels apocalyptic, as though the world has been destroyed and I and the insects and animals are the only ones left. I swear I can hear my blood flowing.

I take a long drag and stare out at the trees, alone with my thoughts in a way I haven't been in years. Fifteen, to be exact. I say the words out loud, "Fifteen years, fifteen years," but the fire of my anger has gone out. Here in the last place on earth where I was truly happy, all I feel is sorrow. Even if I didn't kill my mother, there's no regaining the life I should have had. My parents are dead. Nothing can change that. They will never again walk these rooms, never roam the forest they loved. It guts me to think that in a few years, I will be older than they ever were.

I smoke the cigarette down to the filter and toss the butt out the window, then close the window and go down the back stairs. The kitchen is as dark as a tomb. I make my way to the pantry by feel and open the junk drawer and pat down its contents: pencils, pens, scissors, a rubber band, screws, and other unidentifiable stuff, until finally wedged in the back of the drawer, a flashlight. I pull it out and switch it on and shine the light around the pantry, looking for a can of baked beans or maybe some chili, and score a can of chicken noodle soup. I open the can and dump the soup into a bowl. The broth is greasy and cold, and the noodles are stiff, but I've eaten worse.

I pour a glass of water and carry it upstairs to the sleeping porch so I can keep an eye out for Charlotte and Diana. It's cold, but I don't mind. I've noticed that people make a big deal about the temperature, complaining if it's a few degrees warmer or colder than they'd like, as if the world and its climate revolved around them. I guess when you grow up essentially out of doors, you're more forgiving of the weather. Anyway, until Diana and Charlotte come back and turn on the generator, it's not that much warmer inside.

To the east is the clearing where my mother set up her observation blind. No doubt that's where my love affair with bears began. It's harder to explain why I'm still stuck on bears at the age of twenty-six. All I can think is that I must be like those boys and girls who love dinosaurs and butterflies and grow up to become paleontologists and entomologists.

To the west is the meadow where Uncle Max set up our gun range. Max wasn't really my uncle, but he was my aunt Charlotte's long-term boyfriend, so Diana and I called him "uncle" to tease them. Max was also my first serious crush. With his shaggy blond hair and bright blue eyes and a smile that could charm a grizzly, as my father used to say, I thought he was as handsome as a prince from a fairy tale. Diana and I used to compete openly for his attention. Or perhaps she only pretended to like him because she knew that I did.

Wanting to impress Max is the reason I learned how to shoot. Max and Charlotte and Diana used to go out to the gun range whenever my parents were gone, and while I hated guns, and had no desire to handle a gun or to fire one, I hated being left out even more. So, when Max invited me to come with them a few months before my eleventh birthday, I wasn't about to say no. And after he wrapped his arms around me as he knelt beside me and slid his finger through the trigger alongside mine and pressed me tightly against him to absorb the recoil the first time I fired my rifle—well, I'd have crawled to the ends of the earth across broken glass if he'd asked me to. After that, I sometimes pretended I needed more help than I did. Knowing what I do now about pedophilia and sexual aberrations, his behavior seems more than a little creepy, but back then it didn't set off any alarm bells. I knew he only had eyes for Charlotte.

I wonder now whatever happened to him, if he is still around, if he and Charlotte are still a couple. I know so little about Diana's and Charlotte's day-to-day lives. I don't know if they are stay-at-homes or gadabouts, if they are early birds or night owls, which of them does the cooking or if they take turns, who turns on the generator in the morning and again at night, who makes sure the fuel oil tank is topped off and orders in firewood, if they go to the Cobblestone Bar on Friday nights to listen to Max play the way we sometimes used to do, if they have friends over for drinks or to play cards, or if they prefer to keep to themselves. It's been two years since I've seen either of them. They used to visit a lot more often when I was younger. I guess after I became an adult, they figured I didn't need them.

I tuck the flashlight under my arm and carry my dishes downstairs and rinse them in the sink and put everything back where I found it, then wander the rooms with my flashlight feeling like a burglar until eventually, I find myself standing outside the door to my father's den. His desk is strewn with papers. I can almost smell the tang of the swamp that clung to him constantly, an earthiness that I didn't know I missed until I remembered it just now. People who know my history assume I favored my mother because of our shared love of bears, but my father and I were also close. When I was little and I would wander into this room, my father would stop what he was doing and lift me onto his lap and explain what he was working on as if I were old enough to understand things like profit-and-loss statements and real estate taxes and checkbook balances.

I shine the flashlight over the desk. My father's desk used to be filled with photos. My favorite was a picture he took of me in which I'm sitting in the back of our canoe holding up a shiny rock bass—my first fish—and bursting with pride and delight. This was before I became a vegetarian.

But this desk is no longer my father's, and the photograph is gone. Instead, my flashlight beam lands on a glossy, trifold brochure. *Lost Lake Development*, the heading reads above a picture of a lake that looks identical to ours. Inside, the brochure touts the development's selling points: forty-five miles from Marquette, a pristine wilderness paradise, four thousand acres that have never been logged, five-acre parcels with full lake access, will build to suit.

For the briefest of moments, I think that this brochure is left over from when my parents lived here. Developers would sometimes contact them wanting to build cabins or luxury homes around our lake, and sometimes the proposals would include a mock-up like this. But it's highly unlikely that one of those proposals would still be hanging around, and this brochure looks new. A business card paperclipped to the back along with a handwritten note— *Great talking to you! Hope to hear from you soon!* —that includes the developer's cell phone number. There was no cell phone service over most of the U.P. when my parents lived at the lodge.

I sit down in my father's chair. There's only one reason for this brochure to be front and center on what is now my sister's desk: Diana is seriously considering this proposal. The thought makes my blood boil. Our parents vowed that they would never sell so much as a square inch of our property. What's more, they made Diana and me promise that after we inherited, we would do the same. It seems my sister wasn't listening.

As to why she is considering this proposal, the missing weapons tell the story. The *most expensive* weapons. I'd bet my share of the inheritance that they are not on loan to a museum as I initially assumed. Diana has probably been selling off valuables for years. The lodge is so full of stuff, she could have gotten rid of half of it, and I'd never know. Maybe the lodge needs major repairs, or the property taxes are in arrears and the lodge and the acreage are about to go back to the state. Or perhaps she's been indulging in too much travel or spending our money foolishly in other ways. Either way, it's clear that I shouldn't have signed off on our tax returns without asking questions, should have consulted with one of the lawyer or CPA patients at the hospital to make sure that everything was as it should be, should have been more involved.

But antique guns and Tiffany lamps and Navajo rugs can be sold without my knowledge or consent. There's only one thing my sister can't sell without my signature or my okay: our land. She knows this, and yet she's in talks with a developer. Clearly, there's something I'm missing. I dig through the rest of the papers, and when I find a plain manila file folder with my name on the tab, my stomach drops. Inside is a completed form along with an instruction sheet for filling it out: "Marquette County Probate Court Involuntary Mental Illness Proceedings, Helpful Information & References."

Diana is going to have me committed. *This* is how she is planning to develop our property without my consent. I've seen this happen to other patients, but I never dreamed it would happen to me. An old person suddenly changes his will, a CEO starts making what shareholders believe are off-the-wall decisions, and the next thing you know, they're locked up in the mental hospital, with no say over their affairs. Next up will be a psych evaluation, which— given that I've spent the past fifteen years in a mental hospital—I am certain to fail. All the things that I was hoping to accomplish if I can prove that I didn't kill my mother—going to a university, getting a biology degree, taking up my mother's research, living at the lodge, marrying, maybe one day having children—none of it is going to happen. Diana is going to be my legal guardian again, and I will have no say about where I live or what I do for the rest of my life.

Outside, I hear the crunch of tires on gravel. Headlights sweep the yard. Quickly, I put the papers back as I found them and hurry up the kitchen stairs. I crouch at the top and track their progress by sound: car doors opening and closing, the turn of a doorknob, the kitchen door banging shut, the jingle of car keys on the counter, footsteps across the wooden floor. A screech of metal as someone opens the door to the old-fashioned wood cookstove, a *thunk* as a chunk of firewood is thrown in. Water running into a pot followed by a clatter of metal-on-metal—one of them filling the teakettle and putting it on the stove to heat is my best guess. A shrill whistling a few minutes later confirms it. I imagine them sitting at our big farm-house-style table: Charlotte with her elbows on the table and her hands wrapped around her cup as she blows on her tea to cool it, wearing one of the hand-knit sweaters she used to favor along with a pair of the earrings she makes from bits of recycled aluminum and old jewelry and tiny flat river stones. Diana drinking from the forest green ONLY YOU CAN PREVENT FOREST FIRES Smokey the Bear coffee mug my mother and I found at an antiques shop that I gave her for her seventeenth birthday, wearing a plaid flannel shirt, work boots, and jeans because she always favored practicality over style. They have no idea that I am here. No idea that I know.

The thought fills me with power. I have two choices: I can sneak away after Diana and Charlotte go to sleep. Grab my suitcase and duffel bag and hike out to the highway and thumb a ride to the nearest town. I have no money and no I.D. and no way to access my bank account, assuming Diana hasn't already taken my name off it, but I can borrow someone's cell and call Trevor to come and get me. I can spend the night at his place or perhaps with one of his friends and then move to a women's shelter if Marquette has one while I fight my sister in court.

But there are risks. If I go up against Diana openly in court and I lose, I'll be sent back to the mental hospital with no hope of ever getting out. In theory, I could go into hiding if the judgment goes against me, but then what? With no assets and no job skills, I'd be helpless. Homeless, with the threat of incarceration constantly hanging over my head.

Or I could stay here. If I can find proof that Diana is planning to strip me of my rights in order to develop our property, I might have a chance. My parents both had cameras and tape recorders. If I can take pictures of the developer's brochure and any other paperwork I can find, and better yet, if I can catch them talking about Diana's plan to defraud me and record their conversation, odds are good that the judgment will go in my favor.

And there's another reason for me to stick around: I still need to clear up the discrepancy between my visions and the police report. Reenacting my vision in the place where my parents died is the whole reason I came home. If I leave now, I might never get another chance.

Hiding out in my own home might sound crazy, but I'm not talking about doing this for weeks or months— only as long as it takes to assemble the proof that I need. What's more, I have the perfect set of circumstances to pull this off. It's a big house, with only two people living in it, which means there's plenty of room for me to stay out of their way. The doors to the extra bedrooms are always kept shut, so there's no reason for them to look inside this one and find me or my stuff. Logically, they each use their own bathroom, which means I still have two to choose from. If I only use the bathroom when they're out, and sneak food from the pantry instead of raiding their leftovers, it's unlikely that they would notice their food supplies going down. I don't even snore.

I tiptoe down the hallway to my chosen bedroom and lock the door. Take off my shoes and pull back the covers and climb quietly into bed. The Fates are smiling on me, all right, but not in the way that I expected.

I think again about the raven's message. All will become known, indeed.

13

THEN
Jenny

It's been almost two years since Dr. Merritt delivered his terrible diagnosis, and contrary to my expectations at that time, we're still here. Still going about our daily routines, still living, still breathing. The sky didn't fall, and the earth didn't implode, proving once again the truth of that old adage: life goes on. There have even been a few times when I can honestly say that I have been completely and unreservedly happy.

Naturally, Diana's diagnosis necessitated changes. We'd already moved the baby's crib into Peter's and my bedroom and installed battery-operated security cameras to monitor the room and the hallway ("trail cams," Peter jokingly calls them), as well as a door lock with a keypad to which only we three adults know the combination. We also asked

Charlotte if she wouldn't mind switching to the bedroom next to Diana's, which has a door between them that can be left open like in a hotel suite. Naturally, we didn't tell her the real reason we wanted her close. We said only that Dr. Merritt thought Diana was acting out because she was feeling neglected, and it would help if she would pay as much attention to Diana as she could.

Now, nearly two years on, it sometimes feels as though my sister has taken our request too much to heart. Char and Diana have grown unbelievably close. It's almost as though our roles have flipped, and Charlotte has become the mother while I have become the aunt. Sometimes when I see them with their heads together laughing over a whispered joke or chummily cooking or drawing or playing a board game as if nothing and no one in the world mattered but them, I can't help but feel jealous. Charlotte has always been more exciting than me, more adventurous than me, warmer, prettier, funnier. Possibly even smarter. It hurts to be relegated to the role of lesser sister in my own home. But whenever I start feeling sorry for myself, I remember that Charlotte has essentially put her life on hold for us, and that the extraordinary bond that has developed between my warmhearted sister and my prickly daughter is not a bad thing, and I am beyond grateful.

Today is actually one of those rare occasions when they are not together. It's a gorgeous fall afternoon, perfect in every way; sunny skies with a scattering of clouds and the temperature just the way I like it: brisk enough to wear a sweater but warm enough that we don't need hats or scarves. Peter and I are splitting and stacking the load of firewood he had delivered next to the far end of the barn under a sky so blue, it hurts to look at it. Diana is in the house reading while the baby is in the playpen that we set up for her a safe distance away under a tree. When I was Diana's age, the last thing I would have wanted was to be stuck inside on such a beautiful day, but I understand that when you grow up traipsing the woods with your mother and father day after day, spending time alone indoors feels like a treat.

"Break time," Peter announces as he shuts down the saw. In the sudden silence, my ears ring. He takes a slug from his water bottle, then flexes his fingers and links his hands behind his head and stretches. My heart melts. I can truthfully say that I am more in love with my husband now than I was on the day we married. Whenever I see him swinging an axe or handling a chain saw, I marvel at the wilderness skills this former university professor has acquired. After years of living out of doors, Peter is tanned and fit. I wish I could say the same for me. Diana says I look like I swallowed a bowling ball, which isn't a particularly kind or clever thing for her to say but is exactly how I feel. I got so big so fast, if the ultrasound technician hadn't promised otherwise, I'd have sworn I was carrying twins.

Obviously, this third pregnancy is unplanned. Another surprise: this time we are going to have a son. Peter couldn't be happier. Most of the time I am, too. An unborn baby is nothing but possibility. Will our son be blond like Peter, or will his hair be dark like mine? What color eyes will he have? What will his personality be like? When will he take his first steps, speak his first word, and what will that word be? What talents and interests will he have? What will he become? All prospective parents happily indulge in questions like these. Unfortunately, my happiness will always and forever be tempered by the memory of another little boy who never got to grow up.

"Mama!" the baby calls from her playpen. "Duice!"

The sippy cup of apple juice she was happily sucking down the last time I checked on her is now on the ground a good five feet away. Peter jokes that our daughter has such a strong arm, she's going to grow up to become a major league baseball pitcher. I'll just be glad when she gets big and strong enough to defend herself against her older sister.

"Can you get her?" I sit down on a piece of upended firewood to catch my breath. I'm already feeling the effects of this pregnancy. It's hard to believe that I have to carry this baby another four months.

Peter plucks our daughter from the playpen and swings her onto his shoulders and gallops with her around the yard. She shrieks and laughs. Everyone talks about how difficult children become after they reach the age of two, but so far, our daughter is a perfect angel. Of course, as soon as I have the thought, another intrudes, but I refuse to let it take root. I am determined to love my girls equally, no matter that one is easy to love and the other is not.

A gunshot splits the air, followed immediately by another. I cringe. I know exactly where the shots came from and who made them and why, but I swear I will never get used to the sound. Peter stops galloping and looks off longingly in their direction. Of course, he'd rather be target shooting with my sister and her boyfriend than cutting and stacking firewood with me. Peter's been out to the gun range a number of times, and according to Max, my husband is an excellent shot. They've invited me to go with them as well, but I told them no. I've never touched a gun in my life, and I intend to keep it that way. If it had been up to me, we never would have let them set up a gun range on the property at all. But Charlotte did an end run around us by asking Peter's grandfather for permission without telling him that we'd already said no, and of course, he said yes because he loves guns as much as I hate them.

That said, I laid down two absolute and inviolable rules. First: no guns are allowed to remain on the property. Max can bring his and Charlotte's rifles with him when they're planning to shoot, but he has to take them away again when they're finished. Second: our daughters are forbidden to go to the gun range ever, no exceptions. I don't care that Charlotte and Max think my rules are silly and consider them a major inconvenience; this whole endeavor is one big concession as far as I'm concerned. I get that Charlotte needs someone in her life and something to do besides babysitting my children, and I understand why after Max suggested setting up a gun range, she wanted to make it happen. But I don't like Max, and not only because of the influence he has over my sister. I don't trust him around my daughters. He's too smooth, too self-assured, too proud of his good looks, and far too physical with Diana, lifting her onto his lap and letting her braid his long hair and comb out his beard. It worries me how quickly Charlotte fell in with him. I get that some women are okay on their own and some are not, but that doesn't mean she has to hook up with the first man to show an interest. The only reason we hired Max as our part-time handyman was because Peter wrenched his back when he tripped on a book Diana left on the stairs. Of course, once we'd opened that door, Charlotte launched a campaign to convince us to let Max move in to the empty apartment above the carriage house because he was having trouble paying his rent, but we put our foot down and made sure Peter's grandfather knew how we felt so we wouldn't get blindsided again. I swear, if it were up to my sister, we'd be living in a commune.

"Do you smell something?" I ask. Beneath the dried leaves and fresh sawdust and chain-saw exhaust is something dank and ugly. "I think it's coming from the barn. It smells like something died in there."

"It's an old barn. Something probably did."

"It's really rank. Will you check it out?"

Peter hands the baby to me and follows his nose to the side of the barn facing away from the lodge. There are a couple of missing boards back there that he's been meaning to replace. Most likely an animal crawled inside and couldn't find its way out. Probably a porcupine or a raccoon.

Minutes later, he's back. "You have to see this."

"See what?"

"Just come."

I return the baby to her playpen while Peter opens the sliding door in the front of the barn because there's no way I'm going to fit through the missing boards in the back. Inside, the smell nearly knocks me off my feet. It's all I can do to keep from throwing up, and not because I am pregnant. I swallow hard and pinch my nose and follow Peter past the piles of moldy hay bales and rusty farm equipment to one of the old horse stalls. He opens the latch and steps to the side.

At first, it's hard to comprehend what I'm seeing. A non-scientist would probably conclude from the animals in various stages of decomposition splayed open with their guts laid out beside them that our barn is home to a serial killer. Some I recognize: a field mouse, a striped chipmunk, a baby rabbit. Others are in such an advanced state of putrefaction, it's impossible to tell.

"*My God*. What is all this? Why did she do this?" Because we both know this is Diana's handiwork.

"More important, how did she do this without our knowing it?"

It's a fair question. If anyone were to ask me if Diana

151

had enough alone time to have amassed this macabre collection, I would have said absolutely not; that between tagging after Peter on his rounds, or hanging out in the observation blind with me, or doing whatever it is she does with her aunt Charlotte, she is under constant supervision. Obviously, my sister has massively let us down.

"Can you imagine what would have happened if Diana had done this while we were living in the city and someone discovered it?" I shudder. "Social services would have gotten involved. Diana could have been taken away from us, put into foster care, maybe juvenile detention. My God."

Just thinking about how close we could have come to losing our daughter makes me ill. I understand she only cut open these animals because she wanted to see what was inside of them, and that she did this out of curiosity and not from malice, the same as that first winter when she cut apart her toy animals. It's not her fault that she doesn't understand the difference between a legitimate scientific inquiry and . . . whatever this is.

My stomach twists. "I've got to get out of here," I gasp as the bile rises in my throat. I hurry outside and bend over with my hands on my knees.

Peter follows me out. "Are you okay?"

I take a deep breath and wipe my mouth on my sleeve. "I will be if I can ever get that smell out of my clothes and my hair. How can she stand it?"

He shrugs. "How are we going to deal with it?"

I honestly can't think of an adequate response. One of the things I've learned from reading about psychopaths while waiting in Dr. Merritt's office is that the normal rules of reward and punishment don't apply. Emotionally, Diana operates on neutral, Dr. Merritt once explained, meaning that she simply doesn't feel the range of emotions that guide and moderate most people's behavior. Taking something away from her as a punishment has no effect, because there's nothing she cares about enough to make the threat of losing it change her behavior. Psychopaths also don't feel resentment because they don't care what other people are doing or about what they have. They never experience self-doubt because for them, failure is not a problem. In a psychopath's black-and-white world, she either accomplishes what she sets out to do or she doesn't. If something doesn't work out the way she wanted, she might try something else to achieve it, but in the end, if it turns out that her objective is unobtainable, she simply lets it go and moves on. It's no wonder that all our attempts to discipline our daughter have been a failure.

"I was thinking," Peter says. "Instead of punishing Diana, what if we were to channel her interest in anatomy in a more productive way?"

"Are you suggesting that she become a butcher? Because if you are, it looks like she's already well on her way. Or were you thinking she could become a mortician?"

"I was thinking about letting her learn taxidermy."

"Taxidermy. You're joking." The idea of giving our

eleven-year-old psychopath knives and encouraging her to skin animals and reconstruct them sets off so many alarm bells, I hardly know where to start.

Peter holds up his hand. "Hear me out. I know you hate the taxidermy in the lodge. I'm not crazy about it, either. But taxidermy would give Diana the opportunity to see what's inside animals without coming off as some sort of mad scientist. We could set up a workshop for her in the barn—away from our offices, because of the smell. I'm sure I could find someone to come in and teach her."

I shake my head. "I can't see how legitimizing Diana's bad behavior is going to help her. It seems to me we'd only be condoning it."

"Do you have a better idea?"

I shake my head again because I don't.

"Just think about it. We don't have to make a decision now."

Which is a good thing, because as much as I hate what Diana has done, I hate Peter's solution even more. I go over to the playpen to refill the baby's sippy cup, then follow him back to the woodpile, throwing the chunks of wood he splits against the neat stacks of firewood with far more force than is necessary. *Taxidermy.* I can barely stand to think the word. I've learned to live with the taxidermy in the lodge because I had to, telling myself that as distasteful as these pieces are, they are relics of another place and time. But that's a long way from allowing my daughter to add to the collection.

I throw another piece. It bounces off the barn with a satisfying smack. I think about the carnage on the other side. I picture Diana setting out the live traps she must have found in the barn, turning our property from haven to horror for the hapless creatures who took her bait. Bringing the cages to her secret workshop and killing her victims with her own hands and cutting their bodies apart without a moment's concern for the fact that she had taken a life. Then I imagine her doing this over and over again. If we hadn't discovered her collection, would she have gone on to kill larger animals? Would she have started torturing them first like the boy I read about in one of Dr. Merritt's magazines who cut off the family cat's tail with a knife bit by bit over a period of weeks because he wanted to see how the cat would react?

Maybe Peter is right. Maybe taxidermy is the best way to channel her inclinations. At least she'd be putting animals together instead of taking them apart.

And the sad truth is, it probably doesn't matter what we do in response to Diana's mini massacre because our daughter can't be fixed. Diana is a psychopath and has been since the day she was born. As her parents, it's our job to keep her from going completely off the rails, but in the end, what she does is outside of our control. Maybe Peter's solution will work and maybe it won't. Either way, I can't help feeling as though we're all barreling toward disaster, and my daughter is the one driving this train.

14

NOW
Rachel

I'm trapped, stuck on the sleeping porch for who knows how much longer because Diana and Charlotte are downstairs in the kitchen fixing breakfast and the upstairs floors are creaky and they'll hear me if I move around. I can't sneak down the hall to talk to the ravens for the same reason. I'm cold, I'm hungry, and I have to pee. The smell of frying bacon wafting up the stairs tickles my nose like those vapor trails you see in cartoons, making my mouth water and my stomach growl, and I haven't even eaten meat since I was six years old. And I *really* want a cigarette.

I'm also angry—not so much with my aunt and my sister, though there's plenty of that to go around, but with myself. Granted, the decision to stay hidden for a time was mine. And yet somehow, without her even knowing that I am here, my sister is pulling the strings once again. It's hard to believe that less than twenty-four hours after I've come home, I've fallen right back into our old pattern. Diana always dominated our family. Her wants, her needs always came ahead of mine. I used to think that this was normal, and that my secondary status was because I was the second child, until one of my therapists pointed out that doing everything my sister told me to do, even if some of it was risky or downright dangerous, was my attempt to claim my share of my parents' attention. Until then, I would have said it was more a matter of self-preservation.

So here I sit. The only good thing about being stuck on the sleeping porch is that I have a clear view from here of their studios in the barn. If for some reason they don't go to work today, then my plan to fly under the radar is going to be over before it starts, because I'm pretty sure my bladder is about to turn traitor. The sound of running water from the kitchen doesn't help.

Meanwhile, the clock is ticking. The only question is, will I be able to accomplish everything I need to do before Diana and Charlotte find out that I am here? Last night I almost got sidetracked. I still desperately want to find evidence that my sister is scheming to have me committed, but I can't chase down this new development at the expense of my original plan. Everything hinges on whether or not I killed my mother. If it turns out I did this terrible thing as I have always believed, then Diana can take everything I own and literally lock me up and throw away the key, and I won't care. But if I can prove that I didn't kill her, which is obviously what I'm hoping will be the result now that I have reason to doubt, I will do everything in my power to bring my sister down. The sooner I settle the first issue, the sooner I can move on to the second.

At last, the kitchen door slams. Seconds later Charlotte and Diana cross the stretch of frozen pea gravel between the lodge and the barn. Charlotte's white-blonde hair is as gray as I'd imagined, though my sister's equally blonde hair is now buzzed boot-camp short. They're both wearing jeans and flannel shirts. No jackets because it's a short walk, and not worth the trouble of putting on a coat and hat and mittens and then immediately taking everything off. Whatever they're talking about must be funny because Charlotte suddenly throws back her head and laughs. I feel a familiar twinge. My mother used to say that things weren't always easy for my sister, and that it was hard for her to make friends, and I should be happy that she and Aunt Charlotte were so close. But it hurts to think of the two of them living here happily ever after during all the years that I was alone.

As soon as the barn door closes behind them, I run to the nearest bathroom, then head for my childhood bedroom and throw open the window.

"Hello! Are you there?"

No answer.

I open the window wider and stick out my head. "Hello? Anybody home?" The question is stupid—I doubt ravens even understand the concept of home. But I don't know how else to get their attention.

Still nothing.

I shake off my disappointment and close the window. The ravens will be back. This time of year, instinct demands that they get their nest ready for their chicks. Meanwhile, I have needs of my own.

I go downstairs to the kitchen and stir up the coals in the woodstove and add several pieces of cedar for a quick, hot blaze, then hover over the stovetop as close as I dare without setting myself on fire until the feeling in my fingers returns. The cast iron frying pan that Diana and Charlotte used to cook their breakfast is cooling on the back of the stove. The bacon grease congealing in the bottom looks about as appetizing as gray mud, but I'm so cold and hungry, I don't care what I eat as long as it's hot. I pull the pan over the firebox and open the refrigerator to look for bacon and eggs. I figure I can get away with cooking a hot meal if I fix the same thing for my breakfast that Charlotte and Diana ate for theirs. I've never cooked bacon and eggs before in my life, but how hard can it be?

Not hard at all, it turns out, as long as you're willing to eat eggs that are black on the bottom and bacon that is both half-burnt and half-raw. I score a cup of lukewarm coffee from the bottom of the pot and sit down at my old place at the table so I can keep an eye on the barn—not that I'd have time to put everything back and run upstairs if Diana or Charlotte were to unexpectedly return, but I'll at least have fair warning. I can't begin to describe how bizarre it feels to be back. I spent a lot of time in this kitchen as I was growing up, and not only at mealtimes. Whenever it was too cold or rainy to go to the observation blind, I'd sit at this table doing my schoolwork while Diana sat opposite me doing hers. Occasionally, if Diana was in a good mood and she noticed that I was struggling she would mouth the test answers to me when my mother wasn't looking. More often she would hide my pencil when my mother's back was turned or pinch the back of my neck as she passed behind me on her way to get a drink of water or kick my legs underneath the table until my shins were bruised. Once she took my homework before my mother had seen it and burned it in the wood-stove. When I told her I was going to tell because I'd worked very hard on that essay, Diana said I wouldn't do that if I knew what was good for me and squeezed my neck in that place where if she pinched me too long I'd pass out so I'd know she meant business, so I didn't. I've since learned that when people grow up with a dominant sibling, they tend to be anxious and insecure. It's a wonder I turned out as well as I did.

I fork a mouthful of eggs and push them around in my mouth with my tongue and try not to think about baby chicks as I swallow. I take a bite of bacon and don't think about pigs. By the time I've rinsed my dishes and put everything back where I found it, my stomach is only very slightly queasy, my mind only slightly repulsed at the thought of what is now sitting inside me. I go upstairs to check again on the ravens. Still no sign of them, so I crack open the window and smoke a quick cigarette to get the umami taste out of my mouth, then toss the butt and close the window and go over to the closet.

I push aside my child-sized clothes and shoes to pry up the loose floorboard that covers my secret cubby and reach inside. My fingers brush wood and metal. The touch is electric. Instantly, I am jolted back to the past. I take my rifle from its hiding place and hold it up to the light. That my Remington is still here is a resounding argument in favor of my innocence. Say the police were somehow wrong when they concluded that both my parents were shot with the Magnum. Even then, it's hard to imagine that after I accidentally killed my mother and my father used this same rifle to kill himself, I would have had the presence of mind to pick it up and return it to its hiding place before I ran away.

I sit down on the bed with my rifle across my knees. The gunstock is smooth with age, the barrel more pitted than I remember, but the Remington was used when Max bought it for me. I think again about the first time I shot it, how my nerves tingled in anticipation, the taste of the forbidden as sweet as candy in my mouth. Knowing that I was holding an instrument of death in my hands was empowering. I remember thinking that I could swing the rifle around and point it at my sister before she realized what was happening and shoot her as payback for all the mean things that she had done to me. The thought immediately made me feel ashamed, though not as much as it should have. After that, whenever Diana would say or do something cruel, I would come to my bedroom and shut the door and take out my rifle and hold it. Not that I would ever shoot my sister or any other living creature, but the idea that I could if I wanted to was comforting. Looking back, I think something wild and dangerous stirred inside me that day.

I check now to make sure that the rifle isn't loaded as Max once taught me to do and carry it downstairs to the gun room. The room looks entirely different in the morning light, warm and welcoming with the sun shining through the stained-glass window, throwing pools of colored sunshine on the floor and reflecting off the glass display cases. I used to sit on the Oriental rug in the middle of this room imagining that I was the king's trusted talking lion advisor in the fairy tale depicted in the window—"The Twelve Huntsmen" by the Brothers Grimm, which says all anyone needs to know about my great-great-grandfather's legendary sense of humor. Diana's display case of birds now covers the place where I used to sit. To this day, I don't understand why my wildlife biologist parents let my sister practice taxidermy—to me, taxidermy represents nothing but the waste of a perfectly good animal—but I do love that the gun collection has been restored. My great-grandfather would have been pleased.

I turn my back on the room and position myself in the wide arched open doorway with my feet spread. I have no idea what will happen when I reenact my vision in the place where my parents died; if I will see something new, if the new thing will reinforce what I have always believed, or if I will see something that contradicts it. It's exciting to think that I'm about to find out.

I lift my rifle and point it toward the taxidermy in the great room. I close my eyes and imagine that I am eleven. I am tall for my age, but pudgy. Two long brown braids hang down the middle of my back. I'm wearing jeans and my favorite red plaid shirt—the same clothes that I was wearing when I was found, according to the police report. I point my rifle at the zebra in the great room. I imagine myself pulling the trigger. The zebra squeals, whirls, and falls. I point my rifle next at a gazelle. I'm about to pull the trigger a second time when I hear my parents' voices outside on the front porch. The doorknob turns. Before I can hide my rifle in a dark corner of the gun room and pretend that I was doing something else—

"What are you doing?" my mother screams when she sees me. "Put the gun down!"

I do as she says. There's a big bang. My mother falls. I stand over her looking down. Her mouth is open, and her eyes are closed.

"Rachel!" my father screams. He takes my rifle and looks at me in shock and horror and turns the rifle on himself. There's another big bang—

—and the vision ends.

I shiver. Open my eyes and look down at the rifle in my hands. I feel as though an old friend has betrayed me. I was so sure that conjuring up my vision in the place where my parents died would reveal something new. But if anything, this vision I just experienced was less vivid than those I've had before. Thinner, paler, small. Like watching an old black-and-white movie with the sound turned off.

All will become known, the raven promised, and I believed him. Yet I still remember nothing about that day; not what I had for breakfast, not where I went. I don't know if I went with my mother to her observation blind, or if I followed my father on his rounds, if the day was sunny or overcast, if it was raining or snowing. This was early November, so it could have been doing either or both. I don't know any of these things *because I don't remember.*

I go back upstairs to return my rifle to its hiding place and check the ravens' nest again. Of course, the nest is still empty. I'm beginning to wonder if I only imagined our conversation. Maybe I can't talk to birds and insects. Maybe I really am crazy. Maybe Diana and Charlotte didn't bring me home because they knew that the hospital was where I belonged.

I sit down on the window seat and shake out a cigarette and stare into the forest. The trees are closer than I remember, their branches almost touching my window, as if they know that the lodge doesn't belong here and they're trying to swallow it up. People tend to think of forests as dark and dangerous places inhabited by giants and monsters and fearsome wild beasts, and I can understand why. Bad things happen in the woods in fairy tales and legends. Snow White is abandoned in a forest. Hansel and Gretel get lost in the woods. Red Riding Hood meets her wolf in a forest, and on and on.

But forests can also be magical places where nightingales sing sweetly, and glass castles spring up overnight, and birds and animals are able to talk, and wanderers and travelers find refuge. Certainly, I never felt frightened when I was in these woods. This forest was my home.

And with that thought, a wisp of a memory returns. A genuine memory that is as clear and true as the day it happened. I did shoot my rifle the day my parents died. Of this I am one-hundred-percent certain. But I wasn't in the gun room when I fired it.

I was in the forest.

15

THEN
Jenny

Two feet of packed snow cover, skies more sunny than not, barely a breath of wind, and a temperature hovering around fifteen degrees make this the perfect January day to snowshoe out to the west cliff. Winter is the only time we can access the cliff because of the wide swath of marshland between it and the lodge that at any other time of year is too wet to cross. It's a long hike, about as far from the lodge as it's possible to get and still be on our property, and even under ideal conditions the trek takes well over an hour. But with six inches of fresh snow limning every branch and pine bough and hoarfrost hanging off the trees and drifting through the air like diamonds, the view from the top of the cliff looking out over our frozen valley is going to be worth the effort.

Peter and I have made this trek the past two winters, and now that Diana is twelve and almost as tall as me, I wanted to share this amazing experience with her.

Naturally, she fought the idea tooth and claw because when does my daughter ever do what I want? But I was determined that this time I was going to win. Ever since we set up her taxidermy workshop, taxidermy is all she wants to do. I should have anticipated that my single-minded daughter would get far more caught up in her new endeavor than I would have preferred. We put her in the old milk room in the barn because the poured-cement floor and six-inch cement sidewalls that made the room rodent-proof back in the day will serve the same purpose now, and installed a good ventilation system in the ceiling because the room doesn't have windows, but still: breathing in the odors of death and chemicals hour after hour and day after day can't be good for her. In the end I had to promise that if Diana came with us on this hike, we'd upgrade her set of flensing knives, bribery being one of the few behavior modification techniques that actually works, though you won't find that particular nugget of hard-earned wisdom in any of the "Raising Your Psychopathic Child" how-to books.

"How are you holding up?" Peter calls from the back of the line as we wend our way through a dense stand of tall white pine. Peter and I have been taking turns breaking trail, and at the moment I am in the lead. Breaking trail is a lot more strenuous than following because you have to lift your knees extra high so your snowshoes clear the deep powder and your feet don't get tangled and you end up tripping yourself, but I like going first, seeing the pristine, unmarked snow sparkling away in all directions in front of me, knowing that wherever I choose to place my feet, Diana and Peter will have to follow. The pines in this part of the forest are so straight and tall and uniformly spaced they almost don't look real, as though someone painted them against the sky. The lighting feels artificial as well; sunny yet diffuse because there's so much frozen moisture in the air. Even the sound of our voices feels muffled. Every breath chills my lungs, energizing me in a way that humid tropical air never could. Someone who has never spent time in the far north would probably think we're crazy to be outside on a day like today, but they have no idea how invigorating a winter hike can be. Plus, it's great exercise.

"I'm fine," I call back.

"You sure?"

"I'm fine," I say again, trying not to let the annoyance I feel at having to answer the question a second time creep into my voice. Peter's concern is genuine, if misplaced. Pregnant women are perfectly capable of doing any physical activity they're used to right up until they're ready to give birth, be it horseback-riding, or ice-skating, or acrobatics, or ballet. I've spent years trudging around in these woods, with snowshoes and without; for me, hiking a couple of miles to climb the west cliff is nothing. It's true that my back muscles are screaming from the effort to counterbalance my enormous belly, and my lung capacity is half what it should be thanks to the baby compressing my lungs from below, but I wouldn't feel any differently if I were walking around inside the lodge.

"I'm hungry," Diana says. "And I'm tired. And I'm cold."

"What do you think?" I ask Peter. "Do we have time for a quick break?" Stopping for a few minutes to let her rest and grab something to eat will address two of her three complaints. Ignoring our daughter is never an option.

Peter looks first at the sky and then at his watch. "Five minutes. If we stop any longer, you'll really be cold," he warns her.

I shrug off my pack and pass around bottles of water and three of Charlotte's amazing homemade granola bars. Peter is correct when he says that we can't stop long. We're dressed for the weather with long underwear and insulated snow pants and down parkas and wool mittens and hats and scarves and massive sub-zero boots that would be the envy of a polar explorer, but the best way to stay warm is to keep moving. We'll build a bonfire and rest and warm up with a picnic after we reach the top. Peter is carrying firewood and kindling and newspaper and matches in his pack, Diana has marshmallows and hotdogs and hotdog buns in hers, and I have a wide-mouthed thermos of homemade chili along with the paper bowls and plastic utensils we'll need to eat it. Bringing food with us on this hike is not the problem it would normally be even though we are deep in bear country because all my bears are asleep. Occasionally during the late winter or early spring a hibernating bear will rouse itself enough to poke its nose outside its den if the temperature climbs above freezing, but that's not happening today.

Diana squats down as far as her snowshoes will let her and points to a fresh set of tracks. "Is that a bobcat?"

"Could be," I hedge. Judging by the size and the depth of the prints, I suspect the tracks were more likely made by one of our wolves, but it was hard enough to convince Diana to come on this hike; I don't want her using the wolf as an excuse to turn around and go back.

"I'd like to mount a bobcat. Maybe Max will trap it for me."

"Absolutely not. You know the rule."

Diana knows perfectly well that she is only allowed to prepare animals that have died of natural causes. They can be animals that died of old age, or were killed by predators, or were hit by cars—by far the largest group of the three, especially in the spring and fall, when animals are on the move—and nothing else. "Ethical taxidermy," it turns out our guidelines are called, though we were unaware of the term when we made them. After I told the bookstore owner about Diana's new hobby and asked if she knew of any good books on the subject, she showed me an amazing coffee table book featuring the work of two world-renowned Dutch taxidermists who preserve and pose exotic animals in fantastic tableaus inspired by old masters' paintings. The ostriches and Siberian tigers and anacondas and monkeys and parrots and other birds and reptiles they preserve are strictly sourced from legitimate breeders, animal shelters, and zoos, and have all died from natural causes. The artists even have the paperwork to prove it.

I have to admit that their extraordinary and oddly compelling artistry combined with their ethical approach have softened my opinion. They truly have raised the craft of taxidermy to the level of high art, as evidenced by their gallery and museum showings all over the world. Their work has also shown us the way forward. We're not always going to be around to provide a home for Diana and to take care of her; one day, she's going to have to earn her own living. I can't imagine her working in an office or any other setting that requires her to interact regularly with people. I can picture her living at the lodge and supporting herself doing work similar to theirs. Diana is naturally artistic. Her instructor says she has talent.

But all of that is in the future. At the moment, Diana is a twelve-year-old girl who can't stand to be contradicted. She straightens and tosses her head and fixes me with a glare that could melt a glacier.

"Aunt Charlotte says that rules are made to be broken."

"Aunt Charlotte says a lot of things," Peter says. "That doesn't mean she's right."

I appreciate his support. I wish Charlotte would do more

of the same. I don't care how close she and Diana have become; Charlotte has no right to undermine our authority by encouraging our daughter to disrespect our guidelines and directions. "Rules are made to be broken," indeed.

Diana huffs her displeasure over our united front, but backs off, taking the waterproof camera my sister gave her from her backpack and squatting down again to take pictures.

"I think these are wolf tracks. I'm going to show these to Max. He'll know what animal made them."

And that's the other half of our problem. Charlotte and Max; Max and Charlotte. Diana is always citing them as authorities, as if their opinions are the only ones that matter, never mind that Max is nothing but a con man and a liar. The times I've caught him telling whoppers are too many to count, but two of his wolf stories stand out. In the first, Max claimed that he and a friend were deer hunting when a band of wolves surrounded them. They fired shots into the pack, but the animals kept coming, so Max and his buddy each climbed a tree. Only his buddy slipped and fell, and because Max's rifle had jammed, he could only watch helplessly as his friend was torn to pieces. In the other, Max claimed he got separated from another friend during a hunting trip one January when the weather was severe and game was scarce, and when his friend didn't come back that night, the next morning, he went looking for him. He found his friend's body gnawed to the bone with the carcasses of the thirteen wolves he had killed as he fought for his life surrounding his body. Both stories were so over the top that I checked into them, and sure enough, while both were true, and both happened in the Upper Peninsula, both incidents took place more than a hundred years ago. I figure you can take anything Max says at maybe ten percent of face value, but clearly, my sister and my daughter have drunk the poison.

If Peter is bothered by Diana implying that our handyman knows more about the wilderness than her wildlife biologist parents, he doesn't let on. He blows on his hands to warm them and tugs on his gloves. "Okay. Time to get moving. It's not much farther now. Just to the top of that ridge."

He points to a rock-strewn slope a thousand or so feet ahead. The slope starts as an easy climb but gets gradually steeper until it finishes at an angle of around twenty-five degrees. From this distance, the approach doesn't look all that strenuous, but I know from past experience that it's sufficiently challenging to leave you feeling as though you've accomplished something worthwhile after you reach the top.

"All the way up there?" Diana whines predictably.

"Yep," Peter says cheerfully. "That is, unless you'd rather wait at the bottom while Mom and I enjoy our picnic at the top."

"Daddy's joking," I say quickly before she has time to get upset. "We wouldn't leave you behind. Besides, you have the marshmallows." I grin, though Diana does not.

I collect the empty water bottles and shrug on my pack and move to the head of the line.

"I want to go first." Diana plants her hand in the middle of my back and gives me a shove. It's not a hard push, but between the snowshoes and my belly, I'm so unbalanced that I topple forward and land on my hands and knees.

"Diana!" Peter scolds. He puts out a hand to pull me to my feet because there's no way I'm getting up without help. "Be careful. You could have hurt Mommy or the baby. Tell her you're sorry."

"It's okay," I say quickly. There's no point in trying to extract an apology from a person who has never felt remorse. "I don't mind if she goes first. It will be good for her to learn how to break trail. Let's just keep going."

Diana forges gamely ahead, stumbling and falling more than once as she struggles through the deep powder. Each time she goes down, she gets back up and keeps going. I glance over my shoulder at Peter to share a smile. I'll say one thing for our daughter: once she makes up her mind to do something, she doesn't easily quit.

"Okay," Peter calls to her as the snow cover disappears and the ground turns rocky. "We'll leave our snowshoes here and climb the rest of the way without them."

It's a relief to take them off. I'm much more winded than I anticipated. I'm nowhere close to quitting, but if Peter were to call for a short rest, I wouldn't object.

He moves to the head of the line. I take up the rear, putting Diana safely in the middle between us. We're well away from the edge of the cliff, but I'm not taking any chances.

We pick our way carefully among the boulders. Our cliff is part of the Marquette Iron Range, one of three iron-rich mountain ranges in the western half of the Upper Peninsula, which explains why the boulders are a dusky red. Most of the cities on this end of the U.P. were founded due to mining: Marquette, Ironwood, Iron River, Ishpeming, Negaunee; and some depend on mining to this day. There are copper and gold in the area as well, with hundreds of abandoned mine shafts scattered across the U.P. Peter's grandfather likes to show off a copper nugget the size of a baseball that he claims was found on our property, but I've yet to come across anything bigger than a pebble.

The climb gets progressively steeper. By the time we reach the top, I'm so winded I have to bend over with my hands on my knees to catch my breath before I can even think about taking in the scenery. When I straighten at last, surreptitiously slipping a hand inside my jacket to massage my aching back as I look out over our frozen valley, the view is every bit as magnificent as I remember, a fairy-tale wonderland in every imaginable shade of blue stretching away as far as I can see. Only from the top of this cliff can a person appreciate our acreage's unique bowl shape, which defines our property while isolating and protecting it. The cliff we are standing on curves away to the north and the southeast like a giant scythe, the only break the gap Peter's ancestors cut to allow access to this lost and magical world.

A raven croaks from the top of a tall red pine—*cr-r-ruck tok, cr-r-ruck tok*—a warning to its companions that there are intruders in the forest, as if the crunch of our boots and the sound of our voices weren't enough. Trees crack from the cold. A puff of wind sends the snow swirling down off their branches and onto our shoulders as though we were standing in a snow globe. I think about my bears and Peter's frogs and all the other forest creatures coping with the season in their own way: some sleeping in dens and hollows carved beneath the snow, some like the deer holed up in the cedar swamps, others such as ravens and ermine scavenging whatever they can find on top of the snow crust—everything ecologically balanced and working in perfect harmony. We're so lucky to live here. Truly, our home is a place like no other.

"What do you think?" I ask Diana as I wave my arm to take in the expanse.

"I like it."

Not exactly gushing praise, but considering the source, I'll take it.

Peter walks a short distance back from the edge and begins trampling a circle in the snow for our firepit. "Want to help?" he calls to her as he crumples newspaper and arranges kindling in a circle around it like a teepee. "Come over here. I'll let you light it."

Normally Diana would jump at the chance to play with

fire, so I'm a little surprised when instead she walks closer to the edge of the cliff than I'd like and points to the valley below.

"What's that?"

"Not so close. Come and stand back here with me."

She takes two steps closer to the edge and shades her eyes. "Down there." She points. "I saw something. I think it's a wolf."

"Come back here," I say again as firmly as I can without frightening her. "I'll check it out."

Something in my voice must have told her I'm serious, because for once, Diana does as she's told. I walk carefully toward the edge, testing the snow with each footstep before putting my weight on it, because there's no way to know where the cliff ends. Last year when Peter and I hiked down to the valley to explore the cliff along its base, great curls of snow hung over the lip like I've seen in nature documentaries and in movies. There's no reason to assume that this year it will be any different.

When I've gone as close to the edge as I dare, I lift my binoculars and sweep them over the valley.

"I see it! It's a moose! No, wait. There are two of them. A mother and calf. Great eyes, Diana. Peter—come here. You've got to see this!"

Moose in the Upper Peninsula are almost as rare as the wolves that feed on them. The only decent population is on Isle Royale, an island in Lake Superior that's fifty-six miles from the tiny town of Copper Harbor on the tip of the Keweenaw Peninsula, the northernmost point in the state. Occasionally an Isle Royale moose will get a hankering to explore and cross over to the mainland when the lake is frozen, but the Canadian shore is a lot closer, which means that an Isle Royale moose isn't likely to have traveled all the way here. Odds are this mother and calf are part of a small but growing population on the mainland that has been deliberately reintroduced. It's exciting to think that our property is home to a breeding pair.

Diana tugs at the binoculars hanging around my neck. I hadn't realized she'd come out to join me. I turn to face her.

"I told you to stay back."

"I just want to see." She grabs for the binoculars again.

"Ow! Stop. Be careful, Diana. Give me a minute. The strap is caught in my drawstring."

I pull off my mittens and stick them between my knees to work the strap loose. And then, inexplicably, impossibly, I am turning cartwheels in the sky.

Pain.

Sharp. Insistent. Overwhelming. Everything hurts. My head, my neck, my back, my arms, my legs. My body feels like it's on fire.

I open my eyes. See nothing but sky.

I turn my head to the side. Rocks. Snow. I'm lying on my back in a pile of rocks. I'm not sure why.

"Jenny!" Peter calls from somewhere high above.

"Is Mommy dead?" Diana asks.

"Jenny! Answer me!"

I roll onto my side, wrap my arms around the boulder next to me, pull myself up until I'm almost sitting, hang on to the rock with one hand and prop myself up with the other. The snow is freezing. I don't know why my mittens are gone.

No. I took my mittens off so I could untangle the binoculars' strap from my parka drawstring before I fell.

I fell.

I'm lying in a pile of rocks and snow at the bottom of the west cliff because I fell off it.

I fell, and I am alive.

"I'm okay!" I call, though one of my legs is definitely broken. I can tell by the way my boot is turned too far to the side. I'm not sure about the other.

"Thank God! Are you hurt?"

"I think so. Yes. I can't move my legs."

"Stay there! Don't move. I'll be right down!"

I almost laugh. As if I could possibly do otherwise. But Peter can't climb down to help me. He can't leave Diana on top by herself. And even if they both climbed down, he can't carry me two miles back to the lodge wearing snowshoes.

"Go home! Get the snowmobile! I'll be okay! Just hurry back!" I pour all the strength and confidence into my voice that I can. I don't want him to leave me. He has to leave me.

"All right," Peter calls back after a long silence during which I imagine him weighing all the options and coming to the same conclusion. "Just stay calm. Everything will be fine. I'll be back as quickly as I can."

I let go of the rock and lay back in the snow and close my eyes. My entire body is shaking, whether from the effort to hold myself upright, or from shock, or from cold, I don't know. It's impossible to wrap my head around the enormity of what happened. I fell off the cliff. I'm lying on my back in a jumble of rocks and snow at the bottom. I'm hurt. Probably badly.

On the plus side, I didn't die. On the negative, I still might.

I close my eyes and picture Peter and Diana following the trail we made back to the lodge, Peter running as fast as his snowshoes will let him, Diana struggling to keep up, Peter barely noticing that she's lagging, intent only on getting back to the lodge as fast as he can. I see him ripping off his snowshoes when he reaches the side yard, yelling for Charlotte and Max to look after Diana while he drags the snowmobile out of the lean-to and hitches on to it the sledge that we use for hauling. He jumps onto the machine and roars away, driving much too fast for conditions, struggling to control the snowmobile in the deep powder, wondering all the while if I will be alive when he finds me.

Which I will be. I can't die. I have to get through this for Peter. For our daughters. For the baby.

My hands stray to my belly. The baby hasn't moved since I fell, but sometimes he doesn't for long stretches of time. I poke my belly to provoke a response. If he were a two- or three-month-old fetus floating around inside my womb like a little spaceman with plenty of amniotic fluid to cushion the fall, he'd probably be fine. But this baby is already pushing the boundaries, only millimeters of tissue and skin between him and these rocks. I think I landed on my feet and the weight of my pack pulled me onto my back, and this is why one of my legs and possibly both are broken, but I can't be sure.

I lay still for a long time. The cold creeps through my clothes, through my skin, and all the way into my bones. I unzip my jacket and shove my hands beneath my sweater to warm them. Doing this will cause me to lose body heat faster, but I'm not willing to lose my fingers to frostbite. Not yet. I've read about mountain climbers who faced similar situations. After they were rescued, they said they didn't care that they lost fingers or toes; all that mattered was that they were alive. I hope I don't have to be that brave.

I shiver again. Shivering is good. It's when I stop shivering that I'll be in trouble. That's when I will succumb to hypothermia. It's inevitable. The only question is how bad it will be. As my core temperature falls, my body will shunt my blood away from my skin and extremities to my vital organs—my lungs, my kidneys, my brain, my heart—and I will no longer feel the cold. I have no idea if my body will consider my baby essential or non-essential.

I look up at the curl of snow high above my head, barely visible against the darkening sky. I try not to think about what would happen if it came plummeting down.

A pair of ravens circles like vultures.

I shiver again, but not because I am cold. For the first time since we moved to these woods, I am afraid.

16

NOW
Rachel

I have to go back into the forest. It's not a want, it's a need. I need to go outside, breathe the air, feel the quiet, smell the soil, reconnect with the person I used to be. Now that I know I was in the forest the last time I shot my rifle, I am absolutely convinced that returning is the only way I will get my memories back—all my memories of that terrible day: what I did, what I saw, how I survived the following two weeks. I've lived with this gap in my memory for too many years, telling myself it was okay, and that this was as complete as I was going to be. Never suspecting that the thing by which I had always defined myself might not be as I thought.

I am standing over my mother with the rifle.
The M.E. ruled the daughter did not fire the rifle.

The forest will tell me which is true.

I check to make sure that Diana and Charlotte are still in their studios, then stash my suitcase and duffel bag under the bed and shut my bedroom door and go downstairs to the mudroom for a pair of boots and a warmer coat. The day might look sunny and inviting, but until all the snow has melted and the frost comes out of the ground and the ice in our lake is gone, the air will never truly get warm. My parents used to joke that living in the Upper Peninsula was like living in a freezer.

I pick out a tan canvas Carhartt jacket that reminds me of my father's (and might well have been, it occurs to me as I put it on), add a thick woolen scarf, warm Sorel boots, and stick a pair of mittens in my pocket just in case. The room is so full of outerwear, if Diana or Charlotte comes back while I'm out, I doubt they'll notice that anything is missing. At any rate, I'm not going to be gone long. All I want to do is hike out to my mother's old observation blind, find a dry place to sit, listen to the forest, and wait for my memories to come back. Maybe have a chat with a bird or an insect if any happen to be around.

I sneak out the front door and detour through the woods so I can keep out of sight of the barn until I come to our access road. Every step brings back memories—happy memories from before my life fell apart. This is the time of year when my father used to set up his sugar bush. I loved tagging along when he went out to tap our maple trees and collect their sap. That this thin, colorless, and nearly tasteless liquid could be boiled down into the sweetest and most flavorful sugar imaginable always seemed like a miracle to me. I used to wonder about the Native American who discovered this amazing treat. I imagined him chopping down a maple in the early spring for firewood, though the wood would have been very green and hard to burn. He noticed the sap welling up from the stump, tasted it, and lacking water to make tea because there was no lake or stream nearby, he collected the sap and put it in a pot and put the pot on a fire to heat. Then he got distracted by something—say, a rabbit hopping by or a duck flying overhead—and forgot all about his tea as he went off to chase it. By the time he came back, the sap in the pot had boiled away and turned to sugar, and voilà—a new Native American food staple was born. My father laughed when I told him my maple syrup origin story and said he wouldn't be surprised if one day I became a famous writer.

This is also the time of year when my mother and I used to gather up our rucksacks and her radio antenna and hike out to see how our bears had fared over the winter. A person who didn't know better might think that bears can't come to any harm while they're asleep in their dens, but this isn't always the case. One year when the temperature hovered for weeks near freezing, and the melt-and-thaw cycle that softened the snow during the day and refroze it at night coated the snow cover with a thick layer of ice, three of our bears suffocated in their dens. My mother used to quiz me on the names of the plants we passed while we walked to and from her observation blind, praising me when I got them right and promising that one day, I was going to become an accomplished scientist. Sagebrush lichen. Fairy cup lichen. Devil's matchstick. Cushion moss. Rock cap moss. I even remember a few of their Latin names: *Athyrium filix-femina*, or lady fern; *Dryopteris marginalis* (marginal wood fern); and *Cyrtomium fortunei*, or holly fern, so named because the fronds are as dark as holly leaves (*Ilex opaca*). My father knew some of the names, but not nearly as many as my mother. Diana knew hardly any because she always said that plants were stupid.

Not all my memories are pleasant. There was the time I picked a handful of poison sumac berries along with regular sumac to make the refreshing summer drink my family enjoyed and everyone except Diana got violently ill because she was the only one who didn't drink it; ditto for the *Amanita muscaria* mushroom I sampled on one of my solitary rambles because I saw a fox nibbling it and I thought that meant it would be safe to eat. It turns out *Amanita muscaria* can be eaten by humans, but you have to know how to prepare them; I did not.

The only memory I can't seem to call up is where the trail to my mother's observation blind branches off from the access road. The vegetation has grown so tall during the years that I was away, I have to double back twice before

I find it. This path was originally a game trail that my mother improved by placing boards over a small stream and laying down cedar logs in the boggy places topped with gravel. If I'm lucky, her improvements are still here. If not, well, this is why I'm wearing boots.

A chickadee calls, a clear, two-note mating call instead of its usual *chick-a-dee-dee-dee* chatter. I search the trees until I find both it and its intended. It pleases me that I haven't forgotten how to read the forest. The play of light and shadow on the forest floor tells me what time it is; the diminishing piles of crystalized snow on the north side of the rocks and trees tell me direction. The moss and lichens growing in the tree stumps reveal the forest's history; how long it's been since the tree fell, and whether the tree was broken off in a windstorm or died of old age.

Then I come to the clearing where my mother's observation blind used to be, and my good mood vanishes. The blind is gone. I didn't expect to find it in good repair, but if I hadn't known what this pile of sticks and scraps of milled lumber used to be, I never would have guessed that they were once an important part of my life. I poke at the pile with my foot. Seeing the physical remains of my mother's life's work in disrepair saddens me more than I can say. She should be inside this blind right now, making notes and collecting data, not lying in a pine box in our family cemetery. No matter what happens going forward, the past can never be set right. Even if it turns out I didn't kill my mother and I take up her research on her behalf, her study will be missing fifteen years' worth of data.

I sit down on a fallen log to clear my mind and settle my heart and wait for the forest to speak. Tiny voices: the shush of the wind in the pines, a *thunk* as a pine cone hits the leaf litter on the forest floor, the scrabble of a squirrel's claws against the tree's bark, a scurrying in the leaves at my feet that could be a mouse or a shrew. Larger sounds: the caw of a newly returned crow (only the ravens remain for the winter), the *whump-swoosh* of its wings as it flies over my head, a crashing through the brush that could be a deer. I unzip my coat, stuff my mittens in my pockets, and run my fingers over the deep claw marks on either side of the log I am sitting on. The claw marks tell me that this was one of my mother's bait trees. I loved watching our bears come to feed. It didn't matter how high she hung the meat scraps or how securely she fastened them to the bait trees; one swipe from those giant paws and the meat was gone.

I fed White Bear a piece of bacon in this clearing once, though my mother didn't know and wouldn't have approved if she had. She always said that a good researcher only looked and never touched, and while I understood the reason for her rule, I didn't always do what my mother told me. Most of the time, I only stuck my fingers through the gaps in the observation blind when she wasn't looking and petted whatever parts of White Bear that I could reach. But on this day, Diana and I had come out to the observation blind while our parents were away because Diana was bored and wanted to play Snow White and Rose Red, a fairy tale about two sisters who make friends with a big brown bear who turns out to be a prince. We brought a chunk of bacon to coax in any bears who happened to be around, but before we had a chance to hang it, White Bear came along. Knowing what I do now about a bear's sense of smell, I'm sure he was drawn in by our bacon, but at the time, his showing up exactly when I wanted him to seemed as though it had happened by magic.

We scrambled inside the observation blind and watched him while he stayed near the tree line and watched us back. By this time White Bear was a beautiful five-year-old, the same age that I was at the time, and while he hadn't yet matured to his full height and weight (the largest black bear on record in the Upper Peninsula was seven feet tall and weighed one thousand pounds), he probably weighed at least four hundred.

Diana said that in order to make friends with the bear as the sisters do in the fairy tale, I should feed White Bear a piece of bacon. I took the piece she gave me and pushed aside the canvas flap that covered the opening and went out. White Bear chuffed a hello. I chuffed a greeting back and kept walking. When I'd covered half the distance between us, I tore the bacon in two and put one piece on the ground. I could tell that White Bear was nervous because he swung his head from side to side and grunted. But the pull of the bacon was strong, and I was a patient child, and eventually he lumbered over and picked up the bacon and swallowed it in a single gulp.

I held out the second piece. He took a step back and shook his head and grunted again. A person who didn't know otherwise might have thought that he was refusing to eat it, but I knew he was only trying to make up his mind.

"It's okay," I told him. "I won't hurt you."

At last he opened his mouth and took the bacon from my fingers so gently that I barely felt it; just a slight tug and his warm, bacony breath on my hand. He gulped it down and lifted his nose and sniffed the air looking for more. I held out my hands to show him that they were empty, and he licked the grease off my palms. His tongue was raspy and soft. When my hands were clean, I dried them on my pants and put one hand on his head and scratched him behind his ear. I think my sister was impressed.

I stand up and stretch and look around the clearing where I spent so many happy hours. On the other side of the log is a set of bear tracks—fresh ones, made by an adult, probably a male judging by the spacing and the depth. My pulse quickens. Odds are these tracks weren't made by White Bear; White Bear would be twenty-six now, which is a very long time for a bear to live in the wild even in an area as isolated and protected as ours. But the lure of the tracks is as powerful for me as the smell of bacon was for White Bear all those years ago.

I head out. Most people don't go looking for bears. Most people, if they even think they might see a bear when they're hiking in the forest—say they happen to come across a print, or they stumble on a pile of fresh scat—are going to turn around and go the other way, as they should. Black bears may be among the least dangerous, but if a person who doesn't know better sees a bear and starts to run, not realizing that bears can run up to thirty-five miles an hour, and the bear chases him, there's no way the encounter is going to end well. But I'm not most people.

The prints lead into the woods. The ground quickly turns mucky. Some animals don't like to get their feet wet and make their way delicately through the forest, but bears are like bulldozers, plowing through the underbrush and making their own trails as they go. For me, the ponds and puddles are obstacles to navigate around. This bear splashes right on through. In no time, I am completely out of breath. My boots feel like lead weights and my jeans are soaked past my knees. When I think about all the hours that I spent effortlessly hiking these woods when I was a child, I wish I'd spent more time working out in the hospital's weight room and less time watching television and smoking.

And the difficulty isn't only in following the trail; I'm having more and more trouble finding it in the first place. A depression in a mat of wet leaves could have been left by the bear's paw, or it could be a natural depression. A tuft of hair stuck in the bark of a red pine could have been shed by this bear as it passed through, or it could have been left days or weeks earlier by this bear, or by another. I flounder through the forest hoping the bear will be around the next corner, but when I come to a small pond and walk all the way around it twice with no sign that the bear either went in or came out, I have to admit that I've lost the trail entirely.

I turn around to retrace my steps, pausing first to orient myself, because the tricky part about following your own trail back the way you came is that you're seeing everything in reverse. Any landmarks you noted along the way, whether it was an unusual tree or a distinctive pattern of lichen on a rock, is going to be the opposite of what you remember. Sometimes because of the changed perspective, you won't see it at all.

Nothing looks familiar. Worse, the sun has gone behind the clouds, and the forest is so wet near this pond that moss grows on all sides of the trees, so I have no way to orient myself. I feel a flutter of panic. It hardly seems possible. I, who grew up in these woods, who spent nearly every waking hour tramping them with my mother and father and by myself, don't know where I am. I'm so stupid. I was so happy to be back in the forest, so eager to track down this bear on the off chance that he might be my old friend, that I forgot my parents' number one wilderness rule: presume nothing.

I lean against a tree and shake out a cigarette. My parents used to say that if I ever got lost in the forest, I should find a dry place to shelter and stay put until they found me. But no one knows I'm here, and even if they did, the two people who might conceivably come looking for me are the same two I'm trying to avoid. If I can't find my way back before nightfall, I'm going to be in real trouble. I'm already cold and wet. Once the sun sets, the temperature is going to drop below freezing. As hypothermia sets in, I'll become more and more tired and disoriented as I stumble around in the wet and the dark until eventually, I will fall and won't get up. I picture my carcass freezing and thawing as day turns to night and to day again, rotting where I fell as spring becomes summer and summer becomes fall, being nibbled on by foxes and weasels and torn apart by bears and coyotes until all that's left is a handful of bones. Even my beloved ravens are carrion eaters. I think about the last time that I was lost in these woods. It's hard to believe I wandered for two weeks with nothing to eat, no place to sleep, and no place to get warm. I have no idea how I did it. No wonder Trevor wants to write my story.

A raven calls now: *Cr-r-ruck tok, cr-r-ruck tok, cr-r-ruck tok, cr-r-ruck tok.*

I look up. The raven looks back at me. I have no idea if this is the raven who greeted me or if it is another, if it will talk to me, if it will help.

"Help me," I beg. "Please. I'm lost."

The raven opens its wings and flies off. It lands on a low branch a short distance away and looks back as if telling me to follow.

I toss my cigarette in a puddle and hurry after it. I don't know if the raven is helping me intentionally, or if it's only showing an interest out of curiosity. I want to believe the former. Ravens are incredibly smart. Ravens have been known to imitate a fox or a wolf to attract these animals to carcasses that the raven can't break open because the hide is too tough, or because the carcass is frozen. They've been spotted pushing rocks onto people to keep them from climbing to their nests, and stealing fish by pulling fishermen's lines out of ice-fishing holes, and playing dead beside a beaver carcass to scare off other ravens from a delicious feast. After bears, ravens are my favorite forest creature.

"Which way?" I ask when I come to the base of the tree where the raven landed, and it hasn't moved.

Cr-r-ruck tok! Cr-r-ruck tok! it says and takes off again. But instead of landing on another branch and waiting for me to catch up to it, it keeps going, flying so swiftly that I have to run to keep up, splashing through puddles and stumbling over branches because I don't dare take my eyes off it for longer than a second. I trip over an unseen something and go down on my hands and knees. Scramble to my feet and keep going. I want to call after the raven to tell it to wait, but I don't have the breath.

And then the raven is gone. I stop. The forest is silent.

There's no sound except for my ragged breath. I look for a dry place to sit while I figure out what to do next and spot a large rock beside a stream.

A rock next to a stream.

I am saved. This stream and all the others on our property empty into our lake. If I follow the stream toward its source, at some point it's going to pass through a culvert beneath our access road.

I whisper a thank-you to the raven and step into the water. The water is bitterly cold. I walk straight up the middle because I'm already as cold and as wet as I could possibly be and this is the fastest way to get where I need to go.

When I come to the road after a ridiculously short hike and climb up the stream bank, I'm almost embarrassed to realize that I wasn't nearly as lost as I thought I was. I'm also ashamed of how frightened I felt. I'd love to sit down and pour the water out of my boots and wring out my socks while I catch my breath and regain my equilibrium, but the diminishing daylight urges me to hurry.

At last I see the lights of the lodge. My heart sinks. Lights mean that Diana and Charlotte have finished work for the day and are settled in for the evening. I picture them sitting in front of a roaring fire while their dinner bubbles away on the woodstove, sipping a glass of wine or enjoying a cocktail, and head instead for the apartment above the carriage house. I tell myself it's all relative; that I don't need a hot shower and a hot meal, as much as I might want both. Spending the night in a dark, unheated apartment is a far better option than the one I was facing less than an hour ago.

The apartment is very dark. I put out my hands and immediately run into what feels like a wall of boxes. I pat them down looking for a way around them, and quickly realize that there are boxes everywhere: on a couch, on the kitchen counter, piled against the walls and covering the windows. Diana and Charlotte are clearly using the apartment for storage. The only way I could sleep here tonight would be if I slept standing up.

I find the bathroom and move a stack of boxes off the toilet and do what I have to do and go back outside and head for the barn. There used to be a couple of missing boards on the back side that my mother was always nagging my father to fix. If I'm lucky, he never got around to it.

The opening is as I remember. I slip inside. The barn smells musty and old. Overhead, a piece of tin roofing bangs. I head for one of the horse stalls and break apart several hay bales and score an old horse blanket to spread on top, then tug off my boots and strip off my jeans and socks and spread everything on the hay to dry and roll the blanket around my legs. As I lay down and pull my father's jacket's hood over my head and put on my mittens, I try not to think about the mice and other creatures who might be sharing my bed. Just because I can talk to animals doesn't mean I want to sleep with them.

I fling myself this way and that. The hay pokes and tickles. I'm exhausted, yet it's impossible to get comfortable. It doesn't help that I accomplished next to nothing today. Reenacting my vision in the gun room was a bust. So was the time I wasted in the woods. And it isn't only the fact that I got lost that's left me feeling so unsettled. It's that I was afraid. I didn't want to admit how frightened I was as I was floundering around the forest because I know how paralyzing fear can be, but the terror I felt in the place that I used to love was all out of proportion to what actually happened. I have no idea why I experienced such fear. I'm not sure I want to find out.

All I know is that something very terrible once happened in our woods.

17

THEN
Jenny

We buried our son in a small natural clearing on the hill behind the barn. In spring, the hill is covered with thousands of tiny blue forget-me-nots—a non-native species that Peter's ancestors planted long before anyone knew there was such a thing or that this might one day be a problem. Now their choice seems prophetic. In summer, hay-scented ferns grow up through the flowers so thick and tall you can barely see our boy's headstone. It's a nice woodland glade, certainly a more peaceful resting place for our son than a commercial cemetery could ever be, though I can't help thinking how much nicer this clearing would be if our boy were playing in the dirt instead of lying beneath it.

When I first got the idea for establishing a family

cemetery on our acreage, I wasn't sure if we would be allowed to do this. I've seen these tiny family plots alongside highways in rural areas or surrounded by homes and businesses after urban sprawl has overreached them, and while I always thought they were intriguing and even charming with their rusty wrought iron fencing and tilting headstones, I assumed that they were remnants from the past. I had no idea that people might still be using them.

But it turns out, burying someone on your property is perfectly legal in all fifty states as long as you comply with local requirements—something I imagine the funeral industry would rather people didn't know, since choosing between spending two hundred dollars for a simple pine box in which to bury your loved one on land you already own versus thousands for a typical funeral and a purchased cemetery plot would be a no-brainer for a lot of people if they knew. Obviously, your circumstances have to be just right. You wouldn't want to bury a loved one on your land if there was a possibility that you might one day move, and you'd have to leave them behind. (While exhumation and reburial are certainly an option, there are many more regulations involved with these than there are with burying a body in the first place, to say nothing of the cost.) And if you ever wanted to sell your place, you'd have to tell prospective buyers there's a body buried on the property and where it is, which would obviously affect your property's resale value. But Peter and I aren't going anywhere, and we're not about to sell off so much as a square inch of the land that has been in his family for generations. I like that our son is close by, and that I can visit him whenever I want, and that one day in the far-distant future, I will join him.

During that first year I visited our son's grave every day. I'd sit on the concrete *faux bois* bench I bought at an antiques shop because the bench looks as though it's made of twigs and branches and fits perfectly with its surroundings and tell our boy funny little stories about my bears, or his father's frogs, or something sweet or smart or silly or funny that one of his sisters said or did. Other times, I'd just sit.

I come a lot less often now. Not because after seven years I have forgotten my boy, or because I am too busy juggling the disparate needs of my growing girls to spend time with my son, but because I've come to understand that the hours I spent beside his grave in those early weeks and months were my futile attempt to mend the hole in my heart that was never going to heal. Everyone says I am lucky to be alive; that falling fifty feet off a cliff onto a pile of rocks should have resulted in far worse than myriad cuts and scrapes and bruises and a badly shattered left leg that gives me trouble to this day. A few inches to the left or to the right, and it would have. The deep snow piled up against the bottom of the cliff saved me, but it didn't save my boy.

Peter says the accident was not my fault; that no one could have foreseen what was going to happen, and therefore nothing could have been done to prevent it. But the sad truth is, if we had stayed home that day, our son would be alive. Peter says all that matters is that I am okay, and that as terrible as it was to lose our son, he doesn't know how he could have gone on if he had lost me as well. I know this is his backhanded way of telling me how important I am to him, but I don't like hearing it. How can I take comfort in the idea that if something happened to me, his life wouldn't be worth living? What about our daughters? How could he leave them behind at the very time when they would need him the most? At any rate, I was the one who wanted to bring Diana out to the west cliff to show her how beautiful our valley is in winter. I am the reason our son is dead.

I close my eyes and lean back against the bench and tip my face to the sun and drink in the sweet smell of the ferns. Lately when I visit my son's grave, I've been making a conscious effort to leave the past where it belongs and to reflect on all the good things I have so as not to take the second chance I've been given for granted. Sometimes Rachel comes with me and we take turns naming something we're grateful for, which as it turns out is actually a pretty good way to get inside the mind of a ten-year-old. Charlotte's baked goods rank high on Rachel's list, as does me tucking her in at night and reading her bedtime stories, her father doing art projects with her, the smell of her grandpa's pipe (I had no idea that Peter's father smoked around her when he came to visit), and of course, White

Bear. Rarely does she mention her sister. Rachel knows she once had a brother and that he was killed in an accident and is buried in this clearing and this is why we come to keep him company, but she doesn't know what happened. I might tell her when she's older, or I might not. Sharing the details risks opening the door to too many questions. *How did my brother die, Mommy? Mommy fell off a cliff while your brother was growing inside me and he got hurt. Why did you fall off a cliff, Mommy? Mommy fell off the cliff because your sister pushed me.* No thank you to that.

Because Diana did push me. Diana will never admit it, and Peter didn't see me fall because his back was toward us as he was building our bonfire, but I know what I know. I can still feel Diana's hand pressing against my chest and shoving me backward. I don't think she meant to kill me, though I do believe she wanted to kill her brother. I don't know why. Dr. Merritt says Diana doesn't experience jealousy, so it can't be that. All I know is that she wants what she wants and will do whatever she thinks is necessary to achieve it, which is hardly a logical or satisfying explanation for what could legitimately be considered premeditated murder. I've never told Peter.

Peter has been hinting lately that he'd like to try again for a son, but I told him I'm done. Two children are more than enough, especially when one is as damaged as Diana. Diana is twenty now, still living at home, still doing taxidermy, though her focus has shifted from mammals to birds. Lately she has also begun to paint. I'm glad she's found something that makes her happy. Then again, "content" is perhaps the better word, since Diana never feels happiness or any other emotion. I'm just grateful that the satisfaction she gets from painting and taxidermy seems to have tamped down her rage. She uses words as weapons now, or silence. She still sees Dr. Merritt once a month, though now that she has her driver's license, she goes alone. I have no idea what they talk about. The sessions must somehow serve her needs, because Diana never does anything unless she gets something out of it. I think of the visits as putting a Band-Aid over a scar that has already healed. Talking to Dr. Merritt isn't going to help, but there's no harm in it, either.

The one thing that seems certain is that Diana is going to live at the lodge for the rest of her life. She doesn't need people, never experiences loneliness, never yearns for companionship, and would be horrified at the thought of investing the time and energy required to maintain a steady relationship or, God forbid, a marriage, which is, in truth, a relief, because what would happen if she had children? I remember thinking when we moved to the lodge that this would be a place where she would be able to thrive and grow. I guess I was right.

Rachel, of course, is an entirely different story. It's no exaggeration to say that every moment I spend with her is pure joy. Rachel is the exact opposite of her sister in every way; a kind, considerate, deeply caring child who loves all living creatures with a passion even I didn't have when I was her age. I swear I didn't create this love in her intentionally, though I probably would have if I could. I can see her living with us at the lodge on into the indefinite future after she gets a biology degree and joins me in my research. I'm not pushing her in this direction, because ultimately, what she does with her life is up to her, but I'm pretty sure this is what she also wants. Like me, she's crazy about bears.

A whiff of smoke brings me back to the present. I open my eyes and sit up straight. If there is one thing that I am well and truly afraid of, it's fire. It's bad enough that the lodge is four miles from the highway down a rough dirt road that I'm not sure an engine truck would even be able to navigate; the nearest town with a volunteer fire department is thirty miles away, never mind that we'd have to drive out to the highway and who knows how much farther after that before we could even call for help. Peter and I have talked about this at length and concluded that if a fire ever broke out in the forest, or if the lodge or one of the outbuildings started to burn and we couldn't quickly get it under control, we may as well pile into our vehicles and never look back for all the good it would do us to try to fight it.

I sniff again. Something is definitely burning. My first thought is that Peter and Max are burning trash in our burn barrel, though the smoke doesn't have that toxic plastic smell that comes from burning garbage. I stand up and close my eyes and turn a slow circle and determine that the smell is coming from the forest.

I head out in its direction. At times the odor is so faint I think I only imagined it. Then the wind shifts, and the smell gets stronger again. Briefly, I consider going back for Peter. But if the fire has only just started, or if it is very far away, which I suspect is likely the case because the smell is so faint, then the quicker I can figure out what's going on and determine what we need to do about it, the better.

And there's another reason I don't want to waste time by doubling back—a far more important one: Rachel is somewhere in these woods.

That my ten-year-old daughter is exploring the forest by herself is not unusual; Rachel has been tagging along with her father and me since she was a toddler. She knows her way around this forest almost as well as we do. She also knows what to do in the event that she gets lost, which is to stop walking, find a dry place to shelter, and stay put and wait for us to find her. We've taught her other wilderness survival skills—how to read a compass, how to build a fire, where to find water, which wild foods are safe to eat and which she should stay away from, and she always carries a length of rope, a pocketknife, a Mylar ground sheet, a compass, waterproof matches, and a day's worth of food and water in her backpack. She also asks our permission before she heads out, and tells us which direction she's planning on going, and whether she'll be gone for just a morning or an afternoon or if she'll be out for the entire day, so it's not as though we let her randomly wander. Besides, she'll be eleven in two weeks.

But suddenly our thinking seems horribly foolish.

I push through the trees. This part of our forest is mostly hardwoods, which means there are a lot of dead-falls to climb over and undergrowth to work through or walk around. I take stock of the rest of my family's where-abouts: Diana was in her taxidermy studio the last time I saw her; Charlotte was packing up her jewelry, getting ready to set up at an art fair this weekend in Marquette; Peter and Max were doing chores in the vicinity of the lodge. Worst-case scenario: if it turns out the forest is on fire, I'll find Rachel, run back to the lodge, tell the others what's going on, and we'll toss our go-bags into the Suburban and Max's pickup and head out. Maybe grab a few valuables if it looks as though the fire isn't going to be imminently upon us, though I can't begin to think of which items we should prioritize, and it probably wouldn't be wise to take the time. Nothing is worth saving more than our lives.

"Rachel!" I call every few seconds. She can't have gone far—we ate breakfast only an hour ago. I detour around a blackberry patch because the barbed canes are so inter-twined there's no way I'm going through them, climb over a fallen tree trunk that's as high as my waist because the trunk is so big that crawling under it is not an option, slog through ankle-deep mud because it rained yesterday and the ground is so saturated there's no way to avoid the wet places. Each time my boot gets stuck, I imagine the Marsh King of one of Rachel's favorite fairy tales reaching up through the muck to grab my ankle and pull me under as he did to the princess who bore him the daughter of the story's title. Peter thinks these dark and gruesome fairy tales are completely inappropriate for a ten-year-old, but I loved the original versions when I was her age, and I don't think that reading them hurt me.

I cup my hands. "Rachel!"

Still nothing.

I push forward. The smoke smell grows stronger. My boots are caked with mud. My arms are scratched and bleeding. I'm sweaty and thirsty and my voice is hoarse from shouting, but none of that matters. I have to find her. I have to know that she is safe.

When I come upon an opening in the underbrush that marks a game trail, I take off running down it, expecting to see flames licking the treetops at any second. Instead, as I splash through a mucky area and look down to check my footing, I see footprints. Or more accurately, shoeprints. Two sets, an adult's and a child's, traveling straight up the middle of the trail, neither making any effort to hide their tracks.

I stop. The child-sized set has to belong to Rachel, but this doesn't explain the adult's prints. I have no idea who could have made them. Did Rachel happen upon these prints and decide to follow them? Or is someone following her? The mud is so fresh, and the prints are such a jumble, it's impossible to tell which set was laid down first. I take off running again, trying not to imagine all the myriad and terrible ways in which my daughter might have come to harm at a stranger's hands.

And then in a clearing so small I almost run past it, I see the source of the smoke: a campfire, carefully constructed and conscientiously crackling away inside a ring of stones. A piece of metal grating has been laid across the top. On the grating sits a large pot. Whatever is in the pot is steaming. The sight is so incongruous and unexpected, I hardly know what to think. This campfire has to have been built by the stranger who laid down the footprints. The fact that the fire is going strong says that he or she can't be far.

I resist the urge to call Rachel's name and hang back in the trees. It isn't only the campfire that warns me to be cautious. On the other side of the clearing is a hunting blind, built six feet off the ground among a cluster of slender maples using the trunks as supports. The sides and top are camouflaged with branches. If not for the fire, I probably would never have seen it.

My anger burns. Hunters, trespassers, right here on our land. People audacious enough to build a hunting blind, to make a campfire, to use our property as if it were their own. I'm not naïve. I know people trespass all the time. The Upper Peninsula is so vast and underpopulated a person could squat in an abandoned cabin for years without detection if they chose. I've sometimes worried that something like this might happen to us, mainly because of the impact such an intrusion would have on Peter's and my research. The security gate does a good job of keeping people out from the east if anyone gets curious and decides to see what's at the end of our road, and our acreage is posted with NO TRESPASSING signs all along the highway, but the west side is bordered by state forest. Anyone hiking east from that direction could make their way down our cliff the same way Peter and I used to climb up it and continue onto our land with no idea that they were now on private property.

But there's a big difference between wandering hikers inadvertently passing through and hunters setting up a full-blown camp. Worse, this time of year, there is no game in season because all the game animals are busy having babies. Which means these are not hunters, they're poachers.

Poachers. Using our property, burning our wood, damaging our trees. Killing our wildlife. *Doing who knows what to my daughter.* Did Rachel follow the game trail as I did and discover the campfire and the hunting blind while the poachers were here? Did she innocently walk up to them and say hello, not realizing that what they are doing is illegal, and that making herself known could get her into trouble? Did the poachers run away after she found them, and is this why the fire is burning with no one around to tend to it? Or did they take her with them so she couldn't tell what she'd seen? Are they hiding nearby at this very moment with their hands over my daughter's mouth so she can't cry out to me?

Or are none of these scenarios correct and I'm letting my imagination get the better of me? It's possible that the footprints I saw are not Rachel's at all. Maybe the poachers have a child with them. Maybe the smaller prints belong to a woman. Maybe they're not poachers. Maybe they're merely wildlife enthusiasts and all they're taking is pictures. This camp is not far from the territory that White Bear claimed after he left his mother when he was a two-year-old. Did the hikers wander onto our property and stumble across White Bear and come back and build this blind so they could photograph him? If they did, and word were to get out about the rare albino black bear and curiosity seekers swarm us, eager to see for themselves, my research could be in serious trouble.

There's only one way to find the answer. I step boldly into the clearing, making sure to keep my hands where anyone who might be watching can see them. I scan the edges for movement, a reaction, the reflection off the lens of a camera, the glint of a rifle scope. I wish I had a rifle of my own.

"Hello? Is anyone here?"

No answer.

"Rachel?"

Still nothing. No one calls out to me or tries to stop me. Maybe Rachel is in an entirely different part of the forest. Maybe she doesn't even know this camp is here.

I go over to the campfire and am relieved to see that the pot holds only boiling water, and nothing more. The area beneath the hunting blind is enclosed with wooden snow fencing painted green to disguise it. It looks like a cage. Maybe the people who built the camp really are poachers, and they're hoping to trap baby animals and sell them to the pet trade. This time of year, there are plenty of babies in our woods from which to choose: raccoon and fox kits, bear cubs, even our wolf pups could be targets.

I go up to the fencing and peer through the slats. The interior is deeply shadowed. I can just make out something lying on the ground. It looks to be about the size and shape of a deer.

Then the shape moves, and I see that it is not a deer at all.

"Rachel?"

I literally take a step back. I feel as though I've been punched. It's impossible to process what I'm seeing. Someone put my daughter *in a cage*. I have no idea who, or why.

"Mommy?" She sits up sleepily and rubs her eyes.

"What on earth? Rachel, honey, what are you doing in there? Come over here to me."

She gets to her feet and comes close to the fencing. I stick my fingers through the slats to touch her face.

"Are you all right?"

"Uh-huh." She yawns and stretches. "I fell asleep."

214

Thank God it's only that. She seems unhurt. Which makes the reason for her captivity all the more puzzling.

"I can see that. Are you sure you're okay?"

I keep my voice light. Rachel is a sensitive child. If she doesn't understand that there is something very, very wrong with this picture, I am not about to tell her.

She shakes her head. My heart plummets. "I have to pee," she says.

I don't know whether to laugh or cry. "Okay, then. Let's get you out of here."

I walk the perimeter. If someone put my daughter in this cage, there has to be a way out. The fencing is stretched taut and nailed with staples to the trunks that form the blind's supports. The cage is so secure, it makes me wonder if it was built to contain an adult bear. Maybe the hikers aren't planning only to take pictures of White Bear. Maybe they're hoping to lure him inside and capture him. To what end, I'm not sure. And that still doesn't explain what they did to my daughter.

At last I find a section that looks as though it's meant to fold back on itself as a gate. A gate that is fastened with a padlock.

A padlock. I'm so furious I could scream. Surely, whoever took Rachel as their prisoner can't think that they can keep her here indefinitely, that we wouldn't come looking for her, that we wouldn't scour heaven and earth until we found our missing daughter. I feel like ripping the cage apart with my bare hands, shredding and tearing and burning everything that I can find. These people are *on my property*. They *put my daughter in a cage*. I shudder to think what might have happened if I hadn't found her.

I look around for a hammer or a rock to smash the fencing surrounding the padlock. Beneath a pile of branches, I spot a wooden ladder. The ladder looks identical to one of ours that went missing weeks ago. If the people who built this place and imprisoned my daughter have been sneaking around the lodge stealing our stuff, then they're a lot bolder and more dangerous than I thought.

I prop the ladder against the platform and climb up to look for the padlock key. Then I reach the top rung and stop. On the floor is a blue plastic tarp. The tarp is covered with newspapers. On top of the newspapers, laid out meticulously from smallest to largest, are Diana's flensing knives.

18

Rachel

I wake up in a small, warm, dark place. It feels as though I'm in a cage, or a cave, though somehow, I know it's neither. I don't know where I am exactly, but I know this place is familiar. I've been here before, spent enough time in this place to recognize the contours and the odors immediately. It smells of dirt and something else. It's crowded, but not unpleasantly so.

I also know that I am not alone. Something is in this place with me. Something that's not me. Something alive. I should be frightened, but I am not.

I open my eyes. Instantly, the warm, safe feeling disappears, and reality intrudes. The old barn in which I spent the night is drafty and cold. The hay mound where I slept reeks of mold. It's not dark as in my dream, thanks to the early morning light filtering through the rows of dusty skylights running the length of the barn under the eaves. And it most definitely isn't warm.

Still, the dream lingers. I had a therapist once who was a big fan of unpacking dreams to find their meanings. She said that everyone's subconscious keeps working while they sleep, and that the seemingly random and disjointed thoughts and images my brain conjured up to entertain me during the night were the key to discovering what was keeping me at the hospital. She made me keep a pad of paper and a pencil by my bed so I could write down everything I remembered as soon as I woke up. I could have told her that the reason I wasn't getting better had nothing to do with my dreams and everything to do with my visions, but I didn't.

I don't put much stock in dream interpretation. Even the best and brightest experts don't agree. Freud believed that dreams are the vehicle we use to bury our conscious thoughts. Jung believed that dreams *reveal* our *secret* thoughts, and that understanding them is essential for restoring our "psychic balance," a term that always sounded way too out there to me, though this could have been my therapist's phrasing given that Jung died before New Ageism became a thing.

I have my own dream theory. I believe that dreams are nothing but the recycled pieces of whatever we thought or said or did that day. For example, if you dream that you're being chased by a monster, it doesn't mean that subconsciously you are terrified of dying; it's just the leftover anxiety from whatever went wrong that day taking a different form, whether you forgot to do your homework, or you couldn't find your car keys, or you were late to school or work.

I also believe that dreams are sometimes the remnants of *other* days, and that having dreamed them, we can relive those days again. I believe the dream I just experienced is one of these. Now that I have dreamed it, I *remember* being in a small dark place the day my parents died. Hiding, obviously, though whether this was before or after they died, or whether it was in a closet or in the basement or somewhere else, I can't say. Still, it's a memory. A clue. One more piece of the puzzle that I am trying to assemble. Last night, I went to bed cold and tired and wet and discouraged by how little progress I'd made. This morning, things look a lot better. Since I've come home, I've learned that the last time I shot my rifle, I was in the forest. I also know that something very bad happened in our woods. And now I remember that I spent some unknown amount of time in a warm, dark, safe place. All I have to do is figure out how everything fits.

I unwind the blanket from around my legs and stand up. The barn is freezing. Goosebumps pepper my skin. A line of little drifts along the north wall where the snow blew through the cracks between the boards explains why the barn is so cold. Still, last night wasn't the worst sleep I've had; that honor goes to the night I spent on the floor of a padded cell. A person might think that because the floor is padded it would be relatively comfortable. But when you think about what you're actually sleeping on, including all of the various and sundry bodily fluids that have accumulated in the padding over the years, it's enough to make you wish the floor was concrete. You're not allowed to have a blanket or a pillow, and the staff who are monitoring the ceiling cameras twenty-four/seven won't turn off the lights no matter how many times or how nicely you ask. Beating on the walls and screaming and crying gets the same non-response. The padded room is meant to calm patients after they've had an episode, but in my experience, after a few hours you come out so beaten and worn down from being so completely at the mercy of others, you'd do anything they told you to if only they would make it stop. Never mind the drugs.

I drape the blanket over my shoulders and gather up my clothes to get dressed. My jeans and socks and boot liners are still wet. I shake off the straw clinging to them and put them on anyway, then slip through the gap in the back of the barn to relieve myself. Close by is the cemetery where my parents are buried. I've never visited their graves, though I used to come here with my mother to visit my baby brother. To be honest, the practice seemed odd to me then and still does. I understand that some people find it comforting to sit and commune with their dead loved ones, as my mother used to do with my brother, and I don't begrudge them that. But I don't have to visit the spot where my parents are buried to remember them. It occurs to me now that I don't know how my brother died. Perhaps Diana does.

I zip my jeans and hurry back to the relative warmth of the barn. Mice flee my footsteps. They don't know that I am the last person on earth who would hurt them. I cross to the side facing the lodge and look out through one of the cracks. The lights are on in the kitchen. Smoke curls from the chimney. The windows are foggy with condensation. I can see Diana and Charlotte moving around behind them like ghostly shadows. Warm and well-fed shadows.

I wipe my dripping nose on my jacket sleeve and open the connecting door to their studios hoping to find something to eat: a leftover candy bar, an apple core—and am immediately enveloped in a warmth so delicious it makes me shiver. I feel like an idiot. My parents used to talk about upgrading their offices to electric baseboard heat instead of kerosene space heaters, but when they weighed the small amount of time they spent in their offices against the amount of time they spent in the field, they concluded it wasn't worth the investment. Given that Diana and Charlotte work in their studios full-time, it makes sense that they would have taken the plunge. I wonder if the entire property is now electrified. That first night as I was bumbling my way around in the dark, I never thought to turn on a light switch.

There are other changes. The dividing walls that

separated the offices have been torn down to make one large room. My parents' desks, their papers, their research—the tape recorders and cameras that I was hoping to use to document Diana's scheming—everything is gone. The loss saddens me more than I can say. I'm not sure how I'll be able to take up my mother's research without her records. If I'm lucky, their books and papers are in the boxes in the carriage house. They have to be. I can't believe that Diana would have so little regard for our parents' life work that she would destroy it.

Less intrusive and a definite improvement are the small kitchenette and a door next to it that turns out to be a bathroom. I reheat the leftover coffee in the microwave and scarf down one of Charlotte's homemade granola bars. My parents used to say that Charlotte could have opened a bakery, and I don't disagree. I loved watching her roll out piecrust into a perfect circle on our marble countertop, then adding sugar and flour and a pinch of nutmeg to the blueberries I'd picked for the filling; taking the pies from the oven with a pair of scorched and stained oven mitts, the slits in the tops of the pies bubbling juice like a blue volcano. My father was always threatening to throw away her oven mitts because they were so ragged. Sometimes Aunt Charlotte would throw one of the mitts at him when he teased her like this and say that if he wasn't going to be nice, he wasn't going to get any pie, but we all knew she was joking. A poignant reminder of what my life was like in the early years, back when everyone was happy.

I finish the granola bar and immediately pick up another. If Charlotte is keeping count, I'm in trouble. I grab the steaming coffee from the microwave and wrap my hands around the mug and carry it with me as I explore the room. In front of the row of windows on the north wall is an easel on which sits Diana's latest oil painting: an extreme close-up of a bird's foot along with part of its tail. Even though the painting is not yet finished, the level of detail she has managed to capture is truly astonishing. Every scale on the bird's leathery skin, every barb and barbule on every feather seems to glow. Previously, I'd only seen photographs of my sister's paintings. Now I understand why they have to be displayed behind ropes and glass to keep people from touching them. My sister is a famous artist, though I had no idea how famous she had become until one of my therapists recognized her from a *60 Minutes* interview. She even has her own Wikipedia page. "The reclusive Diana Cunningham," or "In a rare interview," is how the articles about her usually begin. I used to read everything about her I could find until I realized that the articles inevitably brought up the family tragedy. Most stinging was when the articles praised her "selfless sacrifice" on behalf of her "profoundly trau-matized sister," as one particularly uncharitable writer put it. Unless a person also happens to be famous for something that she'd rather not be famous for, I promise they have no idea how discouraging it is to see yourself dismissed so negatively in so few words.

Next to the canvas sits a stuffed bird identical to the one in the painting. Looking at the two together, it's obvious how she achieves such stunning realism. I'm betting that I could match a catalog of my sister's paintings with every bird on display in the gun room—each killed and mounted by none other than my taxidermist sister. I'm assuming her method is a closely guarded secret; at least, I haven't read about her unique blend of taxidermy and painting in any of the articles. I can imagine the PETA people descending on her studio with pitchforks and torches if they knew. The thought of her studio surrounded by screaming protestors makes me smile. If there's one thing my sister can't stand, it's a crowd.

Across the yard, the kitchen door bangs. I grab a third granola bar and a bottle of water and hurry back to the unused part of the barn. Moments later, I hear the studio door open and close. I piece together their scraps of conversation and conclude that Diana's paintings are going to be exhibited at a gallery in New York in a couple of weeks, and she and Charlotte need to crate the last of them to get ready, and Diana will be flying out early to do a series of interviews with Charlotte tagging along as her assistant. It's hard not to feel jealous—especially knowing that not only am I not included in these or any other of their plans, but that Diana wants to set me up where she never has to see or deal with me again.

As soon as I'm sure they've settled in for the morning to work, I slip out the back side of the barn and go the long way around through the woods to the lodge. I return the outerwear I borrowed yesterday exactly as I found it, hoping that neither of them will notice that the boot liners are now soaking wet, and run up the stairs to my bedroom. I take a blissfully hot, quick shower because the lodge has indeed been wired for electricity and the water temperature is not merely lukewarm as I remember, throw on dry clothes, and hurry down the hall to my childhood bedroom, where surprise, surprise—the ravens are sitting on their nest. I open the window and stick out my head.

"Hi. It's me," I say, suddenly shy.

The female cocks her head and fixes me with one shiny eye. *We remember,* she says.

"And do you remember the day my parents died?"

We remember, she says again.

"Tell me. Tell me what you saw that day. What you know."

All will become known, the raven who greeted me on my arrival says.

Remember, his mate adds. *Remember.*

I pull my head back inside. I feel like I'm talking to a pair of toddlers. When it comes to intelligence, ravens are on a par with dolphins and chimpanzees, but this pair are decidedly lacking. It's no wonder I was never able to teach them to talk.

I go over to the closet and take my box of childhood keepsakes off the top shelf. All the objects inside this box were important to me when I was a girl. I'm hoping they'll reveal something now. I spread them out on the bed: a blue jay feather, the bear-tooth necklace my father made from the teeth of a bear that died of old age, a chunk of iron ore I found by the lake. I heft the rock in my hand, remembering how I thought it was a meteorite because it weighed twice as much as it should. A piece of quartz veined with copper. A robin's egg. Clearly, I was a little girl who loved nature.

Other objects link to my sister. The dark blue velvet sack filled with white pebbles I collected from our driveway that Diana and I used to play Hansel and Gretel. The plastic Dracula teeth she found at the dollar store that were perfect for any tale that called for a wolf or a monster. Ours was such a unique childhood, two girls raised in almost complete isolation with only each other for company. Romulus and Remus. Snow White and Rose Red. No Internet. No television aside from the VHS movies our parents let us watch on our old black-and-white cathode-ray television when we were sick. It's not hard to see why we became so skilled at making up our own games.

Shooting was also a big part of our secret life. I loved sneaking off with Diana and Charlotte and Max to the gun range, or into the woods with Diana whenever our parents were away, knowing that every time we did this, we were going against their rules. "Rules are made to be broken," Aunt Charlotte used to say, and I wholeheartedly agreed.

I think again about my visions, and how I always see myself holding my rifle. Like the piece of a memory I dreamed last night, there has to be a reason I see my Remington in my visions. I go over to the closet and open the cubby to take out my rifle, thinking that perhaps I will try to reenact my vision again, but the cubby is empty. My rifle is gone.

Then I notice something in the bottom. I reach inside. My hand closes around something hard and sharp. I take it out to examine it in the light, and shudder.

In my hand is a small, silver flensing knife.

19

THEN
Jenny

I sway. Wrap my arms around the sides of the ladder to keep from falling off. My knees are like rubber. I can hardly breathe. I can't tear my eyes away from Diana's knives sparkling lethally in the sun. Each flash cuts straight to my heart. This is my fault. I did this. I should have seen this coming, should have realized that we would end up here. Should have trusted my instincts and refused to go along with Peter's harebrained idea, should have known that letting our psychopathic daughter learn taxidermy could only end badly. Should have realized that for an expert and prolific taxidermist with absolutely no conscience and zero compassion, preserving and mounting a human would present the ultimate challenge.

Because this is what Diana is planning to do to her

sister. Of this, I have no doubt. The knives, the boiling water, the cage with my daughter locked inside it—Diana lured Rachel here under some pretext, and my sweet, innocent, far-too-trusting daughter willingly went along with it. If I hadn't found her when I did, if I hadn't smelled the smoke from Diana's campfire and come out to investigate, if I'd turned around and gone back for Peter instead of coming straight here, at this very moment, Rachel might well be dead.

"Mommy?"

"Just a minute, sweetie. I'll be right down." Thankfully, my voice comes out sounding almost normal. There will be plenty of time to freak out after Rachel is safely home and I tell Peter what I found.

I climb up the rest of the way and go inside. Plates and cups stacked inside a plastic milk crate; a sleeping bag rolled inside a waterproof bag; a flashlight, a kerosene lantern hanging from a nail. Inside an old beverage cooler are matches, newspapers, and a bundle of cedar kindling tied with twine. All stolen from the lodge, including the wooden ladder that Peter and I presumed Max had taken. The effort that Diana went through to build this place is almost beyond comprehension. Stealing the building materials a few boards and nails at a time so that we wouldn't notice, transporting everything here, constructing the blind and the firepit, and then swearing Rachel to secrecy and bringing her out here by telling her who knows what. All while Peter and I were busy working in the field, naively believing that Charlotte was looking out for our interests back at the lodge and that everything was under control.

I roll the knives inside their flannel carrying case and tie the case shut and slip the case inside my jacket. I know these are Diana's knives because I picked them out myself three years ago for her seventeenth birthday. Diana and Peter and I had been going through a rough patch (if people think normal teenagers are a handful, they should try living with a teenage psychopath), and we wanted to do something special to show her that we really did love her. These five Grohmann flensing knives with carbon steel blades and rosewood handles set us back well over seven hundred dollars, which, when you consider that neither Peter nor I have steady jobs and we are basically living off our savings and his family's largesse, was a huge sacrifice. I can't believe Diana would use these knives on her sister. I can't believe she wouldn't.

What I can't imagine is how she could have possibly thought that she could get away with this. What would she have said tonight when Rachel didn't come home for dinner? When we all fanned out to search for her, would she have led us in the wrong direction, perhaps telling us she'd seen Rachel heading for a different part of the forest than where she told us she'd be? Did she really think we wouldn't move heaven and earth until we found her sister? And what was she planning to say to us when we did?

"Mommy?"

I take a deep breath and grab the padlock key from a nail and stumble down the ladder.

"Did your sister put you in here?" I ask as unconcernedly as if I were asking if Rachel had washed her hands for dinner. My own hands are shaking so badly I can barely fit the key into the lock.

"Uh-huh. We're playing Hansel and Gretel. I'm Hansel," she says proudly and pokes her fingers through the slats. "Do you want to pinch me to see if I'm fat enough?"

"Fat enough—" I look down. The ground around her feet is strewn with candy wrappers.

"Oh, Rachel, honey. This isn't a good game. You need to come home with Mommy right now."

"The witch says I have to stay here until I'm ready to eat."

"You mean Diana? Diana is the witch?"

"Uh-huh. I wanted to be Gretel, because Gretel gets to kill the witch at the end, but Diana said that this time, I had to be Hansel."

"You've played Hansel and Gretel before?"

"Uh-huh. Sometimes we play Rapunzel and I have to stay in the tower until the prince brings the ladder to rescue me. Diana is the prince," she adds unnecessarily, because I've already figured out how these games work. I suppose I should be thankful they haven't been reenacting the version of Cinderella in which Cinderella's stepsisters cut off their heels and toes trying to make the glass slipper fit.

"Well, I'm Gretel, and I'm going to set you free. That's what happens at the end of the fairy tale, right?"

"That's right!"

The padlock clicks open and Rachel scampers out, apparently none the worse for having spent the morning napping in a cage and eating candy. I pull my jacket sleeve over my hand and lift the pot off the fire and dump half the water over the flames, then knock aside the grate and kick apart the coals and douse them with the rest, kicking a layer of dirt and sand over the steaming coals for good measure. I came here to investigate a possible forest fire; I'm not about to be responsible for inadvertently starting one.

"Okay, sweetie," I say when I'm finished. "Let's go home."

She darts back inside the cage. For a moment, my heart stops. Then I realize she's only gone back for her backpack—the backpack with the survival gear that was supposed to keep her safe—and skips ahead of me down the trail. Rachel is so beautiful, so kind and gentle and loving and innocent, it's impossible to imagine how Diana can possibly look at her sister and see nothing but bones and skin. I've tried to put myself inside Diana's head so many times in an effort to understand her until I eventually realized that any such effort is doomed to failure, because I'll never see the world as callously as she does and wouldn't want to. It's as though in lacking the emotions that bind us to one another, she has no heart. I realize she's not alone in this. Some of the things that psychopathic children have done are truly chilling: one little boy decapitated a baby bird with a ruler after it fell out of its nest on a school playground; another told a little girl that he was going to pry out her cat's eyes with a fork, and when she started to cry, he told her he was going to do the same to her. Not unlike throwing rocks at a bear cub to see what it would do or putting a pillow over your sister's face to observe the color change or cutting baby animals apart to see what was inside of them or killing and skinning and preserving your little sister.

But this is the end. I can't do this any longer. No more concessions, no more allowances, no more excuses, no more trying to understand her. I never wanted to choose between my daughters, but Diana has made the choice for me.

"Are you hungry?" I ask Rachel when we come in sight of the lodge.

She shakes her head. Given the quantity of candy she consumed, I'm not surprised.

"All right, then. Mommy needs to call a family meeting. I want you to go to your reading room until I tell you it's okay to come out."

She heads off to the barn without complaint. This isn't the first time we've held a grown-ups-only discussion. At any rate, for a child who loves reading, spending half an hour in a room that's more lavishly stocked than the children's section of many libraries is hardly a punishment.

I find Peter and Max in the side yard filling potholes

with gravel. I go up to Peter and put my hand on his arm. "We need to talk," I say quietly and tip my head toward Max. "Alone."

"Can it wait? We're almost finished here."

"Sorry. No."

He leans his shovel against the barn and strips off his work gloves and sticks them in his back pocket. "Give me a minute," he says to Max. "I'll be right back."

"Actually, I think Max needs to go home for the day."

Peter's eyes narrow. Of course, he knows that my request has something to do with Diana, because what else could it be?

"It's that bad?"

"It's that bad."

"Okay, then. Same time tomorrow?" he says to Max.

"Sure thing. I'll just tell Char I'm leaving." He props his rake alongside Peter's shovel and heads for Charlotte's studio.

"Tell her to come to the kitchen right away, please," I call after him. "Family meeting."

"Righto."

"You want to tell me what this is about?" Peter asks when Max is out of earshot.

"Not yet. Would you please get Diana? I assume she's in her workshop. Tell her we need to talk right now."

I head for the lodge to stir up the fire in the woodstove and fill a pot of water for tea. Chamomile, to settle both my nerves and my stomach. I'm sorely tempted to add something stronger.

When everyone is assembled around the kitchen table, I take the knife case from inside my jacket and place it in the middle. I untie it and unroll it to reveal its contents. Just looking at the knives knowing what Diana was going to do with them makes my skin crawl. These curved knives in an assortment of shapes and sizes are manufactured for a single purpose: removing the flesh from an animal's skin. Hunters use them to get rid of the skin so that they can eat the meat. Taxidermists use them to dispose of the meat so that they can preserve the skin. My daughter, of course, was planning another use for them entirely.

"What's all this?" Peter asks.

"You want to answer?" I say to Diana.

"They're my knives," she says, stating the obvious with a shrug.

I wait for her to elaborate. She doesn't. She has to know where I found these knives, why we are all sitting around the table, that her nefarious scheme is over, and it's time to confess. But if she wants to do this as a game of twenty questions, I can drag out the interrogation as long as I have to.

"And where did I find them?" I prompt.

"In my hunting blind."

Peter raises his eyebrows. "You know we don't allow hunting on the property."

"I don't *hunt* from it," Diana snaps. "I only call it that because that's what it looks like. I use the blind as an observation post. To sketch and to paint."

I let the lie hang unchallenged. The knives do the talking for me. There's no logical reason to bring a set of flensing knives to the forest if all you're doing is drawing and painting. Diana is such a bold and unrepentant liar, I half expect the skies to rain down fire and sulfur on her head, or the ground to open beneath her feet and swallow her up like an Old Testament sinner. A part of me wishes it would.

I walk my family through my morning, beginning with me sitting in the cemetery and ending with the campfire, the pot of boiling water, the hunting blind with Rachel locked in a cage beneath it. Then I tell them what I found inside the blind: the blue plastic tarp Diana had laid over the floor for easy cleanup, the newspapers she'd spread on top to soak up the blood, the knife case open exactly as it is now on our table.

"Rachel told me that she and Diana were playing Hansel and Gretel, and that's why she was in the cage. She said she'd been eating candy all morning because Diana said she had to stay in the cage until she was fat enough to eat. *Fat enough to eat,*" I finish, and look slowly from one family member to the other.

No one speaks. Diana is wearing her poker face, so it's impossible to know what she's thinking. Peter and I have often joked that she could be a champion card player if she wanted to because she has absolutely no tell. There's nothing funny about her lack of reaction now.

"I don't understand," Peter says.

"Don't be naïve, Peter. I think you do."

"You think Diana was planning to kill Rachel, and then what? Eat her?"

"No. I think Diana was going to kill Rachel and skin her and mount and preserve her as if she were a bear or a deer."

He drains of color and recoils as if he's been slapped. Opens his mouth. Closes it. "Is this true?" he asks Diana when the shock has diminished enough to allow him to speak.

She tosses her head. "Of course not. Rachel and I were only playing. She's the one who wanted to act out Hansel and Gretel. I only went along with it because you're always telling me I should be nice to her and do what she wants. Ask her if you don't believe me."

"What about the fire?" I ask. "And the pot of boiling water? And the knives and the newspapers and the tarp?"

"Props. I was only trying to make it fun for her. You know, like the wicked witch."

"I think—" Charlotte begins.

"Not now." I cut her off. "We'll get to your role in all of this in a minute."

"My role—"

"I said *shut up*."

Her mouth snaps shut. I rarely raise my voice, and I never speak coarsely. Our mother had one of the worst tempers I've ever seen, and I determined a long time ago that I wouldn't be like her. But I don't care. I'm done being nice. Diana may be the villain in this story, but my sister is the one who made her wicked acts possible.

"I won't be quiet. You called a family meeting. Well, I'm family."

She points her finger at me and lets loose with a litany of complaints: I'm overreacting like I always do, I'm reading too much into the situation, I think that the way I see things is the only way that's right, I always take Rachel's side against Diana, I'm overprotective, rigid, domineering, demanding, bossy, selfish, and on and on. It's as though she's been secretly storing up all the anger and jealousy that she felt toward me when we were children, and it's come spewing out. I had no idea that she harbored so much hatred.

"You had one job, Char. *One job*. We gave you a place to live, a car, a place to work on your art. We gave your boyfriend a job, let the two of you set up a gun range on our property though you know we didn't want to. All we asked in return was that you supervise our daughters."

"Which I did. For ten years. But Diana is twenty now. She's not a child. She doesn't need supervision. As for Rachel, you're far too protective. Rachel is so hemmed in by your rules she's afraid to think or move without your okay. Do you really think she's as crazy about bears as you are? She's only pretending to like bears because she's desperate to please you. It's pathetic. I'm surprised you can't see that."

Peter holds up his hand. "Okay, okay. Deep breaths,

everyone. This isn't helping. The question is, what are we going to do?"

"No taxidermy for two weeks," I assert. I have much more in mind for Diana, but first, I have to discuss my plan with Peter.

"Two weeks!" she shrieks. "That's ridiculous. You can't do this. I'm not a child, and you can't treat me like one. I just started a new mounting this morning. The skin will dry out if I don't finish it. I can't simply walk away."

"She gave you an explanation," Charlotte says. "Why won't you believe her?"

"One afternoon to wrap things up," I tell Diana. "That's all. I'm serious. After today, you are not going to set foot in your workshop for two full weeks. I'll put a padlock on the door if I have to."

And then as quickly as her anger flared, it's gone. Diana is wearing her poker face again, her "mask," as the psychology books call it, the persona she puts on and off at will to hide who she is. The speed with which her demeanor changes is deeply unsettling.

She sits back in her chair and crosses her arms over her chest. "Whatever. Can I go now?"

"You can go."

She pushes back her chair and heads for her workshop. Charlotte hurries after her. I pour a cup of tea and add a generous dollop of brandy and take a swallow. My hands are shaking.

"You think I'm overreacting," I say to Peter.

"I didn't say that."

"You may as well have. 'Deep breaths, everyone. This isn't helping.' Why didn't you stand up for me?"

Peter reaches for my hand. I push it away. Take another slug of tea. Blink back tears. Bite my lip. Of all the times for Peter to go all fair-minded and equanimous—I wanted him to jump to his feet, to scream at our daughter, maybe even to hit her if that's what it would take to reach her, to show some courage, to take a stand; to somehow react in proportion to what she had done. Instead, he's behaving as if I am the one who's in the wrong.

He reaches for my hand again. "I know you're upset, Jenny," he says as I let him take it. "But maybe Char is right. Diana could have been telling the truth and you misread the situation. I agree that she and Rachel shouldn't have been alone in the woods together, and that Charlotte should have kept a better eye on them, but really—skinning and mounting a human being? You're talking *Silence of the Lambs*. That's pretty far out, even for our daughter."

"You weren't there. Rachel was *locked in a cage*. She'd eaten a bucketful of candy. For all we know, the candy was drugged and Diana was only killing time in her taxidermy studio while she was waiting for Rachel to fall asleep so she could go back and kill her. You didn't see what I saw."

"Okay," he says slowly. "Assuming this is true, what do you think we should do?"

"We have to send her away. We've tried everything.

Nothing has worked. There's nothing more we can do. None of us will be safe as long as Diana is living with us at the lodge."

"You want to send her to a mental hospital?"

"I don't *want* to. But yes. It's time."

It breaks my heart to say this. We tried so hard for so long. Put up with so much. But I can't see where we have a choice. Walking back to the lodge with Rachel, all I could think about was sending Diana away. I am absolutely convinced that this is the right thing to do. But speaking the words out loud hurts more than I would have thought. I understand that we are not the only parents who have had to face the fact that their children are monsters. School shooters, child abusers, kidnappers and rapists and murderers all have mothers and fathers. We did everything we could. We spent a fortune on counseling, moved north so Diana wouldn't be around people, made a home for her where we thought she would be safe. But what about us?

"I can tell you're ready to do this," Peter says, "but I have to be honest: I'm not so sure. Once we start down this road, there's no going back."

Frankly, his indecisiveness surprises me. This is not the first time we've talked about committing Diana. Never in such definite terms, always more along the lines of an eventuality that we might one day have to face, but I'm genuinely surprised he can't see that the day has come.

"Let me call Dr. Merritt. I'll make an appointment for

just the two of us. We can tell him what happened and see what he thinks."

I have no doubt that after I lay out the facts, Dr. Merritt will take my side, but if putting him in the position of decision-maker will help to preserve my relationship with my husband, it's worth it. More important, Dr. Merritt can advise us on the next steps.

"All right. I guess it won't hurt to see what he thinks."

I grab the Suburban's keys from the hook by the door to drive out to the nearest pay phone to make the call before Peter changes his mind. Not until I have driven through the security gate do I pull to the side of the access road and let the tears flow. I feel like such a failure. It breaks my heart to admit that after all this time, and so much effort, we were wrong. My only consolation in all of this is that my dear, sweet Rachel is too young to understand that something unimaginably terrible very nearly happened in these woods.

20

NOW
Rachel

I stare at the knife in my hand. Diana knows I'm here; probably has from the first night I came. I was a fool to think that I was fooling her. Diana has always been smarter than me. More devious. More ruthless. Now she's playing with me as a cat with a mouse, letting me think that I had the upper hand while she's been holding aces all along. I have no idea how she figured out that I'm here. It's possible she saw me eating breakfast in the kitchen yesterday while she was working in her studio. I thought I stayed well away from the windows, but she could have spotted a hint of movement behind the glass, or a reflection that didn't belong, or a shadow. It's possible that when I put the frying pan back the handle was turned in a slightly different direction, or the pan was a few centimeters off. She might have noticed that two eggs and four slices of bacon were missing, or that the coffeepot that had been left nearly empty was now dry, or that her boots and our father's coat had disappeared. Or maybe it's as simple as my therapist calling or leaving a voicemail telling them I'd signed myself out. For all I know, that might have been required.

More important than how Diana figured out I'm here is the message she's sending. *I know you're here. What are you going to do about it?*

What indeed? There are so many ways this could end: humiliation, debasement, physical harm. Not for her, but for me. If there's one lesson I learned as I was growing up, it's that anyone who underestimates my sister does so at her peril.

But I refuse to panic. My sister operates entirely without emotion. So can I. I am not the meek and timid little girl she used to bully. Fifteen years in a mental hospital took care of that. I first learned the power of my convictions the day I stood up for Scotty. I'd gone into the bathroom I shared with seven others to find four of my roommates standing in a circle around him giggling and pointing. This wing of the hospital was restricted to women, so Scotty wasn't even supposed to be there. He was wearing a blindfold and his lips were pushed forward like he was puckering up for a kiss. One of the girls had a piece of meat that was as dark as liver; the hospital often fed us organ meat to cut costs. "Do you want to kiss me?" she asked Scotty after she saw me come into the room and tossed off a grin, no doubt assuming I'd want in on the action. "Yeth," Scotty replied. "I want to kiss you." It sounded like *ah uh ki oo*, but I knew what he said.

I tackled the girl before she could press the meat to his lips and sat on her stomach and shoved the meat in her mouth. It smelled really bad, as though they'd found it in the garbage. I wasn't going to hurt her aside from literally giving her a taste of her own medicine, but I still got a week in solitary for my trouble, which gave me a lot of time to think. Standing up for Scotty felt good. It showed me the kind of person I could have been. I should have stood up to my sister long before now. This time, I will.

I go to my closet and slide my hand along the top shelf until I find a small pillow. It's a sweet little thing, all ruffles and lace and yellow gingham with hand-embroidered chicks and bunnies that Aunt Charlotte said my mother made for me while she was waiting for me to be born, though I have no memory of my mother ever doing needlework. I hold the pillow to my nose. If there are remnants in this cloth of the baby that I used to be—skin cells, baby spit-up, dried-up baby drool—I can't detect them. After I found this pillow in a box in the attic and my aunt told me what my sister had done with it, I saved it against the day that I could somehow use it against Diana. It seems that day has come.

I tuck the pillow under my arm and carry both it and

Diana's knife to the master bedroom. I pause in the doorway before going in. The first and only time I went into Diana's room without her permission, I was looking for our shared book of fairy tales—at least, I thought the book belonged to both of us because Diana and I often read the stories together, though I found out soon enough that she thought otherwise. And while I was careful not to touch anything because I knew that my sister was very particular and she would know if something had been moved, somehow, she knew I'd gone in. After she caught me out, I told her I was sorry and promised that I would never go in her room again, but she said sorry wasn't good enough and that I still needed to be punished. At that time, her preferred method was pinching me on the soft skin of my belly where the marks wouldn't show. According to her rules, if I flinched or cried out when she did this, she got to pinch me again. Even though I knew what was coming, I lifted my shirt when she told me to. It's embarrassing now to think how completely I was under her control. To this day, I have scars on my stomach from her mistreatment.

I go inside. Instantly, I am slammed with memories. This room was a cheerful, friendly place when my parents were alive, with bright colors and fresh flowers and pictures on the walls; a place where I was always welcome to come in and plop down on the bed and snuggle up with my mother and father to read or to talk. Now, without my parents, their bedroom feels cold and spare.

I go over to the bed and place the pillow in the depression where my sister sleeps and stick the flensing knife into the pillow up to its hilt and leave it there, then stand back to admire my handiwork.

Yes. I'm here. What are you *going to do about it?*

Next up: a weapon. I could have kept the knife she left me, but if I needed a knife to protect myself, there are dozens in the kitchen that would do a far better job than this tiny curved scimitar. Better yet is a rifle. I go downstairs to the gun room and search the cases until I find a Remington identical to the one Diana took. I fill my pockets with ammunition and load the rifle and sneak out the front door and through the woods and stash the rifle and ammunition behind a hay bale in the barn. I don't want to use it, but I will if I have to.

I tiptoe over to the connecting door and crouch on my heels outside their studios. Diana is a creature of habit. She used to eat lunch every day exactly at noon. I'm betting she still does.

When the studio door opens and bangs closed precisely at twelve o'clock as I expected, I go to the side of the barn that faces the lodge to make sure that Charlotte and Diana are headed for the kitchen, then open the door to their studios and go in. I'm giving myself half an hour. There are so many things that I could do in this room, from outright vandalism to simple mischief, but I start with the least invasive option. I can always escalate later if I have to.

Diana's desktop is as spare as her bedroom. No family photos, no travel mementoes, no personal items whatsoever. Still, there are enough items for my purpose: a pad of lined paper, three pens and a stapler, a word-a-day tear-off calendar, and a desk lamp. I arrange everything into a mirror image of what it was, then do the same with Charlotte's desk. A part of me feels uneasy, as though I'm being drawn into something bigger than I realize and this is all a giant mistake, but I can't sit back and wait for Diana to make the next move. The only way to prove to her that she can no longer push me around is to get out in front of her.

Things are not as they seem, a small voice says.

I look down. It's a wolf spider, a nondescript, splotchy brown member of the family *Lycosidae*, which is Greek for "wolf." I've never spoken to a wolf spider, because wolf spiders are nocturnal solitary hunters who don't spin webs, and thus people rarely see them. That this spider has come out during the day to speak to me gives weight to what it has to say.

"What isn't as it seems?" I ask, speaking as softly as I can because, despite their name, wolf spiders are extremely timid.

The spider skitters to one side and then the other and waves its front legs as though it wants to get my attention, though it already has it. Or maybe it's just nervous. I stay absolutely still. If I could stop breathing, I would.

Thingsarenotastheyseem, the spider says a second time,

running the words together so quickly that I almost can't make them out before it scurries away.

I purse my lips. I appreciate the effort that this spider went through to deliver its message, but a little more information would have been helpful. I don't know why my conversations with the insects and animals at the lodge are so limited. Getting information from them one scrap at a time is downright painful. It's as if none of them understands the whole and each can supply only one small piece. Interpreting their messages is like trying to put together a jigsaw puzzle blindfolded.

Things are not as they seem.

All will become known.

Remember.

I'm trying to.

Still, the spider's words are clearly meant as a warning, even if they're not as specific as I'd like. I'm missing something. Something important enough for a shy nocturnal spider to come out during the day to tell me that things are not as they seem. I have no idea if this has to do with the question of my guilt or innocence regarding my parents' deaths, or if it has to do with Diana trying to have me declared incompetent, or if the spider was commenting on the war of nerves that Diana and I have embarked upon. I guess I'll find out.

Across the yard, the kitchen door slams shut. I grab a granola bar and a bottle of water and hurry back to my part of the barn. I crouch next to the connecting door.

The studio door opens. I can hear footsteps on the old wooden floor, and Diana and Charlotte talking, but I can't make out what they're saying. I wonder if Diana found the pillow I left for her, if she has noticed that I rearranged her desktop, if she understands the message I am sending.

"So, what are we going to do?" Charlotte asks suddenly. Her voice is so loud it sounds as though she's standing right on the other side of this door. I hold my breath and strain to hear Diana's response.

"Wait," Diana says just as clearly, as if she, too, has moved close to the door and is speaking for my benefit because she knows I'm hiding behind it.

"Shouldn't we call the hospital and let them know she's here?" Charlotte asks. "Maybe ask them to send an ambulance to come and get her?"

"All in good time," Diana answers. "First, we're going to have a little fun."

Fun. I draw back and shudder. My stomach clenches. Hearing my sister speak that word triggers a flood of memories, and none of them good. "This is going to be fun," Diana said the day we played Robin Hood and the rope on which I was supposed to swing over the ravine snapped and I broke my arm. The rope that, when I went back later to check because it seemed inconceivable to me that a brand-new rope should break, had been sliced nearly through with a knife. "This will be fun," Diana said as I climbed into the trunk of Charlotte's car at her command for the ride to the Cobblestone Bar where Max would sometimes play because we were pretending that I was Jack the Giant Killer and Diana was the giant's wife and she was hiding me in her husband's treasure chest, though by the time we arrived, I was dizzy with exhaust fumes and the ride wasn't nearly as fun as Diana had promised it would be. "Watch," she said as we knelt beside the girl who got lost at the roadside park after we found her at the bottom of a steep gully. "This is going to be fun."

I close my eyes. Long-forgotten details of that day bubble to the surface like water from a spring. Details too terrible to consciously retain. I remember that the girl opened her eyes when she heard us talking and blinked as though she was waking up from a nap. I remember she started to sit up, but instead of helping her as I expected her to, Diana pushed the girl down and threw a leg over her and sat on her chest. I remember I watched as Diana pulled the girl's pink scarf from around her neck and wadded up one end into a ball and pushed the ball into the girl's mouth. I remember that when the girl tried to pull it out, Diana grabbed her wrists and told me to hold them above the girl's head and pushed the fabric in farther and pinched the girl's nose until she was still. "Do you understand what just happened?" Diana asked as she stood up and dusted her hands on the seat of her pants and helped me to my feet. I nodded, numb with shock. "You just saw someone die. Wasn't that fun?" I nodded again because I knew that this was what my sister wanted me to do, though when I looked down at the dead girl, I felt sick. I remember that Diana gave me the girl's scarf and told me to hide it inside my jacket and said that if I told anyone I had it, she would tell the police that I was the one who killed her, and so I did.

I did as my sister told me.

I helped kill a girl.

I feel like I'm going to faint. I can't believe I was so in thrall to my sister that I would help her commit murder. My sister should be in prison for what she did, and I should be in the cell alongside her.

And there's more. A postscript to this unimaginably awful thing I did that is so much worse, I can hardly breathe. During the days after the girl died, my mother kept asking me to describe exactly how Diana and I had found her. When I finally broke down and told her the truth, my mother thanked me for being honest and said that she would take care of everything and I shouldn't worry about Diana's threats and that I wasn't in trouble. But later, after I heard my parents arguing in their bedroom about sending Diana away, I told my sister what they said.

I told Diana that my parents were going to send her away. Days later, my parents were dead. I don't know how she did it, but I am one-hundred-percent certain that Diana killed them. Then somehow staged their deaths to look as though my father murdered my mother and killed himself.

All will become known, the raven promised. *Things are not as they seem,* the spider warned. *Remember,* the raven's mate urged.

And now I have. This is my fault. I killed my parents. If I hadn't spoken up out of misguided love for my sister, our parents would still be alive. Diana may have been the bullet, but I was the rifle, the means by which the bullet was delivered.

I swallow hard, gag, and take off for the far end of the barn so they won't hear me lose my breakfast and retch again and again. When my stomach is empty, I raise my head and make my way on trembling legs to the horse stall where I spent the night.

There I see that Diana has left me another gift.

In the hollow where I slept, tied into the shape of a hangman's noose, is a pink scarf.

21

THEN
Jenny

It's Rachel's eleventh birthday, and despite everything that's happened, I am determined that this day is going to be fun. Rachel has selected Tahquamenon Falls as her birthday destination. It's a great choice. The falls are truly magnificent: two hundred feet across and fifty feet high, and with the autumn colors only just past their peak, both the drive and the falls are going to be magnificent. Peter and I took in the falls when we toured the Upper Peninsula on our honeymoon, but Rachel and Diana have never seen them—mainly because the falls are four hours and two hundred miles from our home, which puts them at the upper limit of where we could reasonably go for a day trip.

But now, the idea of spending a long day away from

the lodge feels less like an effort and more like a reprieve. Ever since I found Rachel in that cage, the tension in our home has been unbearable. Peter and I have argued more in the past week than we have during our entire marriage. Always behind closed doors and always out of earshot of other family members, but the strain is taking its toll. No matter how many times and in how many ways I try to convince him otherwise, Peter still doesn't believe that Diana was going to skin her sister. I understand that the very idea sounds outrageous, but he wasn't there. I know what I saw. The sooner Diana is committed to a mental institution, the better. The one thing we do agree on is that we will let Dr. Merritt's expertise and advice guide our decision. Thankfully, our appointment is in less than a week.

Meanwhile, I've been doing my best to pretend that everything is fine. Rachel still has no idea what nearly happened, and as far as I'm concerned, she never will. At the same time, it's all I can do to speak to Diana or to sit down with her at the dinner table. Our daughter is well and truly wicked, I told Peter during one of our many arguments, her heart as black and cold as a lump of coal, and while my words were spoken through copious tears in the emotion of the moment, I stand by them. I understand that Diana can't help what she is, that she is incapable of feeling love or compassion, and that her sole focus on pleasing herself drives her every thought and action. But you can be evil even if you don't choose it.

I've also been having terrible nightmares—so much so that when I crawl into bed at night, I'm afraid to close my eyes. If I could skip sleeping altogether, I would. Always in my dreams I am in some sort of mortal danger: hanging off the edge of our cliff by my fingernails, or taking in great gulps of freezing lake water after our canoe capsizes, or being mauled by one of our wolves or bears. In each instance Diana has the power to rescue me but doesn't. Either she stands at the top of the cliff looking down at me and laughing, or she stomps on my fingers until I am forced to let go, or she tosses the life preserver that will save me in the opposite direction. It's not hard to imagine what Dr. Merritt would have to say about that.

Then there's my sister. Charlotte and I have barely spoken since I discovered Diana's flensing knives in the girls' tree fort. I can barely stand to look at her, knowing what her betrayal almost cost me. There's no way the girls could have built that fort without her turning a blind eye. Peter says I'm being childish and that we'll have to start talking again eventually. I haven't told him that as soon as Diana is gone, I am going to ask my sister to leave.

Peter downs the last of his coffee and pushes away from the breakfast table and picks up the picnic basket beside the door. "Ready?"

"Almost. But leave the basket there for a sec. I still have to put Rachel's present inside."

I go to the pantry and take the vintage Steiff bear I found at Rachel's and my favorite antiques shop from its hiding place on a high shelf. Technically, this is a polar bear and not a black bear, but with a little imagination, a person could easily think it was a certain beloved albino. Rachel's going to love it.

I tuck the bear in a corner of the basket and Peter carries the basket outside.

"Girls?" I call up the stairs. "Come on down now. Your dad's waiting."

As my daughters clatter down the stairs—Diana tall and blond and as thin and beautiful as a model, Rachel short and pudgy with brown hair and eyes and a ravenous sweet tooth—the moment feels so ordinary I could almost believe that we are a normal family. There was a time when I thought that "normal" was a bad word, that there might be nothing worse than being average, and unless a person aspired to something greater, they were dull and unimaginative. Now I crave normality the way Rachel loves her sugar.

Diana yawns and digs at her eyes. "No coffee?" she asks as she lifts the empty pot.

"I put the rest in the thermos. You can have a cup after we're on the road." If we're going to make it to the falls in time to hike to both the Upper and Lower Falls and have our picnic, we need to get going.

Diana drags herself out to the Suburban with as much enthusiasm as if we'd asked her to clean the horse stables. Honestly, if it were up to me, we'd have left her at home, but I couldn't think of a way to exclude her that wouldn't disappoint Rachel.

"I'm hungry," Diana complains after we've been on the road for barely an hour. Already she's kept up a constant barrage of complaints: It's too hot in the car, and when Peter turns down the heat, it's too cold. Peter is either driving too fast or too slowly, she's getting carsick in the back seat and wants to trade places with me in the front; Rachel won't talk to her, Rachel won't shut up.

"We just ate breakfast," I say.

"I didn't."

And whose fault is that? I want to snap, but I don't because of Rachel, and also because arguing with Diana goes absolutely nowhere.

"I don't care if we stop," Rachel pipes up. Of course, she would. Rachel hates conflict. I've read that growing up with a psychopathic sibling can make a child hyper-vigilant, overly dutiful, guilt-ridden, and guarded, which is another reason Diana has to go. I used to believe that being the parents of a psychopathic child was simply the hand we'd been dealt, and that we had no choice but to cope with it as best we could because there was nothing that we could do. Now I know that we could have taken steps—should have taken steps—to control the situation years ago. My only hope now is that it's not too late.

"It's too early to stop," I say. "If we eat our lunch now, we won't have anything left to eat at the park."

This isn't entirely true; I packed plenty of food for both a lunch and a dinner, and we could always stop at a restaurant on the way home if we had to, but I hate the way that Diana's wishes dominate our family. For all I know, she is only saying this on a whim and isn't even hungry.

Diana unbuckles her seatbelt and turns around and crouches on her knees to reach into the cargo area and starts digging through the picnic basket.

"Stop that," I say sharply. I was planning to let Rachel discover her birthday present on her own when we stopped to eat. It would be just like Diana to pull it out now and spoil the surprise.

"Stop it," I say again as she continues to paw through the basket. Even as I say it I realize that I'm going to have to back off because the only way to make her stop is to let her have her way. "All right. We'll stop. There's a roadside park in about thirty miles. We can eat there. Are you okay with that?" I ask Peter.

"Whatever you want," he says, and I can't help but think of another long car trip, so many years ago.

Half an hour later we turn in and park beneath a gorgeous yellow maple. During the summer this park is so crowded it's almost impossible to find an empty table, but tourism in the U.P. falls off sharply after the school year begins and we have our pick. Rachel runs from table to table.

"This one," she says at last, plopping herself down at a table as far as possible from the only other family, a father, mother, and a daughter who looks to be around Rachel's age, who are also enjoying a picnic. The table overlooks a small hill with a creek burbling at the bottom.

Peter lifts the hamper onto the table. "Will you help me set out our things?" he asks Rachel. He looks at me over her head and winks.

"Ooh," she squeals when she lifts the lid and sees her present. She snatches up the bear and cuddles him close and kisses the bald spot on the top of his head. "Thank you, Daddy! Oh, thank you, Mommy! He's perfect! I'm going to call him 'White Bear'!"

"You can't call him 'White Bear,'" Diana says, her voice dripping with scorn. "We already have a bear with that name."

Rachel's face falls. I'm so angry, I could slap Diana. I knew when I imposed a two-week moratorium on taxidermy as punishment for what she was planning to do to Rachel that she would make us all pay, and indeed, Diana has been even more hateful than usual. But attacking Rachel over such a trifling thing as a stuffed bear's name is too much.

"Don't listen to your sister," I tell Rachel. "He's your bear. You can call him whatever you like."

"I'll ask him what he thinks." Rachel whispers into the bear's ear, waits, and nods. "He says he wants to be called 'White Bear,'" she announces with a grin.

Diana only shakes her head. While I'm thankful she backed off, I can't help but sigh. Juggling the interactions between my daughters is a full-time job.

The rest of the picnic goes about as I'd expect, with Rachel running around exploring, chatting with the girl at the other table, feeding potato chips to the chipmunks who come to beg, cajoling her father into carving her and Diana's names into the picnic table, while Diana pokes fun at her or belittles her or criticizes her every move. Now that my eyes have been fully opened to Diana's constant mistreatment, I'm astonished at the extent to which Rachel is able to put up with it.

"That's defacing public property," Diana scolds when Peter pulls out his pocketknife after Rachel shows him where she wants him to carve her name. "You could get arrested for that."

On another day and under other circumstances, I might well have reacted exactly as Diana did because I'm a bit of a stickler for following the rules, but I am not going to do a single thing to spoil Rachel's day.

"It's okay," I say quickly. "There are plenty of other names. No one will care if we add two more."

As Peter is putting the finishing touches on the heart he carved around our daughters' names, a man approaches our table. He looks concerned. For the briefest of moments, I think that he's with the park service and he's going to call us out for defacing the table. Then I recognize him as the father of the other family.

"Excuse me," he says. "Have you seen my girl? She said she was going to check out the nature trail, but now my wife and I can't find her."

My stomach gets tight. A girl lost in the woods. A girl the age of Rachel.

"Rachel?" Peter asks. "You were talking to her. Did she tell you where she was going?"

"Uh-huh. She went that way." Rachel points toward the nature trail.

"You're sure?"

She nods again.

"We looked," the man says. "She's not there."

Peter extricates himself from the table. "Don't worry, we'll find her. Diana, Rachel, Jenny, come on. We'll each look in a different direction and meet back here in five minutes."

"Come with me," Diana says and takes Rachel's hand. "You're too little to go by yourself. We don't want you to get lost."

The idea of my daughters going off into the woods alone makes my blood run cold. "I'll go with them," I say quickly to Peter.

"Emily! Emily!" The forest rings with our cries. The sense of having been here and done this is almost overwhelming. Just last week I called Rachel's name as I hiked through a forest very similar to this one. I tell myself that this situation is nothing like that one. Odds are the girl is fine. We haven't been here long—she can't have gone far. Rachel spoke with her maybe ten or fifteen minutes ago. She can't have come to any harm.

But when we meet back at our picnic table in five minutes as agreed, no one has seen her.

"This is crazy," the girl's father says. "She can't just disappear. I'm calling 911." Her mother is near tears.

Peter pulls me aside. "What do you think we should do? If we're going to make it to the falls and back, we really need to get on the road. But I don't want to leave if someone's child is in danger."

"I agree. If it were my child, I'd want everyone to do everything they could to find her. But this is Rachel's outing. I think we should leave the decision to her."

Peter waves Rachel over and explains the situation. "What do you want to do? Should we stick around and help find her, or should we go to the falls? We can't do both."

"Stay," my kindhearted daughter says without a moment's hesitation. She tugs on Diana's jacket. "Come on. Let's keep looking."

They head for the woods. I trail after them. Diana looks over her shoulder with disgust. I don't care. My sister left my daughters unsupervised and look where it got us.

As we start down a trail that ends at a scenic lookout, a sheriff's patrol car pulls up with its lights flashing.

"Hold up," I call to the girls. "We should go back and talk to the officer, tell him where we've looked and let him direct the search."

"Okay," the officer says after Peter, Diana, Rachel, and I each tell him what we know. "This is what we're going to do. Mrs. Walker," he says to the girl's mother, "I want you to stay here as our point person." A kindness, because she looks ready to collapse. "Everyone else keep doing what you're doing. But stay within earshot and check back here every fifteen minutes. We don't want someone else getting lost." He says this as if it's a joke. It's not funny.

The girl's mother bites her lip. I sit down on the picnic bench beside her and slip my arm around her shoulders.

"It will be all right," I promise. "We'll stay here as long as it takes to find her."

She nods, sniffs. I think I can safely say that I know exactly how she feels. I scan the circle of searchers looking for Diana and Rachel, intending to join them, but my daughters are gone.

Gone.

"Did you see where Diana and Rachel went?" I ask Peter. It's a struggle to keep my voice calm. Nothing happened. It couldn't have.

"They went that way." He points toward the dog run.

And you didn't stop them? I want to scream. *You didn't think to go with them? To tell them to wait for me?* How could he let them go off by themselves? He knows what Diana is like. What she did. I take off running.

"Rachel! Diana!" I call. "Wait for me!"

I run faster. Rachel is wearing her favorite green canvas jacket, but Diana is wearing a bright orange hunter's vest. She should be easy to spot. I sprint across the grass heedless of the fact that this is a dog run, looking for a flash of orange through the trees. I hit the woods and keep going. Branches tear at my hair and my clothes.

"Rachel!"

At last, I see a patch of orange at the bottom of a gully. "Diana!" I call down to her. "Is everything okay? Is Rachel with you? Did you find the girl?"

"Mom! Down here! We found her!" Rachel calls back.

"Is she all right?"

"Just come," Diana says.

The lack of urgency in her voice leaves me cold. I get a bad feeling. Then again, Diana rarely gets excited about anything.

The ground is so steep I have to hang on to the tree trunks and bushes to keep from rolling all the way down it. When I reach the bottom, I see that Diana is bent over something pink. My heart sinks. The girl is lying on her back. Her eyes are open, and her body is still.

I drop to my knees and place my hand on her chest.

"Don't bother," Diana says. "She's dead."

"You don't know that!" I push her aside. The last time that it was in my power to save a life, I didn't know CPR. I do now. I place one hand on top of the other and press down hard on the girl's chest. Two-inch-deep compressions, difficult enough while practicing on a dummy, now seem absolutely brutal in reality. I use my body weight to assist. One hundred compressions per minute. I count them off in my head. CPR is much more difficult than people realize, and a lot more physical. In a third of the cases, the patient ends up with cracked or broken ribs—a small trade-off for their life.

"Go," I tell Diana between beats. "Hurry. Get help. Take Rachel."

The girls clamber up the hill. I deliver two rescue breaths with the girl's head tilted back and her chin lifted, then go back to compressions. For the next minutes, there is only the sound of my breathing as I work to keep her alive. She can't be dead. She can't be.

At last the officer scrambles down the hill. The girl's parents follow on his heels, and behind them, EMTs with a portable defibrillator and a stretcher. The girl is completely unresponsive. I watch the girl's parents watching them work on their daughter for a long sad minute, then turn and slowly climb the hill. Another child dead. Another child I was unable to save.

Peter is waiting at the picnic table with Diana and Rachel. "Are you okay? Diana said the girl is dead."

I collapse onto the bench beside him. "She's gone."

I hate speaking so plainly in front of Rachel. Then again, she's no stranger to death, and not only because of her sister's taxidermy; after all, our beloved bears are omnivores. But this was a person. A little girl like her. I pull her onto my lap as if she were a toddler.

"I'm so sorry you had to see that." I push her hair out of her eyes and wipe the tears from her cheeks and hold her close. "Sometimes bad things happen." I wish I had better words, but nothing is going to undo what she's seen.

"Can we go now?" she asks in a shaky voice. "I don't want to be here. I want to go home."

"I do too, sweetie, but we have to wait until the police tell us we can leave. As soon as they're done talking to us, we can go."

I flash back to another death, to another time when the police questioned my daughter. I shudder to think what they might ask my girls now. The girl was dead when they found her. She had to be.

I see the toddler at the bottom of our swimming pool. I see Diana bent over the girl's lifeless body. I think about her endless lies, her cruelty, her utter lack of feeling and remorse, and am finally ready to admit that the world would be a better place if my daughter had never been born.

22

NOW
Rachel

I can't stop staring at that scarf. Its message is clear: *I killed that girl.* We *killed her. Now I'm going to kill you.*

The irony isn't lost on me. As long as I was in the hospital and had no memory of the day she died, I was allowed to live. Now that I've come home and my memories are beginning to return, my sister has to kill me. But I can't die. I am the only one who knows that my sister is a murderer. If I die, this girl and my parents will never get justice.

I grab my rifle from its hiding place and stick the extra ammo in my jacket pocket and slip through the missing boards in the back of the barn like a soldier heading into battle. I go in through the front door and cross the place where my parents died without a second's hesitation and run through the great room for the kitchen. When Charlotte and Diana came home the first night that I was here, I heard the jingle of car keys tossed onto the counter. I don't remember if the keys were there the next morning while I was fixing breakfast, and I don't recall seeing them during the other times that I passed through the room, but I wasn't looking for them then. I am now. Diana will expect me to run away. She will not expect me to drive. Especially since I never learned how.

I quickly scan the counters, then run up the back stairs to look for them in Charlotte's room. Her purse sits on her dresser. I dump the contents on her bed and find the keys and stick them in my jeans pocket along with all the cash in her wallet. It feels like a lot. The cash makes me feel a thousand times better. With plenty of cash and a getaway car, I have a chance.

I tuck the rifle under my arm and run to my bedroom. All I need are my bear and Trevor's business card, and I'm gone. The books I brought with me from the hospital are for children, and the clothes are all secondhand. I can easily get more. As I imagine the looks on Diana's and Charlotte's faces when they hear the car's engine start and see myself watching in the rearview mirror as they run after me yelling at me to stop, I almost laugh. If they're smart, they'll cut the power to the security gate before I can get to it—Diana upgraded everything to solar after our parents died and one of her fans somehow managed to get in, she told me proudly during one of her visits, and the security system is now state of the art—but I'm counting on the element of surprise to give me the advantage. If worse comes to worst, I'll ram my way through. As for the actual driving, I'm not worried. I know how to start a car and how to put it into gear from watching others. Plus, I'll have four miles to practice.

If I'm making my getaway sound too easy, it's because I don't want to think about all the things that could go wrong. Charlotte's SUV is not the only vehicle at the lodge; there are two others in the carriage house that they can use. Even if they don't catch up to me before I hit the highway, as soon as they can pick up a cell phone signal, they can report Charlotte's SUV as stolen and sit back and wait for the police to nab me. With no driver's license, no I.D., and driving a stolen car, it's not hard to see how that's going to go. Then again, at least I'll be safe from my sister in a jail cell.

Then I open the door to my bedroom and stop short.

In the middle of the bed, propped up on either side of my stuffed bear toy as if they are waving a greeting, are two massive white bear paws.

I scream. I shouldn't. I can't stop myself. My rifle clatters to the floor. I drop to my knees, tear at my hair, squeeze my eyes shut and curl into a ball and bite my hand to stop from screaming again, rock and moan. White Bear is dead—*dead*. The creature I loved more than any other. White Bear, my companion, my brother, my friend.

I take a deep, steadying breath. Open my eyes and lift my head. White Bear's paws are still propped in the middle of my bed, still reaching out to me as if in silent appeal: *Help me. Do something. Get justice. Right the wrong.*

I want to clutch what's left of him to my bosom and tell him how sorry I am for what happened, yet the thought of touching his severed paws repulses me. I hate the taxidermy in the great room. Heads without bodies, bodies without life. Bad enough that Diana killed White Bear but preserving only his paws and keeping them so that she might one day use them against me is positively obscene.

Do something. Get justice. Right the wrong.

I would if I could. But there is nothing that I can do; no way to make this right. White Bear is as dead as my parents. Diana knows I loved this bear more than any other. There was no reason to kill him except to hurt me. This is my fault. My love for White Bear killed him as surely as if I had shot him with my own rifle. Everything and everyone that I love ends up dead.

I get to my feet. I have to assume that she heard me scream. I empty my duffel bag on the floor and dig through the mess for Trevor's business card, then shove the card into my jeans pocket along with the car keys.

The kitchen door slams. Voices, footsteps running up the stairs.

I drop to the floor and grab my rifle and roll underneath the bed and clutch it to my chest. Hold my breath and lay as still as death. I shrink back against the wall as the footsteps come into the room. Diana and Charlotte are so close I could reach out and grab one of their ankles and yank their leg out from under them if I wanted to—but how is that going to help? I'm hardly going to shoot them, and they know it. I could wait and hope that they don't find me, though there's not a chance that they won't look under the bed. Or I can come out on my own.

I leave the rifle behind so I can come back for it later and roll out from under the bed. As I stand up with my hands in surrender my sister's look of triumph makes me ill. She also has a rifle—another Magnum, I can't help but note. Not the rifle she used to kill our parents—that one is shut away in an evidence locker somewhere—but one exactly like it. Her weapon of choice.

"Well, well, well," she says. "Greetings, little sister. Imagine finding you here."

No curiosity, no surprise, no *What are you doing here? How did you get here? Why didn't you tell me you were coming?* as I would have expected. Questions with an accusatory subtext: *You should have told me you were coming; you should have asked me for a ride; you shouldn't have come without checking with me first.* Questions I was planning to turn back on her: *Why did you abandon me in the hospital? Why did you stop coming to visit? Why didn't you want me to come home?* until we came to the only question that matters: *Why didn't you tell me I couldn't have killed my mother?* I want to hit her, scratch out her eyes, choke my sister as she did that girl and scream, *How could you kill our parents?* But I can't. Not yet. Somehow, I have to get her to admit to what she's done.

I focus my frustration and rage on the travesty on my bed. "How could you? How could you kill White Bear?"

"*I* killed him?" Her eyes narrow. She slaps her knee and laughs. "Oh, this is rich. You don't remember." She laughs again.

I squint back at her, utterly confused by her reaction.

"I didn't hurt your precious bear," she says. "*You* did. You shot him. *You* killed White Bear."

"*I* killed him? Why would I?"

I've never killed anything in my life. Diana knows this. I would never shoot the bear that I loved.

She sits down on the bed and pats the covers while Charlotte watches us from the doorway. I sit where she indicates. She picks up one of White Bear's paws and holds it in the crook of her arm and strokes it as though it were a kitten.

"Let me tell you a story, little sister. One fine November day, two sisters were shooting targets at a gun range. The gun range was in a clearing in the middle of a vast forest. The sisters often came to this gun range to practice, though the older sister was far more skilled than the younger and had no need."

She stops and waits for my reaction. I give her nothing.

"On this day, a white bear walked into the clearing. The younger sister believed that this was an enchanted bear, a prince who was bound to remain in that form until a princess's kiss set him free. But the bear was large and fierce. When it saw the sisters, it stood on its hind legs and roared. So, the younger sister shot the white bear to save her sister."

"That's absurd. You know I would never do such a thing." If Diana is trying to trick me into confessing to something that I didn't do, the least that she could do is pick a lie that has a prayer of holding up.

"Do I? *Think,* Rachel. *Remember.*"

I open my mouth to object, then close it. I suck in my breath, because suddenly, I *do* remember. I look at White Bear's mutilated paws and am overcome with shame and horror.

Diana and I *were* at the gun range when White Bear came wandering out from the forest as she described. I remember thinking that he should have been afraid of the noise of our shooting, but for some reason, he wasn't. As he grazed calmly near the edge of the clearing, Diana dared me to shoot him. "It won't hurt him. I promise," she said.

"I can't," I told her. "White Bear is my friend."

"Go on. I dare you. Shoot him in his rear end. It'll be fun."

I shook my head.

"Do it. What's the point of learning to shoot if all you do is shoot at targets? Go on. Shoot him."

"I won't." I started to cry.

"You're such a baby." Diana shook her head in disgust. "If you don't shoot him, I will." She raised her rifle.

"No! Stop! Please! Don't!" I grabbed her rifle barrel and pointed it at the ground. "Don't hurt him!"

She looked at me unmoved and shook her head. "Let me tell you what's going to happen, little sister. Somebody is going to shoot White Bear today. Either you will shoot him in his rear, or I will shoot him in his head. It's up to you."

I cried harder. My sister was bigger than me, older than me. Smarter. Meaner. I thought about all the times she hurt me, all the animals she killed and stuffed. That she *would* kill White Bear if I didn't shoot him, I had no doubt.

"I'm waiting . . ." She raised her rifle. "Ten . . . nine . . . eight . . . seven . . . six . . ." She sighted down the scope.

"Okay! Okay! I'll do it!"

"Five . . . four . . . three . . ."

"I said I'd do it! Please. Please don't kill him."

She stopped counting. Her eyes narrowed. She looked at me not unlike the way that she is looking at me now. Intense, focused, the madness that drives her visible behind her eyes. I knew then as I do now that Diana will do anything, *anything*, to get her way.

I raised my rifle. I had absolutely no intention of shooting White Bear in the rear as she had decreed. I would shoot over his head. Close enough to frighten him away before my sister in turn could shoot him.

I pulled the trigger. The bullet winged over White Bear's head exactly as I intended. He stopped grazing and looked up at me with no more concern than if the bullet had been a wasp or a fly. *Run! Go!* I shouted inside my head when he resumed eating. I couldn't understand why he didn't run away.

"You did that on purpose." Diana's voice dripped with scorn. "Now it's my turn."

"No! Don't! I'll do it right this time, I promise."

"Words, words," Diana said, shaking her head as if she didn't believe that I would really do it.

"I will," I promised, and I meant it. I didn't want to shoot White Bear. But I would to save his life.

"Of course you will. But just to make sure . . ."

She laid her rifle on the ground and knelt down beside me and put her arms around me the same as Max did when he helped me aim my rifle and swung my rifle toward White Bear. My eyes blurred. My hands trembled. My whole body shook.

Diana held me close. Then she slid her finger alongside mine and pulled the trigger.

My bullet hit White Bear in his chest. He raised up on his hind legs and roared. Before I had time to process what had happened or to think of what might be coming next, my sister ejected the spent shell and loaded another. Together, we fired again.

White Bear fell. He didn't get up. Diana let go of me and stood up. I dropped my rifle and ran to White Bear and knelt beside him and threw my arms around his neck. "I'm sorry, I'm so sorry," I whispered into his fur.

Run, he whispered back, which surprised me because I knew that he was dead. I looked up. Diana's rifle was pointed at me.

I shudder, drag a hand through my hair. It's not difficult to imagine what happened next. I must have run into the forest as White Bear instructed. Somehow, I survived the following two weeks. Now I understand why, when I was found beside the highway, I could neither move nor speak. I conflated two traumatic events, the death of my parents and the death of White Bear and ended up with my vision. It's no wonder that reenacting my vision in the gun room didn't reveal any new details; I shot White Bear in the forest. Then after I killed him, my dearest friend used his dying breath to save me.

"You're right. I killed him." It hurts so much to say the words.

"Of course you did. Would you like to see the rest of him?"

I most definitely do not. But whatever she's planning—perhaps she intends to lure me away from the house to a place where the mess of killing me will be easier to clean up—she's basing her strategy on the Rachel she used to know. The one who meekly did whatever she was told and accepted the abuse her sister showered on her without complaint. That little girl is no more. She expects me to say no. I have to say yes.

"Do you really think that's a good idea?" Charlotte says. As if she is honestly concerned with my welfare.

"Of course. Rachel needs to see what she's done." Diana tosses White Bear's paw onto the bed as if it were so much refuse and gestures with her rifle toward the door. "After you."

"Where are we going?"

"I think you know."

And I do. There's only one place he could be. I lead the way down the back stairs and out the side door and across the yard to my sister's taxidermy workshop. I hated this room when I was a child. I've never been inside. I don't want to go in now.

Diana reaches past me and opens the door.

The first thing that hits me is the smell. There's a chemical scent mixed with the faint odor of decaying meat that reminds me of the padded room. The next is the sheer quantity of body parts. Heads, feathers, skins, and paws crowd her worktable alongside paints, paintbrushes, clamps, tweezers, dental picks, scissors, and flensing knives. Q-tips. Cotton balls. Needles and thread. A jar of glass eyes.

And in the middle of the room beneath a white sheet is what I presume is her crowning achievement, her pièce de résistance, my old friend.

We crowd inside. Diana pulls aside the sheet with a flourish.

"What do you think? Isn't he a beauty?"

"I think he'd look better if he had all four paws."

She laughs. "Easy enough to sew them back on. But they got your attention, didn't they? Now say it. Say you killed him."

I hang my head. "I killed him," I mumble. I quicken my breathing as if I'm on the verge of panic, make my hands tremble, pretend that I can barely stand as I edge surreptitiously toward the open door. Let her think that I am so revolted at seeing White Bear's body that I can't bear to be in the room. Let her think that I am helpless. That I'm about to suffer a psychotic break. She doesn't know I have Charlotte's car keys.

"Now tell him you're sorry."

"I'm sorry." It's not difficult to make her believe I am sincere because I am—I'm sorry about White Bear, sorry about that girl at the roadside park, sorry about my parents. Sorry that I was Diana's accomplice in their deaths.

She laughs and nods at Charlotte and tips her head toward the door. Charlotte steps quickly in front of me.

"Going somewhere?" Diana asks. She hands her rifle to Charlotte and grabs my right arm and twists it high between my shoulder blades. I yelp.

"You were right," Charlotte says, shaking her head in evident awe of Diana's perceptive powers, seemingly as proud of my sister's acumen as any parent. "She did exactly as you said she would."

"People are so predictable," Diana says with a weary sigh.

She twists my arm higher. I want to cry out again. It feels as though it's going to snap.

Just as I am certain that my arm is about to break, she turns me loose and throws me to the floor. The ammunition in my jacket pocket scatters. I grab her ankle with my good arm and pull her down with me. We grapple, roll. I do my best to get the better of her, but Diana is taller than me, and stronger. She also has two working arms. Our match ends in seconds with my sister sitting on my chest and her forearm pressed against my throat.

I cough. Writhe and squirm. I think about the girl. I should quit struggling. Let the Universe call me to account. Dying on the floor of my sister's taxidermy studio at White Bear's feet is exactly what I deserve.

"Hold her arms!" Diana commands.

Charlotte props Diana's rifle against the door frame and crouches near my head. She grabs my wrists and pulls my arms over my head exactly as I did to the girl. Diana reaches up and feels along the edge of the worktable and sits back on my chest holding a knife.

Goodbye, I whisper silently to Trevor, to Scotty, to the ravens, to the spiders. To life.

Diana lifts my shirt. Runs her fingers over the scars on my belly and presses the knife against my skin.

When I come to, I am alone. I pat myself down, feel the blood on my shirt, sit up and lift the cloth and look down at my stomach. The cuts don't appear deep.

I get to my feet. Stagger over to the worktable to look for a rag to wipe away the blood and assess the damage. The worktable has been stripped bare. Diana's flensing knives are gone, along with anything else with which I might possibly defend myself when she comes back.

In their place is a mirror. I pick it up and see that the cuts on my stomach are not random as I would have supposed. They're words, cut into my skin in reverse so that when I look in the mirror, I can read Diana's final message clearly:

THE END

23

THEN
Jenny

It's over. Finished. Done. There's nothing left to say. Nothing left to decide. The sooner Diana is locked away in a mental hospital, the sooner we can get on with our lives. I lost something precious the day of Rachel's birthday party: an optimism about the future that I will never regain. Through all of the difficulties and challenges that Peter and I have endured because of our daughter, I've tried not to become bitter or cynical or hard. But now I can see that my optimism was misplaced. As long as Diana is free to go where she wants and to kill when she pleases, no one will be safe.

Rachel insists that the girl at the roadside park was dead when she and Diana found her no matter how many times I ask. I don't believe her. I know there's more she's not telling me, which breaks my heart. I'm used to Diana's lies, but if I can't trust what Rachel says, then I am lost entirely. Everyone says that the girl's death was a terrible tragedy and laments the fact that if she had been found just a few minutes earlier, she might have been saved. I think the only thing that could have saved the girl was if she'd been found by someone other than my daughter.

As Peter pulls to the curb in front of Dr. Merritt's office and shuts off the engine, the first snowflakes begin to fall. Normally, the first snowfall of the season excites me. Today, the falling snow feels ominous; a portent of bad things to come. In a few months, this street will be unrecognizable, with snow piled along the sides higher than my head, the paths shoveled through them leading to this and other businesses like walking through a tunnel. Last winter, the snow was so deep that keeping our access road open was costing us a fortune, so in the end we gave up having it plowed and left our Suburban parked near the highway and drove the four miles back and forth to the lodge by snowmobile. Needless to say, we didn't get out much last year, which is another reason I want to get the situation with Diana resolved. After the events of the past few weeks, I don't think I could handle spending another winter snowed in with her.

I look at Peter. He looks back at me. A gust of wind hurries the leaves along the sidewalk as if urging us to do the same.

"Ready?" I ask because one of us has to break the impasse.

"Ready." He squares his shoulders and opens his door.

I wave at the bookstore owner as we pass her window and follow Peter around to the side of the building and up the covered stairway to the second floor. I wanted to switch therapists after Diana's diagnosis so we could start over again with someone new, but the population in the Upper Peninsula is so small and the subset of therapists able and willing to treat her is even smaller, so we didn't really have any options. Still, I was uncomfortable around Dr. Merritt for a long time. I didn't like that every time he saw Diana or interacted with her, he was judging what she said and did through the lens of his diagnosis.

Now I'm glad we stuck it out. I don't know who else we could have turned to for help. Who else could possibly understand the situation we're in and what we're about to go through. It's not his fault that our daughter can't be cured.

We sit down in our usual chairs. Dr. Merritt's waiting room is as comfortable as the man himself, a worn-around-the-edges, dark wood-paneled, bookshelf-lined oasis where patients can relax and feel safe. Normally, I do. But I can't stop thinking about Rachel. Charlotte is going to take her to Manistique for the day to explore the Big Spring as a do-over birthday outing and has promised that it will be just the two of them, with plenty of one-on-one attention. I think she wants to make up for all the times she let us down. I'm still not ready to forgive her, but I couldn't think of any other way to make sure that Rachel and Diana don't go off together while we're gone. Bringing Rachel with us today was out of the question. I am very good at pretending that everything is fine when it is not, but the idea of going shopping with her after the appointment and getting something to eat while not letting on that anything is wrong—it's exhausting. I don't know what the outcome of this discussion will be, but I do know that Peter and I are going to have a lot to talk about on the way home.

"How're you holding up?" he asks.

"I'm fine," I reply, though we both know that neither of us will be anything remotely approaching okay until today's visit is over. Possibly not even then.

The door to Dr. Merritt's inner office opens.

"It's time," I say without preamble after everyone is settled in our usual places because there's no point in coming at the subject sideways. "Diana needs to be committed."

If Dr. Merritt is surprised by my pronouncement, he does a good job of hiding it. "And you agree?" he asks Peter.

"I do," Peter replies firmly.

I'm grateful for his conviction, even if it took him a while to get to this point. After I found Rachel in the cage and told him what Diana was planning, Peter thought that I was letting my imagination run away with me. But the death of the girl at the roadside park changed all that. I'm a little disappointed that he couldn't see that the safety of our daughter was at risk until something happened to another girl, but I'm willing to let that go in order to achieve our objective. For twenty years, Diana has ruled our family. Now it's time for us to take control.

"May I ask why?" Dr. Merritt's voice is as carefully neutral and non-accusatory as you'd expect of a mental health professional. "Has something happened?"

"I think—we think," I add as I reach for Peter's hand to show that we are in complete agreement. I take a deep breath. "Peter and I believe that Diana has hurt someone. Badly."

I tell him about the incident at the roadside park, and how I suspect that Diana was involved because two weeks earlier, she tried to kill her sister.

Dr. Merritt leans forward with his elbows on his desk and steeples his fingers under his chin. As I describe how I found Rachel in the cage in the woods and Diana's flensing knives and the pot of boiling water, he looks shocked. I feel like shooting an "I told you so" glance at Peter, but I don't.

"Does Rachel know what Diana was planning to do to her?"

"She still thinks they were playing a game. Diana won't admit to anything, either. She says they were acting out a fairy tale, and the knives and the pot of boiling water were props. I think she killed the girl at the roadside park because I foiled her plan to kill her sister. Not out of revenge, but as a substitute, a workaround."

Diana doesn't feel revenge, or hatred, or jealousy, or any of the other emotions that would normally motivate someone to kill. Hers was a crime not of passion but of convenience, which makes what she did so very much worse.

I tell Dr. Merritt everything. About the times when I know that Diana hurt someone, and the times when I only suspected that she did. I tell him how we caught Diana dissecting animals when she was eleven, and how this led to her learning taxidermy. I tell him about the reason we moved to the lodge in the first place, and about the toddler who died in our backyard pool. I tell him things that I have never told Peter. How Diana pushed me off the cliff because she wanted to kill our unborn baby, how before I looked out the windows in our home in Ann Arbor and saw the boy at the bottom of our swimming pool, I saw that Diana's clothes were wet.

"I didn't know she pushed you," Peter says. His voice breaks. "I didn't know you believed she drowned that boy in our pool. Why didn't you tell me?"

What he's really saying of course is *Why didn't you trust me?* I wish I had an answer. Why, indeed? Because I thought I knew better than him? That my maternal love bonded me to our daughter more strongly? That I understood her, and he did not? None of the reasons that I could possibly offer feel as though they are justified. As I list all the unspeakable things that Diana has done, I can see that by protecting her, I've made a terrible mistake.

"I don't think she drowned him," I say, sidestepping his question, "not deliberately, anyway. I think he fell into the pool and Diana didn't know what to do. She might even have tried to pull him out, and that's how her clothes got wet."

I catch myself and stop. I can't believe I'm still making excuses for her. Talk about old habits.

"Or she might have thrown the boy in," Peter says bitterly. He stares at me as if I am a stranger, then takes a deep breath and turns to Dr. Merritt. "So, what do we do next? How do we get Diana committed?"

"About that," Dr. Merritt says slowly, and my heart drops. I've spent enough time talking to him to know that there's going to be a problem. "I have to be honest. I understand what you're saying, and I agree that something needs to be done, but the truth is that having Diana committed would have been a great deal simpler if you had taken this step before she came of age. The law gives parents broad authority over their minor children, and this includes signing them into rehab or to a mental hospital. But once a person is past the age of majority, the laws are weighted heavily in the individual's favor. If you think about the state of the mental health industry in the past, you can understand why things have swung so far the other way. A hundred years ago Peter could have put you in an insane asylum for no reason and you would have had no recourse."

I can't believe it. We waited too long. The opportunity to commit Diana ran out before we were ready to take that step.

"There's nothing we can do?"

"I'm not saying there's nothing you can do. I just want you to be aware of the challenges."

"Which are?"

"The law provides two justifications for taking away someone's rights, which is what you'll be doing if you have Diana involuntarily committed. The first is to protect the citizenry from harm, such as when police impose a curfew in the event of civil unrest. The second is when the law takes away someone's rights to protect that individual from harming him- or herself. It's important to recognize that this latter justification does *not* apply in a case where someone *might* harm someone else, which is your concern. *Parens patriae* powers apply only in cases where the person in danger can't help themselves, such as when the state takes children from their abusive parents. It's also used by family members to exercise legal control over adults with developmental disabilities, or to get a schizophrenic relative off the streets, or to take charge of an elderly parent or a spouse suffering from Alzheimer's."

"So, if we could make the case that Diana was a danger to herself, we could get her committed?" Peter asks.

"That would help. But unfortunately, in Diana's case, it's still not that straightforward. The invocation of *parens patriae* is intended to result in care and treatment, which isn't true for Diana because there is no cure for psychopathy, and no treatment. It all comes down to balancing the powers of the state against a person's individual freedom, and typically judges rule in favor of the individual. I was involved in one case in which social services wanted to commit a homeless, mentally ill psychotic woman because she had been eating her own feces. The American Civil Liberties Union brought in an expert witness to testify that the woman was not a danger to herself because eating feces wouldn't kill her. They won."

"That's crazy."

"I don't disagree. But if you were that homeless woman, you might feel differently."

"So, our hands are tied."

"When it comes to having Diana committed, yes. But there is another approach. If you truly believe that she had something to do with the girl's and the toddler's deaths, you can go to the police. Tell them what you suspect and let them investigate. If Diana is found innocent, you'll have peace of mind. If she's guilty, then the law will do what it's supposed to by removing a dangerous individual from society."

I hardly know what to think. It took Peter and me weeks to agree that Diana should be committed to a mental hospital. Turning her in as a murder suspect never crossed our minds. I can't bear to think of our daughter going to prison because of us. At the same time, I can't bear to think of her hurting someone again.

Dr. Merritt looks at his watch. The gesture is subtle, but the message comes through. He's given us all he can. Others are waiting. Others with problems that need his expertise and his guidance, though I seriously doubt that any of the people in his waiting room are dealing with a problem as difficult as ours.

We stand up, shake hands, promise to let him know what we decide, and go down the stairs. It's still snowing. Two inches have fallen during the time we were parked.

"Do you want to get something to eat, or should we try to beat the weather and head straight home?" Peter asks after he brushes the snow off the car and we get in.

"Let's go home." I don't want to watch others leading their normal, everyday lives while we try to decide whether or not we should hand our daughter over to the police for murder.

Because this is where we are going to end up. I know this with my head, even if my heart is not yet ready to admit it. I'm not alone in my struggle. Parents of psychopaths often have a hard time admitting that their children are dangerous. They deny, minimize, refute, excuse. Even if they are intuitively aware of their child's sinister side, they tell themselves their children aren't evil because they wish or need this to be the case.

But I'm done making excuses. I am not that parent. Not anymore.

By the time we pass the entrance to the Marquette Branch Prison on the south side of the city, the wind blowing off the lake has whipped the flakes into a frenzy. Most residents don't give the prison a thought when they pass. Until today, I hadn't, either. I try to imagine my daughter inside. Diana loves the forest, loves being outdoors. Impossible to envision her living within the confines of a jail cell. I picture her growing more and more frustrated and bored, then becoming violent when her boredom boils over, fighting against her incarceration and breaking rule after rule and negating the possibility of her ever getting out, and push the thought away. Instead, I think back to the day that she was born. Such a happy, hopeful day. Full of joy and possibility. If I had known then what I do now, would I have done anything differently? Certainly, the answer has to be yes.

But I didn't know. I couldn't. All any parent can do is make the best decisions they can using the knowledge that they have at the time. Applying that principle going forward, it's clear what our decision has to be. There is nothing more that we can do for our daughter. This truly is the end.

24

NOW
Rachel

THE END. Two words. Six letters. Oozing with blood and dripping with meaning. Diana has always viewed life as one continuous experiment, the central question not the scientist's *why?* in a quest for understanding but the far more prosaic *what?* born of simple curiosity. What will happen if I put this pillow over my baby sister's face? What if I cut our rope swing nearly through and then contrive for my sister to grab it? What will happen if I put my sister in the trunk of Max's car when we sneak off to the Cobblestone Bar to listen to music? Will she survive the trip, or will she succumb to carbon monoxide poisoning? What if I show her a clump of poison sumac and tell her it's regular sumac? In Diana's eyes, the only reason I exist is so that she can see how close she can come to killing me.

And now her experiment has come to its end.

I use a rag to wipe the blood from my stomach and leave it and the mirror on the worktable. The cuts Diana made are only scratches. Barely enough to break the skin. I don't know why I passed out when she made them. Lack of food and sleep perhaps, combined with the stress of seeing White Bear stuffed and mounted as the centerpiece in her workshop, the ultimate achievement for a taxidermist who had previously preserved only small mammals and birds. My heart aches with the revelation that I shot him, even if I was coerced into doing so and it was Diana's finger that pulled the trigger. I suffered so much at my sister's hands. My parents must have known that something was seriously wrong with their older daughter. They should have done a better job of protecting me. I understand that many parents are unwilling to deal with a problem child and end up denying or minimizing their bad behavior—even becoming so swept up by the dangerous child's charms that they actually favor them over their less exciting and charismatic siblings. But understanding why my parents didn't look out for me doesn't make it right. They should have seen what was going on, should have taken steps to stop it. It should never have come to this. My parents lost everything at Diana's hands. Now I'm about to lose everything as well.

Worse, I've made it easy for her. Diana has four

thousand acres in which to hide the body of a person who it could be argued never made it here. My therapists may have presumed that I was going home, but I didn't tell them where I was going. For all anyone knows, I hitch-hiked my way out of state and into oblivion. Even if someone saw Trevor pick me up, they wouldn't necessarily know who he is to be able to track him down and ask him what became of me. It saddens me to think that my life has had so little impact that Trevor and Scotty are the only two people on earth who might possibly miss me.

I look at White Bear looming over me in an intimidating pose that he would never have adopted toward me when he was alive. It's hard to believe that only yesterday I followed a set of tracks hoping I might see him.

"I'm sorry," I say out loud.

I forgive you, White Bear replies.

It breaks my heart to hear him say this. White Bear may have forgiven me, but I will never forgive myself.

Run, he says.

The same word that sent me fleeing into the woods when I was a child. I would if I could. Perhaps he doesn't realize that we are locked in a windowless room. Or that Diana took every conceivable tool I might possibly use to break free.

"Run where? How?"

Up.

I look up. Directly above White Bear's head is a large, square metal grating. Behind the grating, a massive ceiling fan whirrs. I run to the door and find the switch that turns off the fan, then go back to the workbench and look behind and underneath it for something that I can use to pry off the grating—a screwdriver or a hammer would be ideal—anything that Diana might have missed. But there's nothing.

Then I remember Charlotte's car keys. I once saw my father use a key to pry open a can of paint. I'm not entirely sure how I can use them, but these keys are all I have.

I pull a wooden chair next to White Bear and climb from it onto White Bear's shoulders, straddling his head and bracing myself against it while I sort through the keys on Charlotte's ring for one that looks as though it doesn't belong to her SUV in case it breaks.

Quietly, White Bear warns, though he doesn't have to.

I slide the key between the edge of the grating and the ceiling and lever it back and forth. The grating doesn't budge. White dust rains down as the ceiling material crumbles, and I realize I've caught a break; the ceiling is comprised of a single sheet of thin drywall. I could probably kick through it if I could get my foot in the right position.

I saw away at the drywall surrounding each of the screws that attach the grating to the ceiling until the cover breaks free.

Quietly, White Bear warns again.

I drop the grating onto the pile of rags on Diana's work counter in case Charlotte is posted outside the door standing guard and push the fan to the side. I grab hold of the edges of the opening, climb up onto White Bear's head, pull myself through, and crawl to where the drywall ends and peer over the edge.

No Charlotte. So far, so good, but now what? I am crouching on a wide beam twenty feet above the floor. I can't drop down because I can't take the chance of landing badly and twisting an ankle. The only way out that I can see is a louvered window at the far end of the barn.

I stand up and inch along the beam like a tightrope walker until I come to a small platform beneath the window. It's not wide, perhaps eighteen or twenty inches, but it will have to do. I crouch on the platform and peer through the louvres. This end of the barn is dug partway into the hill where my parents are buried. I'm looking at a ten-foot drop at most. Easy—if I can get through the window.

I wiggle each louvre in turn until I find one that feels close to giving way. If I could get a running start, I'm sure that it would come apart with a single kick. But the tiny platform on which I am standing is too narrow for me to sit, let alone kick at this board with my feet.

I wiggle the board again. It's definitely loose. There has to be a way to break through it. At some point Diana or Charlotte is going to come back to check on me. They might not go inside the workshop when they see that the door is still padlocked, but I can't count on it. I *have* to get away. Now, while my sister still believes that I am secured.

301

I stand up and turn around with my back to the window and try not to think about what would happen if I were to fall. I reach behind my back and grab the louvre directly above the one that is loose with both hands and kick backward blindly. On the third kick, the board goes flying. I squeeze through the opening, dangle by my fingertips, and let go.

My feet hit the ground with more force than I expected. I go down, flailing wildly as I roll down the slope. I jump up and dust myself off and run to the corner of the barn to check the side yard.

A car door slams. I draw back. I can hear voices. One of the voices is male.

Trevor.

He's come back as he promised, but his timing couldn't be worse. He's going to interview Diana and Charlotte. He will have no idea that he's talking to a killer. Worse, Trevor is not going to accept whatever story Diana and Charlotte come up with to explain why I'm not available. He's a reporter. He'll start digging, poking, interrogating, and when he asks the wrong question, he'll be dead.

"Come inside," I hear Diana say. "Charlotte—will you see if you can find Rachel and tell her that her friend is here? She said she was going to visit our mother's old observation blind," she adds for Trevor's benefit. "Poor thing. I'm not sure coming back was a good idea. She's really torn up."

If Charlotte does as Diana tells her to, she's going to

walk right past me. I retreat to the back side of the barn. But I can't stay here. Somehow, I've got to lure Trevor away.

A raven alights on a branch above me.

"Are they still there?" I ask. "Is it safe to come out?"

The raven flaps its wings and flies away. I take that as a yes. I sneak the long way around through the forest and circle back to the lodge until I can see into the kitchen. Trevor and Diana are sitting at the table. Charlotte is presumably staying away to maintain the ruse that she is looking for me. Trevor seems relaxed. I don't know what Diana is saying to him, but clearly, he's buying what she's selling. Diana is a master manipulator. Sometimes when we would go to Marquette, she'd target a stranger, such as a fast-food order taker or a clerk in a grocery store, and whisper to me what she was planning to make them say or do. Later, after they'd done exactly as she had predicted, I'd try to parse out how she'd accomplished it. I desperately want to tell Trevor not to trust her, and to warn him that he is her prisoner, even if he doesn't know it. But as long as they are together, there's nothing I can do.

I slip through the trees and take up a hiding place near the access road. When Trevor leaves—if Diana lets him leave—she *has* to let him leave—he'll drive right past me. When he does, I'll be ready. Hiding and waiting is far more passive than I'd like, but I simply have no way to get his attention. If I show myself, Diana will kill me, and then she'll kill him. Or perhaps she'll kill him first to torment me. All I can do is hope that Trevor is holding to the cover story we devised, that they're only talking about the lodge, about how beautiful it is and how it was constructed, and that he isn't repeatedly wondering aloud how long I'll be gone and why I'm not coming back. A slim hope, since I can't imagine him leaving without seeing or speaking to me first, but I can't bear to consider the alternative. If anything happens to him, and Scotty is left alone in this world, I will never forgive myself. Assuming I'm still around.

As the sun goes down and the lights in the lodge come on, the temperature drops. I try not to think about the abundance of winter coats and hats and mittens in the mudroom. I rub my arms to warm them and creep back to the lodge—because now that it's dark out, they can't see me—and look in the windows. Trevor and Diana are sitting in my parents' chairs in front of the fire. Charlotte has pulled up a third chair to join them. Everyone looks relaxed. If Trevor suspects that something is wrong, he's not letting on. *Go outside, go outside*, I repeat over and over in my head until at last, they get to their feet. Shortly after, the front door opens. I draw back into the shadows as Trevor heads for his Jeep. My heart thumps—unreasonably so, I realize now, because the idea that Diana might never let him leave was ridiculous. Wasn't it?

But Trevor doesn't open the driver's-side door. Instead, he goes around the back of the Jeep to the cargo area and takes out a backpack—his "emergency pack," he told me during the drive from the hospital, which he keeps packed with toiletries and a change of clothes in the event that he needs it when he is chasing down a story—and goes inside.

I feel like crying. He's going to spend the night. I should have known that he wouldn't leave without me. His kindness and friendship are going to get him killed. I don't know what he said to convince Diana to let him stay. All I know is that with every passing minute, the danger increases. If he doesn't leave now—tonight—he's never going to make it out alive. Scotty will lose the only person who truly cares for him, and it will be my fault. I can't let that happen. I won't.

I settle in to wait. It is now dangerously cold. I can't sit down because the cold coming up from the ground will chill me worse than the air, so I pace in a circle until the lights go out. Judging by the size and position of the moon, I'm guessing it's around eight o'clock. Diana might go out to the taxidermy workshop to check on me before she turns in for the night, but I'm betting she won't. Tormenting me by leaving me alone overnight without food and water and a means to use the bathroom is exactly the kind of thing that she would do.

I go over to Trevor's Jeep and quietly open the back door to search the cargo area for a blanket. Everyone in the Upper Peninsula carries emergency supplies during the winter in case their car breaks down or they get stuck in a snowbank. Thankfully, Trevor is no exception. In a corner of the cargo area, I find a lovely woolen blanket.

I pick it up—then my eyes widen. Beneath the blanket is a rifle.

25

THEN
Jenny

By the time we turn down our access road and pass through the security gate, the snow has stopped. If it weren't for the icy accumulation packed into the windshield wiper wells, no one who'd spent the morning at the lodge would guess that at this very moment, Marquette is experiencing a blizzard. Marquette sits on the south shore of Lake Superior, and because of the lake-effect snows, has the dubious honor of being the third snowiest city in the continental United States. Last winter, the city was literally buried under a record-breaking two hundred inches, which translates to a staggering 16.7 feet. M-28 east of the city was closed four times due to blowing and drifting snow—and it's the only way into and out of the city from that direction. Residents are used to snow—

skiing and snowshoeing and ice-fishing and snowmobiling are all popular winter activities, as are more creative outdoor sports such as fat-tire biking and ice golfing—but last winter was bad even by their standards. Cars were buried, schools and businesses closed, roofs collapsed, and the drifts on the Northern Michigan University campus reached the third-story dormitory windows. Peter's grandfather used to say that it took a special kind of person to live in the Upper Peninsula year-round, and I agree.

But while the day has turned sunny, my disposition has not. The discussion with Dr. Merritt was sobering, to say the least. Peter and I have yet to reach a decision, but we both know what that decision has to be. Our daughter has killed twice with impunity. We can't let her kill again.

As if to underscore the point, as we approach the gun range, there is a gunshot. Max shooting by himself, I presume, because Charlotte is away with Rachel for the day. Char will be upset that she missed him. One of the drawbacks of living without a telephone is the difficulty in making plans. Charlotte recently confided that she and Max have been talking about getting married. There was a time I would have argued against it, and I still believe she could do a lot better, but who am I to say what my sister should or shouldn't do? I haven't exactly been a paragon of wisdom when it comes to knowing what's best for my family. Anyway, once Diana is gone, there will be no reason for her to stay.

"Sounds like Max is at the gun range," Peter remarks. "Do you mind if I join him?"

I do mind. I hate the gun range, hate rifles, hate shooting, hate killing. Just the thought of my husband holding a weapon turns my stomach. But if blowing up tin cans will help him blow off some of the morning's tension, I'm willing to grant him this concession. As for me, I want nothing more than to crawl into bed and bury myself under the covers and make this day go away. At the same time, the idea of being alone in the house with Diana fills me with dread.

"I'll come with you. Just to watch," I add when Peter raises his eyebrows.

As he pulls over and parks, another gunshot splits the air, followed immediately by three more.

"That's some fast shooting," he says. "I wonder what kind of rifle Max is using."

I have no idea and couldn't care less. But as we walk toward the gun range, the reason for the multiple shots becomes clear: Max is not alone. There are three others with him. Four people holding rifles silhouetted against the sun. It looks as though the gun range has been invaded by an army.

Peter squints. "It's Charlotte and Diana," he says after a moment, which doesn't make sense because Charlotte took Rachel to Manistique and Diana isn't allowed to set foot on the gun range. "And is that *Rachel*?"

"Rachel is with them? *My God*."

I don't know which is more shocking: that my eleven-year-old, animal-loving daughter has been coerced into learning how to shoot, or that the twenty-year-old psycho-pathic daughter I am about to turn over to police as a murder suspect is standing next to her holding a rifle.

We take off running.

"Mom? Dad? What are you guys doing here?" Diana says when she sees us. "I thought you were going to Marquette for the day."

"Obviously." For a moment, I am so stunned I don't know what else to say.

Then I do. I whirl on Charlotte. "How could you? How *could* you bring my girls here? How could you let them *shoot*?"

"It's okay," Max breaks in. "The girls know all about gun safety. And your Rachel is a pretty good shot. A total natural."

I can't believe Max is so cavalier. In addition to a con man and liar, is he also an idiot? When I think of all the times that we made allowances for him for Charlotte's sake, I realize that my daughter's isn't the only bad behavior I've indulged.

"How *could* you?" I berate my sister again. "You *know* how Peter and I feel about guns."

She tosses her head. "Of course I do. Why do you think we only bring the girls here when you're gone? What are you doing back so soon, anyway?"

"Don't put this on me. You knew. *You knew* I would never approve, yet you did this anyway."

"It's only target practice. It's not as though we're

teaching them to hunt. But even if we were, lots of kids know how to shoot. You're too protective. You need to give them a chance to make mistakes. Children need room to breathe in order to grow."

"Says the woman who's never had kids."

"Not fair. I don't have to give birth to know how to raise them. You're not a bear, yet you claim to understand *them*."

"It's not the same thing at all, and you know it."

I stop because I can feel myself slipping and I don't want to lose control in front of my girls. Rachel looks positively terrified. As for Diana, as always, it's impossible to know what she's thinking.

Max smirks. I don't know if this is because he's enjoying seeing Charlotte and me going at it like a couple of boxers, or if he's smirking out of nervousness. It doesn't matter. The smirk is enough.

"As for you, take your stuff—all of it—the rifles, the ammunition—and don't come back."

"You're firing me?"

More like throwing him out.

"You can't do that!" Charlotte exclaims. "I won't let you."

As if she could stop me.

"I'm not going to say it again. Max—pack it up and clear out. Diana, Rachel—leave your rifles here and get in the car. As for you . . ." I turn to Charlotte and stop. I take a deep breath, think about the lasting impact of what I was about to tell her, which was to leave with her no-good boyfriend and never come back, and dial it back. "You can do what you want."

Charlotte looks at me steadily for a long moment and turns her back. I feel like crying. If only she had respected our rules, none of this would have happened. Going behind our backs and deliberately doing something we've forbidden, teaching my daughters to disobey us, *putting a rifle into the hands of a psychopath and teaching her how to shoot it.* I'd laugh if the whole thing wasn't so terrible. I brought my family here to keep them safe. Now my sister has done the opposite.

We drive to the lodge in silence. As Peter pulls up and parks, I turn to the girls in the back seat. "Straight to your rooms, both of you. Stay there until we say you can come out. Your father and I need to talk."

Diana opens her door and heads off in the direction of her taxidermy workshop. Then, evidently remembering that the workshop is padlocked, she heads for her painting studio in the barn.

"Let her go," Peter says. "Rachel? Are you hungry?"

She shakes her head and runs off toward the woods. For a moment, I am stunned by her disobedience.

"Rachel!" Peter calls as he starts after her.

"Let me handle it," I say. "She's going to the observation blind, I'm sure of it."

As I hurry after her down the trail, gradually, my equilibrium returns. I don't blame Rachel for running into the forest. It's my comfort place, too. I hate that she had to hear and see all that she did.

Then again, she's not entirely innocent. She's eleven. Old enough to know right from wrong. When Max or Charlotte or Diana suggested that she come with them to the gun range, she could have said no. It appalls me to think that my daughter has been so corrupted by the adults in her life that not only has she learned how to shoot, according to Max, she's good at it as well.

As I near the clearing, I hear Rachel talking. She sounds as though she's carrying on a conversation. Most likely she's talking out her troubles with an ant or a fly. Rachel has an amazing imagination. Some children conjure up an imaginary friend to keep them company, but Rachel has an entire forest full of creatures she purports to know and love. I hang back in the trees. I won't interrupt unless she needs me; I just want to be sure she's all right.

Then I see who—or rather, *what*—Rachel is in conversation with, and my heart drops. She's not talking to herself, or to an imaginary insect or animal as I supposed. She's talking to White Bear.

I can hardly believe it. White Bear is eleven, a powerful, mature adult male, with teeth and claws like daggers. His thick white fur shimmers and ripples in the sunlight. I want to call out to her, to tell her to get away, to stop what she's doing before she gets hurt. This is a wild animal. Even if she has interacted with White Bear before, there are no guarantees that she can do so safely again.

And yet even I can see that she seems to hold some sort of power over him. There are a few rare people who have a special bond with wild animals who are able to interact with them to an extraordinary degree, and evidently, this is true of Rachel. I hold my breath as she sits down and pats the ground beside her. When White Bear sits at her command, I am in awe of my daughter. I am also terrified for her. White Bear towers over her. He could kill or maim her as easily as he can rip open a termite nest, yet he sits quietly beside her, as charmed by her murmurings and caresses as if he were a cat or a dog. The scene feels as enchanted as a fairy tale. I hold my breath so as not to break the spell. Whether Rachel's extraordinary ability to communicate with animals is something she was born with, or it's because of the unique way in which she was raised, clearly, there's something magical about my daughter. Earlier, when I saw her holding the rifle, I knew it was never in her nature to want to shoot it. I blame Charlotte. My sister has no idea how fragile our family is, how much work it takes to keep up the façade. I realize we never told her about Diana's diagnosis. But she's so enamored of my daughter now I doubt she'd believe me if I did. Either way, it doesn't matter. Charlotte is the poison, rotting my family from within.

I remain close by until White Bear wanders off and Rachel starts for home, then follow her at a distance. Because I realize now that the real danger isn't from White Bear. It's not even from her sister. It's from mine.

26

NOW
Rachel

Trevor's rifle is the same make and model as mine. My great-grandfather used to call this Remington "the most-loved hunting rifle in America," and I'm definitely loving this one now. I crawl over the back seat into the cargo area to look for ammunition. I search everywhere, inside a canvas sack that turns out to hold fishing gear, under and inside every paper bag, every tackle box, every nook and cranny, but can't find any. What kind of hunter carries a rifle but no bullets? Granted, there's no game in season this time of year, but a stray bullet or two stuck in the edges of the floor mat would have been nice. I check my jacket pocket hoping to find a lone remaining bullet lodged in a corner, but the pocket is empty. Still, it feels good to hold a rifle in my hands. Diana and Charlotte won't know it isn't loaded.

I tiptoe across the front porch and ease open the door and sneak through the great room and go up the main stairs, then creep down the upstairs hallway, sticking as close to the walls as I can so the boards are less likely to squeak. I don't think Diana would put Trevor in my childhood bedroom, and I don't think she'd put him up in the room with the sleeping porch either, since White Bear's paws are presumably still on my bed, which leaves six bedrooms to choose from.

My bed. My Remington is beneath it. I slip inside the room to exchange Trevor's useless rifle for mine, but my Remington is gone. So are my suitcase and duffel bag and stuffed bear toy and White Bear's paws. Diana has removed every indication that I was here—proof that if my sister gets what she wants, I will never leave the property alive.

I make my way down the hall, pausing outside each bedroom door to listen for breathing, or the creak of bedsprings. But in the end, it isn't sound that tells me where Trevor is, but the smell of wet wool. I hope one day to be able to tell him that his life might have been saved because of his wet feet.

I tiptoe to the bed and put my hand over his mouth.

"Shh," I whisper when his eyes jerk open. "It's me. Don't talk. We have to leave. Now. Are you good with that?"

His eyes widen, dart around the room, then look up at me and relax. He nods. I take my hand away.

"Jesus, Rachel—you scared me," he whispers back. "Your sister said you'd gone to your mother's old observation blind, but then when you didn't come back, she admitted that you'd had a breakdown and she'd shut you in her workshop so you wouldn't hurt yourself. I couldn't leave until I knew you were all right, so I talked her into letting me spend the night. What's going on?"

Trevor wouldn't leave without me. He wanted to stay until he was sure that I was all right.

He put himself in danger for me.

"I'll explain everything later. Right now, we have to get out of here. Grab your things and let's go. And don't make any noise."

I watch a range of emotions roll over his face: uncertainty, doubt, incredulousness. I get it. A crazy person who he just sprang from a mental hospital, whose sister claims has had a nervous breakdown, has snuck into his room carrying a rifle expecting him to go with her without asking questions. I'm not sure what I'd do if our circumstances were reversed.

Down the hall, someone coughs.

"Please," I whisper. "The rifle is yours. It's not loaded. I found it in your Jeep. But we have to hurry. It's important. You have to trust me."

"Okay," he says at last. He throws off the covers and sits up. "I trust you."

He eases off the bed to put on his shoes and his jacket, then grabs his backpack and follows me into the hallway. We navigate past Charlotte's bedroom and down the main stairs and wind our way through the great room. Behind me, there is a *thunk*.

"Sorry," Trevor whispers. "It's so dark in here."

"Who is it? Who's down there?" Charlotte calls from the top of the stairs.

"It's me," Trevor answers before I can stop him. "I couldn't sleep. I was just going outside for a smoke. I stubbed my toe is all."

Trevor doesn't smoke, but Charlotte won't know that.

"Stay there. I'll turn on some lights for you."

"No need," Trevor says quickly. "I'll be fine."

He clumps noisily to the front door and makes a show of opening it. I follow him silently in the shadows and dart outside before Trevor shuts the door just as noisily. We run for the Jeep.

"Don't start the engine," I hiss as he opens the driver's door and tosses his backpack onto the back seat. "Not until we're out of earshot."

He puts the Jeep into neutral as I open the passenger door and brace myself against it to push. It's harder than I imagined, especially when we come to a slight rise and the Jeep rolls to a stop. We're not nearly as far away from the lodge as I'd like, but we pile in anyway. I twist around in my seat as Trevor peels down the driveway and turns onto the access road.

"Do you see anything?" he asks.

"Nothing. Thank you," I add as the lodge recedes in the distance. "For believing me, and for trusting me."

He grins. "Well, when a beautiful woman shows up in my bedroom in the middle of the night carrying a rifle, I figure the smartest thing is to do what she says."

I blink. Did Trevor just call me beautiful?

"So, are you ready to tell me what's going on?"

"Diana wants to kill me." I hate putting it so bluntly, but there's no easy way to say it. "Possibly both of us, now that she knows you're helping me."

I think again about the danger I put him in, how if anything were to happen to him, it will be on me.

"She wants to kill you? Why? What did you do to her? This doesn't make sense."

"I know. I'm sorry. I promise it does, but first, we really need to get out of here." It's one mile to the security gate, three miles after that to the highway. To freedom.

Only when we come to the gate, it doesn't budge. Normally, it would swing open automatically as we approach.

"Stay here," I tell Trevor as I open my door and get out to see if I can open the gate manually.

"Can I help you?" a tinny voice says over the intercom as I approach. A voice belonging to a person who has no intention of helping; who doesn't do a thing for anyone unless it benefits her.

Diana.

27

THEN
Jenny

Peter and I have barely spoken in the days since the incident at the gun range. Not because we are at each other's throats—if anything, we are more united than we've ever been—but because there's nothing left to say. For the first time in a very long while, we are in complete agreement: As soon as Diana is out of the picture, Charlotte has to go. There's no reason for my sister to stay on. Her job, which she performed so miserably, will be over. We've focused on Diana and her needs far too long. Rachel is only eleven. We need to get rid of the corrupting influences in her life so we can create an atmosphere in which she can flourish. It's not too late to make up for lost time. Assuming the state lets us keep her.

It breaks my heart to think that she helped Diana kill

the girl at the roadside park. Emily Walker was twelve years old, according to her obituary. An excellent student who loved horses and playing basketball. No siblings. Survived by her parents and a host of grandparents and aunts and uncles and cousins. Killed by my daughters' hands—both my daughters, because Rachel has at last told the truth. Her account was doubly hard to listen to knowing that the repercussions of turning Diana in for murder will also fall on Rachel. I have to believe that the authorities will realize she was coerced into helping, and she is too young to fully understand what she was doing, and that Diana is solely to blame, and that Rachel won't be charged. I can't lose them both.

Meanwhile, I can't stop thinking about the Yang boy. William would have been fourteen now, and ready to start high school, or if he turned out to be as gifted as his parents, perhaps he already would have. As for what would have become of him after that, there's no way to know. He's frozen in time, forever a toddler, the promise of his life snuffed out at my daughter's hand. He and his parents deserve justice. Handing Diana over to the law and letting the court system determine her fate is the only way to make this right. Meanwhile, I can't help thinking that if Diana had been called to account for the first death, there might not have been a second.

Then there's our boy. Our unborn son who never drew a breath. As I lay on my back in the rocks and snow waiting for Peter to come back for me, during the ride back to the lodge and then in the back of the Suburban as Peter raced for the hospital in Marquette; throughout the examinations, the X-rays, the tests, the consultations with specialists, the helicopter airlift to the University of Michigan teaching hospital in Ann Arbor because my leg was so badly shattered the doctors in Marquette had no idea where to start—during all of that time, I knew that our son was gone. Giving birth to a baby that has already died is as dreadful as it sounds. Peter and I saw him before they took him away. He was perfect and very small, with all his body parts in the right places and with the correct number of fingers and toes, tiny fingernails, delicate eyelashes. His skin was not as blue as I expected, more translucent, luminescent, an extraterrestrial, a moon baby, a child of the stars.

William Yang. Emily Walker. Our not-yet-named boy. Three deaths. All tied to Diana. With the weight of all of that pressing down on us, it's no wonder that Peter and I are utterly spent.

We're washing dishes at the kitchen sink when Diana runs into the side yard.

"Mom! Dad! Come quick!" she calls.

My heart drops. For the briefest of moments, I think she's killed someone else. I throw open the window.

"What is it? What's wrong?"

"White Bear is dead!"

"What? How?" I drop the dishrag in the sink and run outside.

"Hurry!" Diana says as she runs up to meet me on the porch. She grabs my hand. "You have to come! Rachel shot White Bear!"

"Rachel shot White Bear? Why would she do that? That doesn't make sense."

"Just come."

Charlotte clatters down the back stairs and runs out the kitchen door to join us. "What's going on? I heard shouting."

"Rachel shot White Bear," Diana says again.

"Is she all right?" Peter asks.

"I don't know! Just come!" Diana says.

We take off running. I can't imagine how this could have happened, why Rachel would shoot her favorite bear, where she would even get her hands on a rifle since we sent Max packing a full week ago and he took the rifles with him. Just days ago, Rachel was playing with White Bear as if he were her pet. There's no way she could hurt him. Diana is lying. It's a trick. To what purpose, I have no idea. I can't help but note that the emotion she is exhibiting more closely resembles excitement than worry.

But when we come to the gun range, I see the awful truth. White Bear is lying on the ground, a pile of unmoving flesh and fur. My throat closes. My one-in-a-million bear should have lived for at least another dozen years, sired cubs, possibly even another white one. Now there truly will be no more.

"You see?" Diana says, again with that odd mix of

detachment and excitement. "I told you. Rachel killed him."

"But why would she? And where is she?"

"She went that way." Diana points into the woods.

I take off for the trees. Diana must have shot White Bear and is trying to pin the blame on her sister. It's the only explanation that makes sense. Rachel saw her do it, and she ran away.

Behind me, I hear Charlotte and Peter arguing. "This is your fault," Peter says. "If you and Max hadn't insisted on setting up a gun range, this never would have happened."

"Don't blame this on me," my sister retorts. "You enjoy shooting, too."

I leave them to it. All I care about is Rachel. My heart breaks for her. Rachel is no stranger to death—nature is as red in tooth and claw as the poet says, and animals eat and are eaten all the time—but the deep connection she had with this bear puts his death on a whole other level. If Rachel did this, she's going to be a wreck. I know how it feels to take on the responsibility for another's death. And the devastation I felt over the Yang boy's death is nothing compared to how I would have felt if he had been my closest friend. Of course she ran into the woods to hide. The forest is the only place where she will feel safe.

Behind me, there is a gunshot. I whirl around.

Peter is lying on the ground. Diana and Charlotte are standing over him. Both of them are holding rifles.

I blink. For a moment, I am too stunned to move. I don't know which of them shot my husband. All I know is that the gaping hole in his chest makes it clear that he is dead.

I scream. Run to Peter's side and fall to the ground and gather him in my arms and rock him as if he were a baby. As if he were still alive. I look up at my sister and my daughter in disbelief and shock and horror.

"Why? Why did you do this? *Why?*"

"You were going to send Diana away," Charlotte says. "I couldn't let you do that. This is our home."

She puts her arm around my daughter and looks at her with a mix of pride and love and affection, and something else. "Ownership" is the only word I can think to describe it. As if my daughter belongs to her.

"You never loved Diana," she goes on. "You always favored Rachel."

Rachel. I scramble to my feet. "What have you done with her? Where is she?"

"You see?" Charlotte says to Diana. "I told you she only cares about your sister."

Diana shrugs as if all this talk of love and caring is an annoyance. "Enough." She raises her rifle.

I fall to my knees at her feet. The barrel is inches from my chest. "Diana. Darling. No. Don't do this."

"You were going to send me away," she says. "Rachel told me. She heard you and Dad talking."

"Rachel— No, no. That's not true. I mean yes, your

326

father and I talked about it as a possibility after—after that girl at the roadside park died. But we know you had nothing to do with that. This is your home. I promise no one is going to send you away."

I focus all my attention on Diana, try not to look behind me at my husband. "I love you," I say.

She has to believe me. If she kills me, Rachel will be an orphan. Unless Diana is planning to kill her as well—I swallow hard.

"She's lying," Charlotte says. "Go on. Shoot her. One murder each. That's what we agreed. Do it."

My throat seizes. *Charlotte* killed my husband. Not Diana. My sister made a devil's bargain with my daughter, and now my daughter is going to kill me.

Diana raises her rifle and sights along the scope.

"I'm sorry," I say. "I'm sorry you thought I didn't love you. I've always loved you. I still do." Pouring everything that I am feeling into what may well be my last words, knowing that the words are true.

Time slows. We remain as we are, a delicate balance. And my daughter pulls the trigger.

28

R achel?" Diana's voice prompts.
"Should we answer?" Trevor asks.

I shake my head and point toward the security cameras that top the gate. I don't want to give her the satisfaction of seeing us panic. I feel like one of the beetles my sister used to make me catch so she could pin them in a shoebox and watch them squirm.

"She can see us?" Trevor mouths.

I nod. "She can hear us, too," I whisper. "My family has a tendency to overbuild. We need to get out of range."

Trevor grabs his messenger bag from the back seat and slings it over his shoulder. I grab nothing, because I have nothing to grab. The idea that I am leaving everything behind is oddly freeing.

The security camera looks down on us like the eye of God. But the cameras are fixed in place. Once we're out of range, Diana will have no idea which way we're headed. I let the cameras see me leading Trevor away from the gate and toward the south, then cut a wide arc through the woods, cross to the north side of the road, and double back toward the cliffs. Let Diana think we're going to ground in one of the densest areas of our acreage hoping to use the trees for cover. I have a better plan.

"Where are we going?" Trevor asks.

"To the lake. We can't climb over the gate—not with all that wire. And the cliffs between here and the road are too steep. The only way off the property is to go around them. There's a section of fencing that sticks out into the lake where the cliff ends that we'll have to swim around, but once we do that, we're home free."

"Wait. That water was only recently covered with ice. It might still be. You do realize how crazy this sounds?"

"I do. Please. You have to trust me."

I wish I could give him more. His reporter's brain has to be overflowing with questions. But there simply isn't time. I also don't say anything about what we'll have to deal with after we swim around the fence. It's three miles to the highway. Hiking through the forest in soaking wet clothes with the air temperature barely above freezing, hoping that we won't die of hypothermia before we get there, doesn't exactly inspire confidence. Never mind that the last time I hiked through the forest,

I got lost. It's a terrible plan, but this truly is our only option.

"All right. But once this is over, you're going to owe me big-time."

I don't disagree. If I'd had any inkling of the danger I would be walking into, I never would have come home at all, let alone gotten Trevor involved. At the same time, I feel as though this is my last chance to make things right. Saving Trevor from the situation I got him into won't balance the scales of justice, but it will help.

We start off. It's tough going. The base of the cliff face is littered with boulders, the forest that butts up against the cliffs dark, tangled, wet. At least the difficult conditions will work in our favor. Diana is thirty-five, Charlotte well over sixty—so Trevor and I have youth on our side. Before Diana finds us—*if* she finds us—she's going to have to work for the privilege.

"How are you holding up?" I ask.

Trevor is more fit than me, so what I'm really asking after isn't so much his physical condition as his mental one. I'm sure when he came to the lodge expecting to interview my aunt and my sister, he didn't anticipate that the day would end with him fleeing for his life. But when it comes to mental strength, I have the advantage. I've been locked up, subjected to electroshock therapy, spent weeks in solitary, been hosed down with cold water along with a host of other humiliations. I've been forced to undergo hypnotherapy, I've been sleep deprived, drugged.

I may not be his equal physically, but I'm pretty sure I've got him beat when it comes to endurance.

"I'm fine. Don't talk. Just keep going."

And then, as we slog our way through the dark into the unknown, a curious thing happens: memories of how I survived those two lost weeks begin to return. I see myself running through the forest knowing that something was chasing me, but not knowing what it was or where I should go. I remember I found a warm, dark place to shelter in, as in my recent dream, where I felt safe. My therapists once hypnotized me to try to help me regain my memories of those lost weeks. I guess they should have set up a reenactment. Because with a clarity that is almost frightening, suddenly, I remember *everything*.

I remember that after Diana forced me to kill White Bear, I ran away as he told me to do, dodging and feinting through the forest like a frightened deer, until I came to a tall cliff not unlike the one we are walking beside now. I remember I wanted to climb it, but I couldn't. Then I saw a small opening halfway up the scree, a bear's den, the same den where my mother told me she and my sister first saw White Bear. I scrambled up to it, sobbing as I climbed because I knew that White Bear wouldn't be inside the den when I got there because I had killed him.

Only the den wasn't empty. Another bear had taken it over, as bears sometimes do. The bear was sleeping. I crawled inside and snuggled against him and cried.

The following days are less clear. I remember it snowed,

but the bear kept me warm. Occasionally the bear would stir and open one eye and look at me sleepily and close it again. I remember I ate snow for water. I knew that doing this would lower my body temperature because my parents had taught me many survival skills, but I was counting on the warmth from my companion to raise it again. I was very hungry. Most of the time, I slept.

Then one day, a raven called: *Cr-r-ruck tok, cr-r-ruck tok, cr-r-ruck tok, cr-r-ruck tok*. I opened my eyes. The raven called again. *This way*, he said to me in words that, somehow, I could understand. *You can't stay here. I'll show you where to go.*

I crawled to the opening. Outside, it was very bright. The snow was gone, and the day was sunny and warm.

Follow me, the raven said, and so I did. I slid down the rocky incline and followed the raven until we came to the access road. I started back toward the lodge, but the raven flew away in the other direction, so I went after him and slipped through the security gate and followed him to the highway. It seems impossible to me now that a child so weakened by hunger and trauma could have walked those three long miles, but obviously I did because the police report says a passing motorist found me lying beside the road, though I don't remember.

All will become known, the raven who greeted me said. The same raven who helped me when I was a child? I'd like to think so. I glance over my shoulder at Trevor and grin. I can't wait to tell him my memories have come back.

He's going to have one fantastic story. Assuming we live to tell it.

"What? Why are you smiling?"

"I'll tell you later."

Then the morning sun breaks over the top of the cliff, and I realize we have a new problem.

"Faster," I urge. The forest is now bathed in sunlight. It's early spring, with no leaves on the trees. Even if I wasn't wearing a red plaid shirt beneath my jean jacket, our movements would be easy to spot. I glance over my shoulder. We've been hiking for nearly half an hour, and there's still no sign of Diana. Yet I can't help feeling that I've made a mistake. It feels as though we're walking into a trap. My sister was never this easily fooled. She's let us get this far because she knows something I don't. Perhaps she's opened the gate and driven through it and is waiting for us to come around the other side. Perhaps she's stationed Charlotte at the end of the fencing with a rifle. Perhaps she's planning to shoot us as we swim. If so, once again, I will have made it far too easy for her to dispose of our bodies.

Despite my misgivings, we press on because what else can we do?

A raven calls from high over our heads. Is it trying to get my attention? Ravens have excellent vision. It's possible that this one can see my sister. That it wants to help us get away. A raven saved me once; perhaps a raven will save me again.

"Where is she?" I ask. Let Trevor think I'm musing aloud and talking to myself.

The raven sounds its alarm call and flies off toward the access road.

"Hurry," I say. "She's coming." I don't tell Trevor how I know.

We run. The ground turns mucky and wet. I hate that we're laying down such an obvious trail. The only thing we can do is stay out ahead of her—out of range of the rifle she is undoubtedly carrying.

Then I see a bear's footprint in the muck, a big one, a single hind footprint much larger than a man's. Our bears are not naturally aggressive, but this one has just woken from his winter's sleep. He's going to be hungry. Grouchy and unpredictable. Bad enough that we're in danger from my sister. If we cross paths with this bear, there's no telling what it will do. The bear is heading toward the lake. The only way we're going to avoid it is if we go in the opposite direction it's traveling, back toward its den.

Back to its den.

Of course. It's movement that gives a person away. Whenever a person is being chased through the forest, their best option is to go to ground. Until now, I had no idea where we could hide. Now I do.

"Stop. Wait. Change of plan." I point to the tracks and explain what I'm thinking.

Trevor's eyes are wide. "You want to hide in a bear's den?"

"Just until the coast is clear. It'll be fine. The bear is going to the lake to drink and to feed. It won't go back to its den for hours, if at all."

I want to add that hiding in a bear's den worked for me before, but there's no time for that now. If we're going to make it to the bear's den before Diana catches up to us, we need to hurry. I realize that to Trevor, our escape no doubt seems chaotic. First, I tell him that we can drive away, then that we need to hike along the base of the cliff and swim around the end of the fence, and now I'm leading him back toward the lodge with the promise of refuge inside a bear's den. Even to me, the plan sounds crazy. Or perhaps the truly crazy thing is that I am so certain it will work.

"You're serious," Trevor says.

I nod. "It'll work. I promise."

A promise I hope I'll be able to keep.

29

Are you sure this is the right way?" Trevor asks twenty minutes later as we slog through yet another boggy area that sucks at our boots like quicksand. "Can you still see the trail?"

"This is it."

I don't tell him that I lost the bear's trail some while ago. But I'm not worried. Ever since we turned away from the lake, the raven has been flying a short distance ahead, alighting on a low branch while it waits for us to catch up, then flying on again just as it did two days ago when I got lost. Anyone else might think that the raven showing up when he did is a coincidence, and that he's flying through the forest without any particular purpose or intent, and that his actions have nothing to do with Trevor and me. But I know otherwise.

I'm also not worried about the question of whether or not the den is going to be big enough for both of us—a concern that Trevor has also expressed. When bears excavate a den, they make it the same size as they are, which makes sense if you think about it, because why hole up for the winter in a cavern bigger than you that will only rob you of precious body heat? Judging by the size of this bear's footprint, there's no question we'll fit. The only question is what kind of den this one will be. After a bear reaches adult size, as this one surely has, they return to the same den year after year unless another bear happens to get there first. Some dig their dens into the side of a cliff, such as the one in which White Bear was born. Some are dug into the root systems of a tree. Sometimes a bear will use a small cave as its den or dig into the side of a sandy hill. If they're really hard up, they'll even bed down for the winter in a small depression out in the open. Obviously, I'm hoping for something warm and dry.

Cr-r-ruck tok, cr-r-ruck tok, the raven calls as it lights on yet another branch. Only this time, when we catch up to it, it stays still.

I hold up my hand to call a halt and turn a slow circle looking for disturbed earth or a clump of branches where they shouldn't be and find the den beneath a pile of branches near the exposed roots of a large white pine. I pull them aside.

"Here we are. Home sweet home."

"How—"

I shake my head and crawl inside. I'm not about to tell Trevor how I found it.

He crawls in after me. It's a tight fit. The den is also much closer to the access road than I would have liked, and in fact, from here I can see a section of road clearly. But I have to believe that the raven knows what he's doing; that this is the only place in the forest where we will be safe.

"And if the bear comes back?" Trevor asks after we've pulled all the branches that we can reach in front of us to camouflage the opening.

"He won't. He just came out of hibernation. He's as hungry as a—well, you know. He won't come back until he's eaten, if then." Bears are hardly this predictable, but I'm hoping Trevor doesn't know this.

"Anyway, I've done this before. This is how I survived those weeks that I was lost. I sheltered in a bear's den. *I remember.*"

I tell him everything: how my sister made me shoot the rare albino bear I had befriended, how I ran into the woods after I killed him because I was afraid that she was going to shoot me, how I found the den and crawled inside, how the sleeping bear kept me warm. I don't tell him that it was White Bear who warned me to run away, or that a raven eventually led me to safety.

"Incredible," he says when I finish. "Wish I had a pencil."

"Don't worry. Once this is over, I promise I'll give you an exclusive."

We fall into silence. I shiver.

"Cold?" he asks. He extricates his arm from between us and slips it around my shoulders and leaves it there.

"I'm okay. It's just—"

I stop. Because the thing is, telling Trevor about my flight through the woods the day my parents died has brought back more memories, a jumble of images and emotions that don't yet quite make sense.

"Just what?"

"Shh. Let me think."

I close my eyes, let the sounds and pictures that flood my brain take form and coalesce, and shudder. The account I related to Trevor is not quite correct. Because after I shot White Bear and ran away, but *before* the raven led me to the bear's den, I went back to the gun range. I don't know why. Possibly I did this because the farther I traveled, the more I couldn't believe that White Bear was really dead. Perhaps I wanted to go back to check. I realize now that this was a dangerous and reckless thing to do considering that my sister was presumably still at the gun range with a rifle, but at the time, I wasn't thinking clearly. As I drew close, I heard voices. I dropped to my hands and knees, then crawled through the underbrush as close as I dared to watch and listen.

I saw my parents and Diana and Charlotte. Everyone was pointing at White Bear and yelling. My mother looked toward the woods and called my name. But before I could answer, Charlotte shot my father. My mother screamed and ran to my father and threw herself on top of him. Diana pointed her rifle at our mother. My mother was on her knees. "Do it," I heard Charlotte say clearly. My sister pulled the trigger.

I feel like I'm going to throw up. *I was there*. I saw everything. I witnessed my parents' murders. It's no wonder I conflated the death of White Bear with the deaths of my parents. Three deaths in quick succession would be enough to drive anyone to the brink, let alone an eleven-year-old child. I marvel at the fragility of memory, how my brain corrupted the memory and put me in the scene as a participant instead of an observer. But now I know the truth. *I remember.*

"Cold?" Trevor asks when I shiver again.

I nod dumbly. He draws me closer. I lean into him, rest my head against his shoulder while I absorb the enormity of what I just learned. I always knew my sister was evil. Knew that when she chose to be the witch when we played Hansel and Gretel, or she wanted to be the wicked step-mother in Snow White, or the evil queen in Sleeping Beauty, that these roles suited her nature. But I didn't realize that Charlotte was just as bad. I used to think of Charlotte as my sister's lackey, her faithful servant whose only wish was to serve. After I got older and I learned about various personality disorders at the mental hospital, I even felt sorry for her. Clearly, she was suffering from dependent personality disorder: difficulty making everyday decisions, such as what to eat or what to wear, a tendency to be passive and to allow others to take the initiative and assume responsibility for major areas of their lives—it all fit.

But now I truly understand the depravity of her servitude. Charlotte killed my father. I saw it. My aunt and my sister deserve each other more than I realized.

What they don't deserve is to go on living in my home. I have to tell the tale of two murderesses living happily ever after at the lodge while the people they murdered lay beneath the forget-me-nots on the hill.

I think about the words Diana scratched into my belly. I have to live. I am the only one who can bring them to justice.

Because *this* is how their story ends.

30

We wait in the den a very long time. My back aches and my butt hurts and my legs tingle and my feet are numb. Trevor is crouched beside me with his arm around my shoulders and his head kinked to the side because the den is too small for him to sit up straight. His neck has to be killing him as much as my legs are hurting me, yet he doesn't complain, doesn't offer up recriminations or second guesses, doesn't question what we're doing or why. He trusts me.

I wish I was as certain of myself. I can't help worrying that Diana isn't tracking us as I presumed and she has something else entirely in mind. When I think back to all the times I thought I knew what she was going to do and didn't, all the times when I believed that I had gotten out ahead of her and then she got the better of me, I can't help but doubt. I feel trapped and vulnerable. I can't stop thinking about Scotty. I wish I'd told him goodbye.

The minutes crawl by. At last, there is the crunch of tires on gravel. I make an opening in the branches covering the den's entrance and peer out. A dark green Jeep identical to Trevor's drives slowly past. Perhaps it *is* his. I can't remember if he took the keys. Minutes later, the Jeep returns from the direction in which it disappeared and drives past again. I don't know if this is because Diana knows where we are, and she's cruising up and down the access road to torment us, or if she's still searching. I suppose we're about to find out.

"Do you think she knows we're in here?" Trevor whispers after the Jeep drives past a third time.

"There's no way to know. Sit tight. Better to wait too long than not long enough."

"There's no need to whisper," Diana suddenly says. My heart leaps, then freezes. "We know you're in there. Next time you want to hide, don't wear a red shirt."

Trevor squeezes my shoulder as if to say it's not my fault and puts a finger to his lips. I wish he weren't so generous. I got us into this mess. Now it's up to me to get us out.

"Stay here," I whisper. "It's me she wants. Don't let her see you. Whatever happens, don't move."

I push aside the branches and crawl out.

Diana is waiting with her rifle. I put my hands up in surrender and move to the side to draw their attention away from Trevor. The Jeep is parked on the road. Charlotte leans against it with a rifle in her hands, looking for all the world like Bonnie to Diana's Clyde. Aiding and abetting my sister's pending crime.

"Okay. You found me. Now what?"

Diana gestures with her rifle. "Now your friend."

"Trevor? He's not here. He climbed over the fence to get help." I toss my head in what I hope is a convincing show of defiance. "You shouldn't have disabled the gate."

"Why don't we make sure?" Diana fires into the den twice in quick succession.

Charlotte gasps. It's all I can do not to scream. I clench my fists, bite my lip. If I give the slightest indication that I know Trevor is inside, she'll shoot him again.

From the den, there is no sound. No movement. Trevor is dead. I got him killed. Now I'm going to die.

"Check it out," Diana says to Charlotte. Charlotte picks her way past us through the underbrush and gets down on her knees and looks in.

"It's empty," she says, her voice tinged with wonder. She sits back on her heels and shakes her head. "He's not here."

I can't believe it. Of course Trevor is inside. Dead or wounded, I don't know. But he must be alive because if he were dead, why would Charlotte say he's not there? She's covering for us. She hasn't gone over completely to the dark side. She still has a conscience.

"Whatever," Diana says with a shrug. She gestures with her rifle toward the road. "Walk."

I don't move. If I do as she says, I will never leave the

property alive. I have no idea how badly Trevor is wounded, if he will make it, if he will escape. I hope he's okay, and that he will investigate my parents' murders and mine and write the truth about the tragedy that destroyed my family. I hope Diana buries me beside my parents. I hope . . . I hope . . .

No. I can't give up. This isn't over until I can no longer draw a breath.

I toss my head again. This time, my defiance is real. "No. I'm not going anywhere until you tell me everything. You owe me that."

"I owe you nothing."

"*I was there*. I saw you and Charlotte kill our parents. I came back after you killed White Bear and was hiding in the forest. *I saw you*."

"So, you saw us. So what? What else is there to know?"

"I want to know how you and Charlotte convinced the police that our parents died as a murder-suicide. I watch a lot of true-crime shows. That's not easy to pull off."

"Oh, it's far easier than you might think," Charlotte breaks in. "Especially when your partner in crime is as clever as your sister."

Is she *proud* of the role she played in my parents'—her own sister's—deaths? Or is she only pretending to be on Diana's side to mislead her?

"After we killed them, we loaded their bodies onto an ATV and brought them back to the house and staged the scene in the front hallway," Charlotte continues. "Your mother had been shot with Diana's rifle, so we shot your father's body with the Magnum as well to make it look as though the same rifle had killed them both, then wiped off our prints and put his prints on the rifle and left the rifle beside him. We even wiped our hands on his palms so the police would find gunshot residue on them. We couldn't do anything about the blood at the gun range, but we figured if the police found it, they'd assume the blood belonged to White Bear. Which is exactly what happened."

"People are stupid," Diana says. Considering how easily she and Charlotte were able to deceive trained professionals, in this instance, I have to agree.

"Diana was going to track you down and kill you as well," Charlotte prattles on. "We looked a long time before we gave up and called in your mother's murder. Later, after you wandered out of the woods and wound up in the mental hospital and we realized your memories were gone, killing you was no longer necessary."

Until now, she may as well have added. Charlotte's perfunctory account of my parents' murders leaves me cold. How could she live with herself all these years knowing what they'd done? I spent fifteen guilt-ridden years in a mental hospital because I believed I'd *accidentally* killed my mother. How much worse would it be for someone who'd killed deliberately? There's so much I want to say to her, so much I want to ask. *Why did you kill my father? What happened to you? When did you change?* The Aunt Charlotte I remember was fun-loving and kind. She read me stories, took me sledding, taught me how to bake and to draw. Impossible to believe that she has become so corrupted by her love for my sister that she would help her hunt me down to kill me with no more care or concern than if I were a rabbit. And yet here we are.

"Why are you doing this? What did I do to you? I loved you," I say. Charlotte is still the weak link. She lied about Trevor to protect him. She has to help us now.

"Enough," Diana says. She gestures again toward the access road. "Move."

"I won't," I say, not only because I still have questions but because the moment I do as she tells me, I am dead. "This isn't finished. I have to know *why*. Why you're doing this. Why you killed our parents. Why you killed that girl at the roadside park."

"Why not? She was nothing to me."

"And Max? Does Charlotte know you killed him as well?" Playing my last card as the final missing piece of memory slides into place.

Charlotte's face drains of color. "Wait. What are you saying?"

"I'm saying that I remember *everything* I saw that day. Diana killed Max. After she shot White Bear, Max came running into the clearing—I imagine because he heard the gunshot. They argued, and Diana shot him."

"I don't believe it." Charlotte looks toward Diana. "Tell me this isn't true."

Diana shrugs. "Of course I shot him. He was going to ruin our plans. I hid his body in the woods before I lured my parents to the gun range, then went back later and buried it." She smiles. "Our little family cemetery is much more crowded than you know."

"How *could* you?" Charlotte screams. "I *loved* you. I *killed* for you! Now I find out that as . . . I was doing that . . . my boyfriend was lying dead not fifty feet away? I loved him! We were going to get married!"

She points her rifle at my sister. Her hands tremble. "You're evil. Horrible. Despicable. I can't believe I ever loved you."

"Oh, please," Diana says, her voice dripping disgust. She raises her rifle and shoots before Charlotte or I can react.

Charlotte falls and lies still.

I can't believe it. Charlotte is dead. I've just witnessed another murder.

And I'm next.

Then from the corner of my eye, I see movement. At first, I think it's Trevor. He's alive. Diana's bullets only wounded him and, weakened by pain and shock and blood loss, he's crawled out of the den looking for help.

Only it's not Trevor. It's the bear. Huge. Powerful, healthy, and strong. Every bit as big as I'd imagined. The bear swings its massive head from side to side and chuffs and takes a step toward my sister. I want to let it kill her for all she's done. But I am not my sister.

I point. "Behind you. The bear. It's come back."

Diana smiles her disbelief.

"I'm serious. *Look.*"

She turns. The bear rears up on its hind legs and paws the air, then drops to all fours and chuffs. She shoots. It stands up on its hind legs and claws at its chest and roars. Drops to all fours and keeps coming.

Diana shoots again. Still the bear keeps coming. I don't understand. She killed White Bear with two well-placed shots from my Remington, yet multiple shots fired from a rifle that's larger and more powerful won't bring this bear down.

I watch, utterly riveted, as the bear who should have been dead continues to run toward my sister. Its fur becomes lighter and lighter. Diana shoots again and again. Yet the bear keeps coming. By the time it leaps onto my sister and sinks its teeth into her throat, the bear is completely white.

I cover my eyes. Wait for her scream. Instead, a raven calls.

I open my eyes. The bear is not white. My sister is not dead. It's an illusion. Another vision. A trick of the light. There's only me, one very dead black bear, and my sister shooting like a madwoman into its carcass.

I dive for Charlotte's rifle without thinking and flatten myself behind her body and shoot.

Diana falls.

She doesn't get up.

"Trevor!" I cry when the forest falls silent. I run to the den and look inside.

But the den really is empty. Charlotte wasn't lying. Trevor is gone.

I fall to my knees, put my head in my hands. I was so sure Trevor was inside, so sure Diana had killed or wounded him. Nothing makes sense. Maybe none of this is real. Maybe I really am crazy. Maybe I belong in a mental hospital after all.

And then Trevor is standing over me. He reaches down and pulls me to my feet.

"Arc you okay?" He brushes the hair from my face and takes me in his arms and looks down at me. I read worry, care, concern, and something else. Something I'm not yet ready to put a name to.

"How did you? I don't understand—"

"After you crawled out of the den and you and your sister were talking, I didn't feel safe, so I broke through the back. There was a low spot behind the tree, so I rolled into it and pulled some branches over me." He looks down at his clothes. "It was a little wet."

"I can't believe you're okay."

"I'm sorry about your aunt and your sister."

"So am I."

I look at Charlotte's ruined body, think about how she tried to help me, think about how she killed my father. She wasn't fully evil. Neither was she entirely good. I think about how easily I shot my sister. Maybe we're all a little of both.

I pick up the rifle from where I'd dropped it and turn it over in my hands. I recognize the scuff marks on the gunstock. It seems somehow fitting that the Remington I used to shoot my sister is mine. My sister was a killer. Now I am a killer, too.

"Don't worry," Trevor says. "I saw what happened. It was self-defense. I'll tell the police that. In fact . . ." He reaches into his jacket pocket and takes out his digital recorder.

"Seriously? You got everything on tape?"

"I wouldn't be much of a reporter if I didn't." He grins. "Come on. Let's get out of here."

We start walking toward the lodge. "First order of business is to restore power to the security gate. Then we can drive out to the highway and call 911."

Cr-r-ruck tok, cr-r-ruck tok, the raven calls in warning. I whirl around.

Diana has rolled onto her stomach and propped herself on her elbows. Her rifle is pointed at Trevor.

"Get down!" I yell and give him a shove. We tumble to the ground. The bullet that would have killed him passes over our heads.

Diana quickly ejects the cartridge and loads another. I jump to my feet. Swing the rifle that Charlotte never got the chance to fire in her direction and take careful aim and pull the trigger.

The bullet hits exactly where I intended. I wouldn't have expected otherwise. I am a very good shot.

31

FIVE YEARS LATER
Rachel

After everything was over, I tried living at the lodge by myself. Everyone said I shouldn't. They said that too many bad things had happened there, and too many people had died, and the best thing for me to do would be to sell out and move on. Some thought I should leave the U.P. entirely. Get as far away from my past as I could and make a new start. When I asked them where exactly they thought I should begin this new life and what I should do and how I should go about it, the answers were a lot less specific. The only thing that everyone seemed to agree on was that I shouldn't live at the lodge.

So, of course, I had to prove them wrong. It wasn't only stubbornness that made me want to give it a try. This was my home. The lodge and the acreage have been in my family for generations. I loved living here before every-thing fell apart, and I had many happy memories. My mother's work was here, and I was hoping to take it up. My parents are buried here, as is my unborn brother.

I lasted a week. Part of the problem was the way my memories threatened to overwhelm me, as everyone had predicted. But the bigger reason was me. After Diana killed Aunt Charlotte and I in turn shot her, I felt unmoored. Unsettled. Intellectually, I knew that I was free to do as I wished, yet I couldn't seem to move on. I think I was so used to believing that I was worthless, it was hard to accept that not only did I have a future, I deserved one.

The other problem with living at the lodge was that it seemed as though my parents weren't ready to leave. Whenever I walked into a room or turned a corner, my mother and father would be reading in their chairs by the fire, or filling the wood box, or cooking dinner, or talking about something they'd seen or done or learned that day. Sometimes I'd catch them laughing over something silly that I did, such as when I forgot to turn on the pump and the water tank ran out, or when I didn't realize that before you could build a fire in the cookstove, you had to open the damper in the chimney and the kitchen filled with smoke. Other times I'd catch them with their arms around each other kissing. At night, I'd hear them talking softly in their bedroom when they thought I couldn't hear.

After a week, I took a room in a motel. I stayed there three months. Still, I went back every day. I *wanted* to learn how to live in the place where I grew up, wanted to take up my mother's research not only out of love and respect for her and for her memory, but because I truly love bears and I love what she was doing. I knew I should put the ghosts of my parents to rest, but instead, I'd talk to them when I was feeling lonely or when I needed advice because the birds and insects and animals had stopped talking to me.

I didn't tell anyone that I was struggling. But somehow, Trevor knew. When he offered to stay at the lodge to help during the transition, I said yes. One thing led to another, and five years later, here we are.

"I'm hungry," our daughter says now as we crouch inside the observation blind watching a female black bear and her cubs feed at the bait station a dozen feet away. "Can we go home, please?"

Our daughter always says "please" and "thank you." She's a very well-mannered child. My mother would have loved her.

"Just a little longer," Trevor says. "Mommy and I are hungry too, but Midnight will tell us when it's time to leave."

Midnight isn't a particularly original name for a black bear, but our daughter was only two when she named her. For that matter, White Bear wasn't a particularly original or creative name, either. Midnight is a female, four years old, the same age as our daughter, the only survivor of a litter of three that was born the spring that I took up my mother's research. The smallest cub drowned when he fell off a log as the family was crossing a stream, and the other died after the wound she suffered when she fell out of a tree became infected. It's a tough world when you're a bear.

By the time Midnight has led her brood into the forest and we've hiked back to the lodge, our daughter is almost asleep on her feet. We go in the side door. The kitchen is warm and welcoming. A pot of what smells like beef stew simmers on the stove. A smaller pot beside it contains a vegetarian version for me.

Scotty sits at my old place at the kitchen table. "Ursa!" he calls when he sees me and flaps his hands. Lynette—Scotty's babysitter, therapist, and teacher, and our chief cook and bottle washer, as she likes to call herself—smiles and ruffles his hair. We pay her a small fortune to live at the lodge and look after Scotty, but when I think about all the years that Scotty suffered in the mental hospital, and how the halfway house that Trevor found for him wasn't much better, she's totally worth it.

"Would you like me to put the kids to bed tonight?" Trevor asks when we've finished eating.

We call them "the kids" though our daughter is four and Scotty is forty-three. Scotty loves it. Normally I enjoy putting our daughter to bed and reading bedtime stories to her the way my mother used to do with me, but climbing stairs is difficult for me. Our second child is due any day. Another girl. Raven is looking forward to having a sister.

"Would you? That'd be great."

Trevor lifts our daughter onto his shoulders and gallops up the stairs. Lynette follows more slowly with Scotty. "Mrs. Eklund," Scotty calls her. Though it comes out sounding like *mi-eck-lun*, even Raven understands.

I rinse our dinner dishes and stack them in the sink, then sit down in my mother's chair in front of the fire. Never could I have imagined that one day I would be living at the lodge with my growing family, that I would marry the aspiring journalism student whose hunger for a story would ultimately set me free, that we would make a home for his brother and my best friend, that I would get my biology degree from Northern Michigan University as my mother had always wanted, and that my husband would be offered a teaching position at the same university thanks to the Pulitzer-nominated article he wrote about my family for *The New York Times*.

Sometimes it bothers me that Diana's second-degree murder charge in Charlotte's death was reduced to manslaughter. But the prosecutor explained that letting a case go to trial was always a risk because of the possibility that the jury will return an acquittal, whereas accepting a plea bargain guaranteed that my sister would spend the next fifteen years in prison.

I also worry about what she'll do when she gets out. She lost the use of her right arm when I shot her in the shoulder and can no longer paint. I can't help thinking that because I took something that she loved away from her, she's going to come back and take something I love from me. Our lawyer says Diana could possibly be charged in the deaths of the girl who died at the roadside park or the boy who drowned in my family's swimming pool, and that if she's convicted for one or both, this could extend her jail time, though he admits these are long shots. There's also Trevor's tape recording in which she admits to killing our parents, which you'd think would be a slam dunk, but for some reason it is not. It's a good thing we have ten years to figure something out.

Meanwhile, I am content to sit in this chair enjoying the fire while White Bear stands behind me with his restored paws extended as in a blessing. Happiness settles over me like a cloak. Sometimes I think it's all too much; that here in this beautiful hunting lodge, doing meaningful work that I love with the support of a husband I never dreamed I would have while raising my growing family, I've been given far more than I deserve. Then I think about everything that I went through to get to this point and decide that if the Universe is trying to make up for all that I lost, it has a long way to go.

But most of the time, I don't dwell on the past. I don't even think about the future. Instead, I choose to live in the present and focus on all the good things I have.

Because why shouldn't my fairy tale have a happy ending?

ACKNOWLEDGMENTS

I owe a huge debt of gratitude to the many passionate and talented people who made this book possible:

Ivan Held and Sally Kim, my publisher and editorial director at Putnam. Your unfailing belief in me and in this novel means more than I can say.

Mark Tavani, whose keen editorial insight and deep understanding of the complexities of human nature elevated this novel above what I could have imagined.

The Putnam team: Alexis Welby, Ashley McClay, Katie Grinch, the production staff, the art department, sales, and promotion, along with a special shout-out to Danielle Dieterich, who came up with the title—thank you for making such a beautiful book!

Huge thanks also to my agent, Jeff Kleinman, without whom I wouldn't be the author I am today. Every author should be blessed with an agent as dedicated and passionate as he is. I'm honored to call you my friend.

Thanks also to Melissa White, my foreign rights agent at Folio Literary Management, for putting my novels into the hands of readers all over the world, and to my first readers, Kelly Mustian and Sandra Kring, without whose insight and encouragement, I'd be lost, as well as to my writer friend Steve Lehto, who generously shares his knowledge of both the Upper Peninsula and Michigan law.

Most of all, I want to thank my husband, Roger, and my mother, Marian Walker, as well as my children and the rest of my family and friends for their unflagging encouragement and support. Writing is such a solitary endeavor, it's easy to get caught up in the worlds that we're creating in our heads and forget the things that matter most. You all keep me grounded, and for that, I am truly grateful.

And finally, a quick shout-out to all the real-world and online friends who entered my contest for a chance to be a character in my novel, but who didn't win: Adele Woskobojnik, Amber Martensen, Amber McLean, Amy Klco, Amy Moss, Ana Gaby Anaya, Angelika Wojciak, Ann Elder, Ann Holt, Anne L. St Onge, April Arotin, Arlene Brown Stein, Barb Woods, Bernadette Bender Buszek, Beth Ann Hiatt McFalls, Beth Vollbach, Beverly Purdy, Brian Wilson, Bruce Wallis, Carmen Murphy, Caroline De Ruyck, Charlene Temple, Chris Williams, Christopher Aumick, Cortney Casey, Dan McDougall, Danis Houser, Danny Bartolotta, Darcy Giovannetti, Dawn Nacker, Dayna Edwards, Dean Lever, Debi Krogstad, Deborah Wall McGraw, Doreen Fresco-Sparkes, Elaine Breault, Erica Trowbridge, Esther Mudge, Gail Tobias Smith, Geneva Robertson, Gigi Harris, Gloria Caswell, Hailey Fish, Haley Georgi, Heather Dobberstein, Heather Hope-Thomas,

Helen Lindstrom, Iris Gernhuber, Jackie Wilson Fredenburg, James Agnew, Janet DeCastro, Janet Rudolph, Janice Rydzon, Jeanine McIntyre Dunaj, Jennifer Knapp, Jennifer Lasslett, Jerrle Gericke, Jessica Drayton Frost, Jessica Sampson, JH Bográn, JM Barton, Jo Hansen, John Thomas Bychowski, Joni Cross Massad, Julie K. Koleszar, Justine Janora, Karen Dybis, Karen Ford, Karen Schwartz, Karynn Ellis Anderson, Kate Courtney Scollin, Kathie Antrim, Kathleen Fannon, Kathryn Dalheim, Katie Mignogna, Kay Kendall, Kelly Martin, Kelly Mustian, Kristopher Zgorski, Laura Barens, Leslie Carlson Davis, Lilian Brugel, Linda Ciochetto, Lisa Brendemuehl, Lisa Romeo, Lisa Roy White, Lissy Pritchard, Lori Hunt, Lori Twining, Lorraine Fallis Bergevin, Luzmarie Alvarez Allen, Lynn Parker, Lynn Sinclair, Magdalana Basel, Maly Kue, Marge Sawyer Crawford, Margo Parmenter Zieske, Mariah Lalonde, Marlys Pearson, Martha Dalrymple, Mary Carol Webber O'Malley, Mary Jane Snider, Maureen Tuohy, Melanie Hoo Swiftney, Melissa Maxey, Michael Hackett, Michael Knapp, Michele Kinney, Michelle Murphy, Mike Walker, Millie Naylor Hast, Missy Jenner, Myla Bilello, Nancy Nowak Messina, Nick Garlinghouse, Nita Joy Haddad, Norman Garver, Pam Killebrew Alessandro, Patty Patano, Patty Renfro Wonderly, Patty Sundberg, Paul Lahti, Penny Nantell, Pia Nielsen, Rebecca Burnton, Robin Agnew, Rosanna Lanza, Sandy Fields, Sarah White, Shana Silver, Shasta Burzynski, Shawn Reilly Simmons, Sherri Trbovich, Sherry Neuder Bradow, Shirley Barrett, Steven Bartley,

Susie Barajas, Tara Humphrey, Terry Beedom, Tina Pelrin, Tracey S. Phillips, Trina Hayes, Trisha David, Wendy Harrison, and Yolanda M. Elkins.

I'm sorry you won't see your name in my book! Oh, wait . . .

Read on for a sneak-peek at Karen Dionne's
bestselling novel . . .

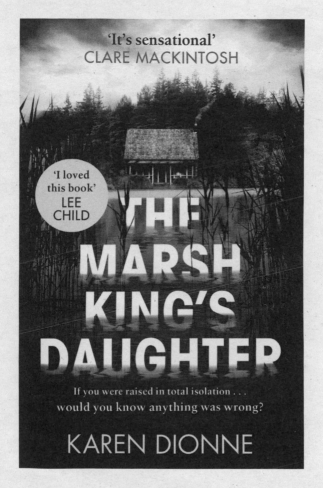

HELENA

⸺

If I told you my mother's name, you'd recognize it right away. My mother was famous, though she never wanted to be. Hers wasn't the kind of fame anyone would wish for. Jaycee Dugard, Amanda Berry, Elizabeth Smart—that kind of thing, though my mother was none of them.

You'd recognize my mother's name if I told it to you, and then you'd wonder—briefly, because the years when people cared about my mother are long gone, as she is—where is she now? And didn't she have a daughter while she was missing? And whatever happened to the little girl?

I could tell you that I was twelve and my mother twenty-eight when we were recovered from her captor, that I spent those years living in what the papers describe as a run-down farmhouse surrounded by swamp in the middle of Michigan's Upper Peninsula. That while I did learn to read thanks to a stack of *National Geographic* magazines from the 1950s and a yellowed edition of the collected poems of Robert Frost, I never went to school, never rode a bicycle, never knew electricity or running water. That the only people I spoke to during those twelve years were my mother and father. That I didn't know we were captives until we were not.

I could tell you that my mother passed away two years ago, and while the news media covered her death, you probably missed it because she died during a news cycle heavy with more important stories. I can tell you what the papers did not: she never got over the years of captivity; she wasn't a pretty, articulate, outspoken champion of the cause; there were no book deals for my timid, self-effacing wreck of a mother, no cover of *Time*. My mother shrank from attention the way arrowroot leaves wither after a frost.

But I won't tell you my mother's name. Because this isn't her story. It's mine.

1

"Wait here," I tell my three-year-old. I lean through the truck's open window to fish between her booster seat and the passenger door for the plastic sippy cup of lukewarm orange juice she threw in a fit of frustration. "Mommy will be right back."

Mari reaches for the cup like Pavlov's puppy. Her bottom lip pokes out and tears overflow. I get it. She's tired. So am I.

"Uh-uh-uh," Mari grunts as I start to walk away. She arches her back and pushes against the seat belt as if it's a straitjacket.

"Stay put, I'll be right back." I narrow my eyes and shake my finger so she knows I mean business and go around to the back of the truck. I wave at the kid stacking boxes on the loading dock by the delivery entrance to Markham's—Jason, I think is his name—then lower the tailgate to grab the first two boxes of my own.

"Hi, Mrs. Pelletier!" Jason returns my wave with twice the enthusiasm I gave him. I lift my hand again so we're even. I've given up telling him to call me Helena.

Bang-bang-bang from inside the truck. Mari is whacking her juice cup against the window ledge. I'm guessing it's empty. I bang the flat of my hand against the truck bed in response—*bang-bang-bang*—and Mari startles and twists around, her baby-fine hair whipping across her face like corn silk. I give her my best "cut it out if you know what's good for you" scowl, then heft the cartons to my shoulder. Stephen and I both have brown hair and eyes, as does our five-year-old, Iris, so he marveled over this rare golden child we created until I told him my mother was a blonde. That's all he knows.

Markham's is the next-to-last delivery of four, and the primary sales outlet for my jams and jellies, aside from the orders I pick up online. Tourists who shop at Markham's Grocery like the idea that my products are locally made. I'm told a lot of customers purchase several jars to take home as gifts and souvenirs. I tie gingham fabric circles over the lids with butcher's string and color-code them according to contents: red for raspberry jam, purple for elderberry, blue for blueberry, green for cattail-blueberry jelly, yellow for dandelion, pink for wild apple–chokecherry—you get the idea. I think the covers look silly, but people seem to like them. And if I'm going to get by in an area as economically depressed as the Upper Peninsula, I have to give people what they want. It's not rocket science.

There are a lot of wild foods I could use and a lot of different ways to fix them, but for now I'm sticking with jams and jellies. Every business needs a focus. My trademark is the cattail line drawing I put on every label. I'm pretty sure I'm the only person who mixes ground cattail root with blueberries to make jelly. I don't add much, just enough to justify including *cattail* in the name. When I was growing up, young cattail spikes were my favorite vegetable. They still are. Every spring I toss my waders and a wicker basket in the back of my pickup and head for the marshes south of our place. Stephen and the girls won't touch them, but Stephen doesn't care if I cook them as long as I fix just enough for me. Boil the heads for a few minutes in salted water and you have one of the finest vegetables around. The texture is a little dry and mealy, so I eat mine with butter now, but of course, butter was nothing I'd tasted when I was a child.

Blueberries I pick in the logged-over areas south of our place. Some years the blueberry crop is better than others. Blueberries like a lot of sun. Indians used to set fire to the underbrush to improve the yield. I'll admit, I've been tempted. I'm not the only person out on the plains during blueberry season, so the areas closest to the old logging roads get picked over fairly quickly. But

I don't mind going off the beaten path, and I never get lost. Once I was so far out in the middle of nowhere, a Department of Natural Resources helicopter spotted me and hailed me. After I convinced the officers I knew where I was and what I was doing, they left me alone.

"Hot enough for you?" Jason asks as he reaches down and takes the first box from my shoulder.

I grunt in response. There was a time when I would have had no idea how to answer such a question. My opinion of the weather isn't going to change it, so why should anyone care what I think? Now I know I don't have to, that this is an example of what Stephen calls "small talk," conversation for the sake of conversation, a space-filler not meant to communicate anything of importance or value. Which is how people who don't know each other well talk to each other. I'm still not sure how this is better than silence.

Jason laughs like I told the best joke he's heard all day, which Stephen also insists is an appropriate response, never mind that I didn't say anything funny. After I left the marsh, I really struggled with social conventions. Shake hands when you meet someone. Don't pick your nose. Go to the back of the line. Wait your turn. Raise your hand when you have a question in the classroom and then wait for the teacher to call on you before you ask it. Don't burp or pass gas in the presence of others. When you're a guest in someone's home, ask permission before you use the bathroom.

Remember to wash your hands and flush the toilet after you do. I can't tell you how often I felt as though everyone knew the right way to do things but me. Who makes these rules, anyway? And why do I have to follow them? And what will be the consequences if I don't?

I leave the second box on the loading dock and go back to the truck for the third. Three cases, twenty-four jars each, seventy-two jars total, delivered every two weeks during June, July, and August. My profit on each case is $59.88, which means that over the course of the summer, I make more than a thousand dollars from Markham's alone. Not shabby at all.

And about my leaving Mari alone in the truck while I make my deliveries, I know what people would think if they knew. Especially about leaving her alone with the windows down. But I'm not about to leave the windows up. I'm parked under a pine and there's a breeze blowing off the bay, but the temperature has been pushing upper eighties all day, and I know how quickly a closed car can turn into an oven.

I also realize that someone could easily reach through the open window and grab Mari if they wanted to. But I made a decision years ago that I'm not going to raise my daughters to fear that what happened to my mother might also happen to them.

One last word on this subject, and then I'm done. I guarantee if anyone has a problem with how I'm raising my daughters, then they've never lived in Michigan's Upper Peninsula. That's all.